# A Necromancer's Guide to Grave Mistakes

Copyright © 2025 by Melissa Wright

All rights reserved.

No part of this book may be reproduced in any form or by any electronic or mechanical means, including information storage and retrieval systems, without written permission from the author, except for the use of brief quotations in a book review.

Cover Illustration by Fernanda Suarez

Cover Design by Katie Anderson

Line Art by Grace Crandall

Courtyard Illustration by Bella Bergolts

Character Illustration by Hannah Latham

# A Necromancer's Guide to Grave Mistakes

MELISSA WRIGHT

*For Janice*
*You know what you did.*

## CHAPTER 1

If Ella had learned anything from grave robbers, it was that she only needed a hole big enough to drag out the head. Digging was the worst part—Ella was half a foot shy of the customary six-foot depth herself and couldn't possibly manage to empty an entire plot before dawn. At least this time the dirt was still loose, likely owing to the superstition that treading the earth before a fresh marker stone caused ghost pox.

She flung a rain-soaked shovel of dark soil over the ledge, and the small gray mouse standing near the lip of the muddy pit coughed pointedly. Ella ignored him.

If Ella had been granted the position of High Cinder like her father wanted, she would have been standing alongside the grave with an army of kingsmen at her command. A lantern would lead her processional, and Ella would supervise, stately and dignified, as they dug up her late father's scribe. She would not be wearing a muddy frock and borrowed boots.

But Ella was not in the king's employ, nor even the king's favor, and her stepfamily had tried to make certain she never would be. So there she stood, shovel in hand, in a moonlit graveyard beyond an abandoned church on the outskirts of a kingdom that didn't show her the slightest regard. And she would keep digging, with nothing more than a bitter grudge, a pair of censorious undead rodents, and a squat, slightly less censorious undead badger for company. In the rain, no less—which was not owing to any conspiracy or ill-treatment but was just poor timing.

The mouse chucked a pebble into the hole, then leaned forward dramatically as if listening for the *plink* at the end of the drop.

Ella paused in her digging to look at him, one hand planted heavily on her hip. "I have told you before, Fritz, and I will hold all progress to tell you again: attempts at rushing me will not get you out of the rain any faster. I have a job to do, and it takes skill and concentration, and no little amount of cleverness."

A chunk of earth took that moment to slide from the ledge, its wet plop punctuating Ella's declaration and spattering mud up the front of her pinned skirt and, somehow, directly into a nostril. She wiped at her nose with the back of her hand.

Beside Fritz, Cybil released a chirp of laughter, and the pair exchanged a few quick gestures before chittering in unison as they performed a mocking imitation of Ella's entire speech. Ella's shovel slapped against the pooling water as the undead mice rolled across the grass, laughing. Magnus, the badger who had completed a good deal of their digging before the rain had begun, spat a half-chewed strawberry stem into the trampled grass beside him without comment.

Ella's mouth set in a determined line. She was going to get the scribe out of the coffin so she could put things right by her father and never have to spend another moment thinking of the king, his court, or inheritance law ever again. And she was going to do it all without being thrown into the stocks.

It was a quarter hour later before the shovel edge thudded against a wood plank and longer still before Ella realized what a mess she'd made of it. An efficient grave robber would dig down to where the head was located and pull the body out without disturbing the whole site. Ella was neither a grave robber nor efficient. The only treasure the buried man held for her was information. Evidently, however, he'd been buried in the wrong direction because all Ella could reach were his feet.

She glanced at the badger where he watched from above with new interest. "Do you suppose this is merely the work of a poor burial or something more sinister?"

Magnus shrugged.

Ella knelt to peer through the hole she'd knocked in the thin wood. "Nothing to be done for it now."

A brief shuffling noise was the badger's only response before he tossed the rope down. Ella tied it around the man's stockinged ankles, then climbed gracelessly out of the pit. At the top, she settled onto the ledge, braced her boots against the opposite edge of the hole, and pulled.

There was a mud-muffled *thump* as the man's ankle came off and the rest of him fell the distance they'd gained. Ella leaned forward, she, Magnus, and the two mice squinting down at the body. Cybil chittered sage advice, which Ella promptly ignored. Ella did not have time for wisdom. She only needed not to get caught. Reaching into the pit, she looped the rope farther up the man's leg, then hauled his body out of the hole by leaning flat on her back... where the corpse landed on top of her.

As Fritz and Cybil agreed that some humans were just too stubborn to be taught, Ella shoved the man's body off her own, then knelt beside it. "There," she said. "Not too worse for wear."

Magnus gave her a skeptical look but was gracious enough not to glance toward the lone foot at the bottom of the hole.

Ella waved away the badger's concern. "He's better off up here than down there in any case."

The corpse was heavier than Ella had expected. She'd only seen her father's scribe briefly, from a distance and alive. She had not expected him to possess quite so much muscle. He wore the garb the king preferred for his close staff, an embroidered tunic and leggings, much out of date for current fashion. The undertakers performed a bit of magic of their own, preserving the appearance of the body a great deal, but it did nothing to restore things such as broken bone, and Mister Hicks had been struck by a fast-moving carriage. Fritz moved closer, searching the man's neck for chains of office, while Cybil stood on her hind legs and sniffed the air before closing in.

When the pair finally finished their inspection, they decided the man smelled sufficiently of ink and parchment. The moon was high, her lantern was low, and the watch would soon make their rounds. Ella decided the assessment would have to be enough.

She stood, nearly slipping on the slop they'd made by digging, then drew the supplies out of her bag. Fritz and Cybil lined up beside Magnus, the lot of them taking on a more solemn air. It was not an easy thing to be dragged back from death, and no one understood the gravity of what was about to take place more than them.

Ella forced down a familiar pang of guilt at the thought, then laid her light cloak over the man's missing foot before threading thin braided string between her fingers. Her voice was low when she sang the words upon the corpse inside the circle formed as she placed the string, and lower still when she leaned over to smear dark ash down his face and throat. She straightened, stepped back, and hoped very hard that the magic would work the way it was meant to.

"Stick," she demanded.

Magnus lifted the hazel branch toward her. Ella took it without removing her gaze from the body. She continued the chant, dragging the tip of the branch through the damp soil to mark a wider circle around the rope.

Twine to keep him in. Hazel wood to keep her out.

The rain had slowed to a drizzle, but Ella's hair and gown were heavy and dripping. When the circle closed, the cold damp was devoured by warmth, distinct and dangerous. Ella's focus tightened on the corpse. The man's throat began to glow like a coal beneath the bellows. It was where Cinders got their name.

The magic directed through the hazel wood appeared like an ember on the charred tip. And the undertaking never became less momentous.

The glow raced outward, toward sternum and chin, then briefly flared before fading away. Ella spoke the binding word, and the spot that had glowed went unnaturally dark, cauterized.

The corpse coughed. No longer a living flame, but not entirely extinguished. Somewhere in between the living and the dead.

Ella glanced at the badger; his teeth were bared. She widened her stance, just a fraction, and wished she had worn better-fitting boots.

The corpse sat up, several clods of earth and what looked to be a ceremonial pin rolling off him to land on the ground.

"Good evening, sir."

He blinked.

"It is so kind of you to assist me, and when the weather is so dreadful."

He nodded sloppily, seemingly confused by her pleasant smile and conversational tone.

Ella did not release her gaze. "I wonder if you might be able to tell me your name."

The man, for he was beginning to resemble such more by the minute, stared at her.

Ella shifted a step closer, her boots coming to rest right against the line in the sod. "What may I call you?"

"Henry," he said, voice a bit rusty but intelligible enough. "Henry Hicks." Then, "Why are you smeared in mud?"

"Henry," Ella repeated, relieved that she had finally found her Mister Hicks. "I had an uncle named Henry. He lived in Dorchester for a time. Dreadfully rainy every time we visited. Some days it just feels like the rain follows me wherever I go." She inched closer, coming to kneel before the demarcation so that she might face him directly. "Tell me, Henry, how long have you been in the employ of the king?"

"Since I was a boy. We're one of the families he keeps on. Did you have a fall, miss? You've got mud..." He trailed off as if a gesture might have accompanied the words, though his arm did not move.

Ella adjusted the material of her skirt, proper-like, as if they were sharing evening tea before the fire and were not in a damp and moonlit graveyard. In her experience, conversation accomplished more than interrogation. "Can you tell me if you ever worked with Cinder Morgrave?"

The man's full eyebrows drew together.

"He may have gone by the name Emeri. A friendly sort, but terribly distractible. Always so deep in his work. Tall, thin, sandy hair and sandy skin."

His head cocked sideways a bit, possibly on purpose. "What would a Cinder want with me?"

"Well, scribe work, of course."

"Miss"—the man looked slowly through the graveyard before his gaze came back to hers—"I'm a tinsmith."

Ella's stomach dropped. She tried desperately to keep the devastation wrought by his revelation from her expression; it was never a good idea to upset a newly unearthed corpse. Swallowing against the lump trying to overtake her throat, she asked, "Why would a tinsmith be dressed in the clothes of a king's man?"

Henry tried a glance downward at said wardrobe, his neck wobbling perilously in the attempt as the magic and his body found equilibrium. "Oh. Erm..." He looked back toward Ella, one of his fragile hands lifting to roam over the fabric of his tunic. "These are Harold's."

"Harold?" Ella's voice had gone shaky.

"My cousin." The man pointed a finger somewhat loosely in her direction. "You think I'm Harold. Because he was the High Cinder's scribe."

Ella pressed her lips together hard, then drew a deep breath through her nose. She did not weep or wail or raise her head to shout at the sky. She did not pound her fists into the earth and stomp her feet. She said calmly, "I did think that the case, especially given the shared surname." It was a bit too soon to mention that he'd been in another man's grave. "And how, again, was it that you came to be wearing your cousin's uniform?"

"Oh, that's easy."

Ella waited.

"It was on account of someone trying to murder him." Henry's expression fell, the finger he'd been gesturing with seeming to follow some invisible line of thought through the air. "Hang on." He glanced once more at the churchyard, nothing much to discover except the pit behind him and a freshly carved marking stone, which, naturally, he did discover. The crown did not generally employ fools. Henry's eyes met Ella's, glistening in the moonlight and more alive than they had any right to be. "Is that why I smell of lilies? Have I—have you—" He emitted a sickly little mewling sound. "Aw, no, miss, no. You've gone and necromancered me."

Ella crossed her arms, then forced them back to her lap in the most nonthreatening way she could manage, which was difficult given that she was nearly out of reach of her own self-control. And she had to keep herself in control, because when her emotions grew unruly, so did her magic. "Henry, I need you to stick with me on this for just a bit longer, please. Where is your cousin now? It is extremely important that I speak with him."

Henry ran a hand over his breastbone, then made a horrified and accusatory face, perhaps because he realized there was no beating heart inside or because the bone was slightly askew. "How should I know? I was busy being dead."

In the distance, a dog barked, and Ella hoped very much that the man she'd just awoken did not notice the undead mice nearby having an animated discussion about how Ella was running out of time before the watch made their rounds. She resisted the urge to glance over her shoulder; she'd been on edge since a tall copper-haired guard had watched her a little too attentively at the market the week before. Ella had not liked the way he'd looked at her.

She leaned closer, careful not to cross the boundary mark until she'd had time to anchor the man properly to her magic. "Henry. Where was Harold last?"

Drawing his eyes off the church in the distance, Henry said, "Don't know. That was why the pair of us would switch clothes —so that Harold might be able to sneak away and meet secretly with Silas. Never told me where, just that someone was aiming to do away with him because he was a witness."

Ella felt a little twinge at the name, but as a name, it was common enough and surely not the single Silas whom Ella knew —the Silas whom everyone in the kingdom knew. "A witness to what?"

Henry shrugged. "Harold was too afraid to tell me, never mind that they might come after me too, should they think I was in on it, what with switching our clothes. But it had to be bad, didn't it, for Silas to be wanting to meet with him."

There it was again, that name. But Harold being in hiding was a problem, possibly the worst problem that Ella had acquired since she'd dug up the wrong corpse. She didn't have time to dwell on it. She had to find her father's scribe so that she could drag the location of Emeri Morgrave's last will and testament out of the man before the king picked the next High Cinder and Ella lost what little she had left. The scribe was more than her father's assistant; he was the only reliably organized aspect of Emeri's work. And he had been the last person to see her father alive. "Who was the *someone* aiming to do away with your cousin?"

Henry shrugged again, and his shoulder tipped at an unlikely angle. He did not seem to notice. "No one knew that yet, but Silas was trying to find out. He had a theory, and he had vowed to keep Harold safe. Can you imagine? All that trouble for a scribe."

Ella sat back on her heels. There was something off about the awe in Henry's tone, the way his eyes went all dreamy, and Ella did not like it one bit. The last thing she needed was anyone important—or worse, connected to the king or his court—to be tied to her problem. They would be duty-bound to report her. She would never succeed. She would be punished, and the closer the mess was to the king, the worse it could get.

"Henry," she asked, "who is Silas?"

"Well, the king's son, of course. Harold was being protected by Prince Silas himself."

## CHAPTER 2

Outside The Spinster Inn—named so after its proprietor decided to thumb her nose at the society who mocked it thus, in turn and with no small part irony making the site suddenly fashionable for the very ladies and gentlemen who spurned said proprietor—Ella drew down the hood of her cloak, then gave the pump handle a few swift pumps to rinse any remaining trace of soil from her hands. It was nearly dawn, and the inn staff had already risen, busy about their tasks to start the day, but Ella had been so filthy that she'd run out of water in her attic room above the inn. In a few hours, when the highest of society got around to leaving their houses, Ella would have to face her stepmother, the way she did every Tuesday, and resist the urge to bludgeon the horrible woman with bucket and mop. Restraint was much harder without a decent night's sleep.

Ella had pondered her situation, Henry's words, and the sheer quantity of bandages she was about to require the entire walk back to the inn. She had managed to come up with only one solution. It was not a solution her father would have praised, or advised, or even approved of. But she had nothing else. If she didn't do it, Ella would have even less than nothing, thanks to the woman her father had married the year before his death. She did not have the luxury of choice.

The problem was, Ella's plan involved a prince. As High Cinder, Emeri Morgrave had worked directly for the king since before Ella was born, but it wasn't as if his position had given Ella unfettered access to the king and his family. She hadn't been party to their extravagant ceremonies and had not been permitted to fraternize with Prince Silas, demonstratively so, even as a child. Of course, it hadn't stopped her from trying. When Ella had grown older and was refused attendance at society events and royal balls, it became clear there was no point in the attempt. Necromancers would never be accepted into good society. They were a tool, a quiet necessity, and the only of their kind shown any deference, the only permitted by kingdom law to even practice the craft, were those titled Cinder by, and in service to, the king—men and women who had been trained by Ella's father.

The nearest Ella had been to the king was the day she had petitioned for her father's title. Dressed in mourning, Ella had stood tall and pleaded her case, without the signed order of succession that would be included in Emeri's missing will. King Julian and his court had laughed her off the throne room floor. The prince, Ella had not encountered in years. Oh, she had seen him from a distance, of course, as any peasant might. She had even imagined, on occasion and over the years, that the prince's gaze had sought her out in a crowd. Ella had always turned away, lest he believe she was fawning after him like all the rest. Even thinking of it, she could not help but feel a bit betrayed by how her imaginings portrayed the prince. But she did not truly know him, and should she pass him in the street, were he not dressed in palace finery, Ella might not realize that she'd encountered him at all. Which did not bode well for her plan.

She dried her hands on the length of her apron and tied her hair back with a bit of ribbon, giving a nod to one of the stable boys as he ran past.

What Ella had seen about Prince Silas was that he had grown into a man, dark-haired and light-skinned, his long-legged figure always draped in royal shades and glinting with gold and jewels. What she'd heard about Prince Silas was that he was just about the sort of man she'd expected him to come up as—pompous, arrogant, drunk, and often lewd. A skirt chaser and layabout. Fairly good at cards. She'd heard other things as well, but she wasn't certain she should give the more outlandish stories credit —bards did need to make a living, after all.

*Prince Charming*, their songs called him, owing to the second or third of his seven names being Charmon and that it was said he could charm the pantalettes off a—

"Ella!" shouted one of the maids from somewhere beyond the kitchen entrance.

"You could have warned me," Ella hissed at the scrawny gray dove perched on the lip of the archway. "George!" The undead bird shuddered, apparently having been woolgathering. Ella gave him an admonishing glance—being the lookout was his job, after all—and called, "Coming!" in the direction from which the angry shout had come. She tossed her cloak over a hook near the back entrance to the tavern that adjoined the inn, then picked up the pair of heavy wooden buckets at her feet.

"You're late," Grace said, not glancing up from her dough work as Ella strode past. "The Spinster's on the hunt for you."

Nodding to one of the kitchen girls, Ella set the buckets by the hearth, then poured one into the cauldron and half the other into the sink. "What is it this time?" she asked Grace.

"You're to go to the market and order extra chickens for tournament day, there's a stray dog in the stable she suspects someone has been feeding, and one of the guests left a mess of broken glass outside the cellar door."

"How am I supposed to stop her ostler from collecting strays? I'm only the maid."

Grace lifted a shoulder as she rolled the dough expertly thin. "Don't ask me; I'm only the cook."

"Maybe you should threaten to stop feeding the man, then."

Grace laughed. "Wouldn't hurt him a bit, I'd wager, with all the horsebread he's stowed away. Perhaps you should try swatting him with your broom."

"I'll start with sweeping by the cellar and see where it goes from there." Ella leaned over Grace's shoulder on her way to grab the broom. "What's on the menu today—ginger biscuits? Make an extra special one, please. It's Tuesday."

The corner of Grace's mouth lifted. "Only the best for your stepmother. I'll be sure to set one aside just for her." The pair exchanged a knowing glance before Ella, hands full, used her bottom to swing open the well-worn door.

The morning was reasonably warm, and though everything was still a bit damp from the night before and would be harder to clean, it felt as if the weather would soon clear. After sweeping up the mess by the cellar, Ella used a shovel to dump the glass into a bin then leaned the shovel and broom against the shed. She entered through the low door, grabbing a handful of dried peas to drop into her pocket for the mice before coming to stand over a lumpy bundle of cloth across the straw-strewn floor. She reached above the mass to yank aside the linen that covered a broken slat in the shed wall. The resulting strip of light cut across the narrow, slumbering face of the tavern's most regular entertainer. He winced, smacking a hand over his eyes before scissoring two fingers open to peer at her.

"Ellenora, no."

She knelt close. "Come on, Finley. Time to earn some coin."

His fingers opened wider to reveal deep brown eyes. "How much coin?"

"Enough. It's delicate work. I need information on the prince."

Finley snorted and rolled over, pulling the end of his jacket over his head as he muttered, "The prince."

Ella tugged the cloth back down. "I'm serious. He's involved in a matter about which I need information. Quickly."

Finley's head tilted side to side, his lips moving in a mockery of her words not unlike the performances Cybil and Fritz had been giving of late. Ella supposed it was what she got for letting them chew a hole through the tavern eaves to watch the goings-on inside. Regrettable they'd not taken up juggling instead.

Finley said, "Listen to you, talking to me like you're some royal lady. About a prince. Do you know how hard it is to find a prince?"

"From the stories you tell, one would think you found princes fairly regularly." She pressed a palm to the floor. "I don't have time to haggle; I've too many chores to finish. Skip to the part where you accept the job."

His mouth turned down. "This is the reason you can't keep suitors. You know that, don't you?"

"I can ask Rory instead."

Finley rolled to his back, slapping a palm to his chest, fingers splayed. "How dare you? You would hire my sworn nemesis? My most unworthy adversary? The enemy of my heart?" When Ella didn't respond, he said, "Fine. Two crowns."

"Done."

"Wait! Two crowns whether I'm able to secure the information or not."

Ella stood. Two crowns would polish off her meager savings, putting her right back where she'd been the day her stepmother had thrown her out on the streets. She would be risking everything she'd gained for a single chance. There would be no funds left to find information from Rory or anyone else, let alone cover the month's food and housing. But if Ella didn't secure her father's will, and quickly, she would be something far worse than merely hungry and penniless. She'd be... well, there wasn't even a word for what she'd be. *Ruined*, perhaps, colossally and in ways that were hard to imagine. Though *ruined* seemed to imply an end. Ella's devastation would feel more relentless.

She nodded once, firmly. "Meet me before the supper crowd

so I can fill you in. And, Finley, I need you to understand that this doesn't go past the pair of us. Not a single word."

He reached forward to pat her shoe reassuringly. "Ellenora, I think you overestimate how much I speak of our relationship. I've made quite a habit of not admitting to even knowing you."

She grinned, kicking his hand away. "Saucebox."

"Nipcheese." He rolled toward the wall once more. "Now leave me be. I have a seventeen-minute ballad and three tankards of ale to recover from before my chores."

***

THE BREAKFAST ROOM at The Spinster Inn was a large open space that echoed with the clatter and clink of every plate and glass. It was sunny and overly warm and just the sort of spot where society loved to gather at too-close tables to overhear the latest gossip. To be seen serving in such an establishment would be the ruin of any lady's reputation. To be a maid living above the let rooms, death to her reputation and dishonor to her family.

"Not a concern for our Lady Locke," Ella muttered as she carried a platter through the crowd. Her stepmother had made clear to society that Emeri's daughter was no longer a part of their esteemed family, nor their household. In fact, she'd gone as far as to hint that Emeri had never truly fathered "the child" at all.

A charity case. That was what the beast had called Ella, and the reason Lady Locke had given for her weekly visits to the inn.

Tall and lean with a sturdy bosom and just the sort of elegance expected of a lady with connections to the king's High Cinder, Lady Louisa Locke had been about as well-stationed as one could get without marrying into the royal family. That was, before she drove Ella's father into an early grave.

Ella slammed the dish onto the table with a bit too much

force, nearly knocking pickled salmon over the rim. "Stepmother."

"Lady Locke," Lady Locke reminded her, nose pinched unattractively at the dish.

Ella did not give the woman her gaze, turning instead toward Lora and Lena. The pair wore new gowns. Lora tucked back her shoulders, plainly showing off the heavy jeweled broach attached to her spencer, also new. "Stepsisters."

"Ellenora," Lady Locke snapped. "We have discussed the proper way to address my family." At the look Ella shot her, Lady Locke's voice dipped. "You would not want me to complain to the Spinster, would you?" Her wide red lips slid into a spiteful line. Covering her gloved fingers with a delicate napkin, she shifted the plate farther from her place, then dusted a nonexistent speck off her glove. "I suspect it would be very difficult to find a new place of employment, particularly given the current economy."

"I can see that you're exceedingly concerned with economy. The special is liver. I can bring it to you on a plate or in a soup. Or, if you prefer, I could take a handful and shove it—"

"Chocolate," chirped Lena.

"Scones and sugared fruit," said Lora. "With tea. Oh, we are famished. We've been to the shops, you know. Terribly taxing, that. Truly, nothing makes me so hungry as being pressed by too many choices. The colors alone this season!"

"And chocolate," Lena said, tipping her voice toward Ella as if she might have forgotten.

Ella's gaze never left her stepmother. Then, beneath the din of breakfast dishes and high-society conversation came the unnatural rattling *hwaah* of an undead dove. A shadow crossed in front of the window, then darkened the doorway. Lord Locke, Louisa's brother and a man Ella hated singularly, stepped into the breakfast room. He wore a black suit, not the uniform Ella had become accustomed to—none of the necromancers would be dressed for duty, not when they awaited the appointment of their new High Cinder. Outside, George's beak pecked against the broken bell beside his nest, warning Ella too late.

Ella's hands began to tremble.

Lady Locke said, "You know what I want, Ellenora. Give me the documents, and you can come home."

Lord Locke removed his hat, his dark eyes scanning the room. Ella snapped her focus toward her stepmother before the magic wanting to commit violence against Lord Locke could slip free. "As your daughter?"

Lady Locke's face went hard, her gaze trailing over Ella's frock. "How could I? After you've sullied yourself so in front of the entire kingdom. Of course not. Honestly, that you would even ask that of me." She let out a small bark of disgust. "But you may come back and do the same sort of work you're doing here. We will always have a place for you below stairs."

Ella leaned near. "We both know handing you that document would be a death sentence for me."

The corner of her stepmother's lips twitched. "That could be arranged, if you prefer."

"I prefer you make your order or leave."

Her stepmother made a little hum of mirth in her throat instead. "If wishes were horses and all that." She made a production of noticing her brother across the room, as if she'd not been awaiting his arrival. "Oh, and there is Lord Locke. What good fortune."

From the other side of the small round table, Lena cleared her throat delicately. "Chocolate?"

"Very well," Ella said from between gritted teeth.

Lora muttered, "What a foul mood she's in this week," as Ella returned to the kitchen.

Every Tuesday, Ella had to stand in front of the women who had taken everything from her and pretend she still had a chance to take it back. Pretend that though they had taken her father, her home, and every last coin with the pockets they rested in, they had not taken her spirit. Never mind Lady

Locke's brother. Bad enough was that the union of the Morgrave and Locke families—both littered with forebears skilled in necromancy—was meant to have been some brilliant strategy to benefit the kingdom, but worse was that the only living Locke with magic was currently attempting to manipulate the king. To turn him against the last of the Morgrave line. To corrupt the very office Ella's father had devoted his life to.

Ella's father had made certain Lady Locke knew of the document directing possession of his title and estate to his only daughter. She had known since the day they were married, and it was all that saved Ella from a much worse fate. Without signed and sealed proof of the succession, the king might award Emeri's property to anyone. Even Lady Locke was at risk if her brother did not succeed. She wasn't coming into the inn to be cruel. The woman was odious but not so much that she'd waste time that might be spent on her own pursuits. No, Lady Locke was only making certain Ella stayed in her place. She thought the work and suffering would wear Ella down, that she would become so desperate she would hand over her inheritance and beg to be taken in. Little did she understand what Ella had already endured.

The Lockes believed that the only reason Ella had not already handed over the will was Lady Locke's threat to turn evidence against Ella's father, to dishonor his memory and destroy his name. Should there be any hint that the document was missing, as it truly was, then Lady Locke would immediately act to steal Emeri's possessions forever. She wanted all he owned, and anyone with a claim to it dead and forgotten. Fortunately, Lady Locke wasn't aware that Ella had already tried to appeal to the king without the document in hand. Certainly she'd heard there'd been an embarrassment at court, but only in relation to the position of King's High Cinder. If a Locke discovered the truth before Ella could secure evidence against them, it would all be over.

The door to the kitchen swung shut behind Ella, and Grace glanced up from her spot by the stove. "That bad?"

Ella shook her head. The hot tears that might have threatened when she was young would not come; the only thing left to burn in her was anger.

Grace nodded solemnly, drawing out a napkin-wrapped bundle from the pocket of her apron. She placed two perfectly round biscuits onto a delicate plate then slid it toward her friend. If one supposed a wicked stepmother might catch on to the discomfort she experienced every week after a trip to The Spinster Inn breakfast room, one would be greatly underestimating the cunning of its cook.

"What is it this week?" Ella asked, voice low. She hoped it was headaches. That one had kept the lady Locke from both court life and her spending spree for nearly a week. She hoped it was something in which Lord Locke would share.

Grace reached forward to pat Ella's hand. "Best you not know. This one's a bit more experimental." Grace glanced over her shoulder. "The ostler is trying out a new remedy on his gelding, and I was able to borrow a bit."

"You do realize we need her to remain alive?"

Grace took hold of the meat knife and threw Ella a wink. "Only until the property is safely back in your name."

## CHAPTER 3

It was only a short four days before Ella got her chance at the prince. She had traded her best pair of shoes to pay for a considerable supply of bandages and was working past supper, scrubbing the kitchen linens in a shallow laundry tub and muttering to Magnus about quality lye and fat mixtures, when Finley popped up behind her and shouted, "Got him!"

It nearly startled Ella off the soapy block she'd been standing on. She shot an anxious glance toward Magnus. The badger held very still.

Finley did not seem to notice. "The prince!" he explained.

Ella tossed a cloth over the badger's head as she ran more linen through the wringer. "What do you mean *got him?*"

Finley crossed his arms over his chest, the puffy jacket he wore puffing even further with the move. His dark skin had a glittery sheen to it that was a complement to the bright threads in the fabric. It was possible he was meant to be costumed as a jester, but sometimes Finley just liked conspicuous tinsel. "He's foxed. Swine-drunk. Sprawled behind The Cross and Cup, weeping and snotty and sobbing." Finley shook his head. "Embarrassing really. What's royalty coming to when they can't even hold their chins?" He leaned an elbow on the railing beside the washtub.

The badger beneath the linen shrank back.

"He's incapacitated?" Ella asked. "And only a few blocks away?"

Finley nodded, expression smug. "I was thinking of questioning his guards once he's gone to sleep."

Ella was not trained to be a maid. She was trained to be a necromancer. Her magic might be too strong, too unpredictable, but her competence in every other area of the post was sound. Including interrogation. She draped the last of the linens over the rail. "I have a better idea."

Finley's eyes went wide, but before he could argue, Ella had dried her hands, tossed her apron onto the rail, and was reaching for a cloak. She said, "I'll ask him myself."

Which was how a ragged washerwoman and a locally infamous balladeer came to be tucked behind a stable wall, peering at a drunken prince limned in torchlight like a dramatic painting by a master.

"Kind of pathetic," Finley whispered. "Look at him there, those fine and fancy clothes soaking up the muck. More than two crowns alone in that cravat wadded on the floor, I'd wager."

"Where are his guards?"

Finley's chin tipped toward the far end of the stable. "Posted out front. Guess he wanted to sob without an audience."

"This seems too easy."

His gaze slid sideways. "Too easy for what? You said you only needed to talk to him."

She shrugged. "I do." She studied the prince where he sat in the long, dimly lit passage, his back against a post and his boot on the edge of a stall door opposite him. Gone were the lines of the gangly youth he'd been. "But they don't just leave princes unattended like that."

They had once, when he'd been younger, and it had not ended well.

Finley turned to face her fully, his shoulder resting against the slat wall, voice low. "Crying in the dark outside a dung-covered horse stall?"

"No," she said. "You're right. Special case."

"I mean it," the prince grumbled drunkenly. "Upon pain of death! Do not enter this stable! I shall not be disturbed until daybreak! Do you hear me, Roberts?"

"Yes, Highness," said a deep male voice.

"And the rest of you?"

"Yes, Highness," came a chorus from outside the doors.

Ella shook her head. "Seems a bit unprofessional, overall. You'd think they'd want this sort of thing kept at home, behind closed doors. Not very seemly for a kingdom official."

"Eh," Finley said. "It's not like princes have to audition for the part."

"True." Ella leaned to peer past the other stalls.

"He's cleared out the whole stable. No one's brave enough to go back inside." Finley's face scrunched. "Likes to call out 'upon pain of death,' evidently."

Prince Silas was so much larger than he used to be, so much less a boy and more a man. Aside from the sobbing, in any case. Of course he would be after all this time. Ella wasn't sure what she had expected.

"All right," she said. "Let's do this."

Finley straightened. "Us? No. You promised two crowns for bringing you information. I delivered the whole hog. I'm not going to be involved in—" He gestured vaguely at her. "Whatever this is."

"Saints," she whispered. "Why does a man need a jaw like that?"

Finley's attention immediately snapped back to the prince, who had shifted so that his head dropped against the post and his long, bare neck was exposed. It was an impressive jaw but a spectacular neck. Finley cursed. "I'm definitely going to help you, aren't I?"

"It will make an excellent story later."

"As if I could tell it."

"I'm grateful, Finn, truly. Two more crowns once my inheritance is settled. Ten, even."

He sighed heavily. Then, "Wait, where are you going?"

Over her shoulder, Ella whispered, "Entertain the guards. I'll whistle when I need you."

---

PRINCE SILAS, King Julian's eldest son and heir to the kingdom, was heavier than he looked. Not being bold enough to question him right there in the walkway, Ella had crept through the narrow space behind the row of stalls then climbed through a feed slat into the stall near where the prince had settled to weep.

He was a good bit into a long moaning sob when the sound of male laughter echoed outside the stable where Finn was distracting the guards. Two stalls down, a mare nickered, and Ella used that moment to reach through the stall door, grab hold of a single polished boot, and drag the prince, leg-first, inside.

He struggled, of course, but she was fast, he was drunk, and she had the advantage of surprise. The gag was easy, because the first thing he'd done was open his mouth. The restraints, a good bit harder, because evidently not all princes were as soft as the tales vowed. His forearms were corded with muscle, his fingers long, and the strength in any number of his limbs threatened to overturn and pin her to the ground.

There was just so very much of him. But Ella had worked alongside her father for years. And a drunken, sappy royal had nothing on the angry dead. She leapt to standing, staring down at a man who'd just realized he'd been trussed like a gamebird about to go on the fire. "Good evening, Highness."

He stared up at her, eyes wide, mouth also wide owing to the rag shoved inside, any trace of familiarity or boyishness gone. Tying him up felt somehow worse given that she was, in effect, a complete stranger, but Ella could not deny the comfort of knowing he could not possibly recognize her after so many years. Between that and the drink, he would not easily be able to identify her later. He made a—possibly—shocked grunt of—likely—protest through the gag.

Outside the entrance to the stable, the guards laughed and sang along with Finley's bawdy song. Inside the stable, it was warm and smelled of damp straw. The prince's hair was very dark, his eyes were very blue, and his disheveled jacket revealed a clean, well-starched shirt. He smelled as if he'd been doused in expensive bourbon, which was not the sort served at The Cross and Cup.

Ella knelt before him. "You should really find better guards. But, for now, I need to ask you a few questions."

If a man could look properly incredulous and insulted around a gag, he would have. As it was, it came across more like wounded pride than anything else.

"I am going to remove the rag, but I need you to understand how very, *very* disappointed you will be if you attempt to call for help. Also, it would be cowardly, as I'm merely a washerwoman and you're a big, strong prince. I have a friend outside who sings songs about such things, and I would not hesitate to tell him every word."

His eyes narrowed.

She nodded. Times were desperate. Ella reached forward, and when he flinched and dodged, she whispered, "Do not make me regret this, Highness."

The moment the rag was free, he lunged sloppily forward. But Ella had been ready, her spare hand quick with the rope. She had a knee on his chest and the rope taut, but before more force was necessary, a squat shape lumbered out from the shadows and released a terrible hiss.

The prince attempted a backward shuffle, bootheels scraping straw where it was strewn over the stall floor, unable to gain purchase. "What is that?"

"A badger."

The prince's hands were balled into fists, and where the rope bound his wrists, his skittering had pressed his fingers to her stockinged leg beneath the edge of her pinned skirt. If she was not careful, she would lose her advantage. If he was not careful, he'd have a hand full of Ella's thigh.

But his gaze only flicked from the badger to Ella, then back. Voice thick with drink, he asked, "What's he going to do?"

"Who, Magnus? He's just going to watch. Things get boring for him these days." Ella always forgot her friends looked particularly terrifying in the dark because a bit of that spark still lingered in their eyes. Plus, there was the decay. It wasn't the sort of thing she would normally employ in such a manner, but when Magnus came closer, baring his fangs in a toothy little snarl, Ella could not help herself. Turning her face away so that the prince could not make out her grin, she said darkly, "I only let him have the ones who don't behave."

Magnus let loose dreadful growl.

It was truly impressive; he must have been practicing. Ella had to press her eyes closed and beg the saints for composure.

The prince's fists went slack, his fingertips light against Ella's leg as he stared at the undead badger. "It's true," he whispered, then his eyes rose very slowly to meet hers.

In the dim strips of light that made it through the slats in the stall, Ella stared back at him. "What's true?"

"They say there's a witch in the alleys who can raise the dead."

Ella pressed off him hard, her skirt falling back into place as she stood over his bent form. "I'm looking for Harold. Word is you're keeping him hidden."

"Oh," he said, in the way a person did when the utterance carried far more weight than merely simple surprise.

But outside, the laughter had died, and the sound of scuffling boots and a man in a too-puffy jacket and festival mask attempting to shove through a narrow opening came from behind the stall. Magnus slid back into the shadows just as Finley's feathered mask sprang into view.

Finn crawled on hands and knees through an opening near the stall floor. Gaze lifting, he let out an anguished swear. "Ellenora, no. Ropes? You cannot tie up *a prince*."

From his place at Ella's feet, Prince Silas slurred, "You'll never find him without me." Then his head lolled and he fell loudly to sleep.

# CHAPTER 4

"We cannot cart him back to your apartment," Finley argued the entire time they carted the prince back to Ella's apartment. They had to. Because the prince might not have remembered *who* Ella was, but he understood *what* she was. Few in the kingdom possessed magic, and practicing without license from a High Cinder, Head Undertaker, or any number of the king's agents was forbidden. Magic was strictly governed, only to be used in service to the crown and under direction of said agents. Being a necromancer might be looked down on by society, but the disobedient power that sometimes spilled from Ella could have her locked away.

Finley did not know Ella possessed magic or that she was secretly practicing necromancy. So she'd had to lie, as well as bribe him with the last of her good hair pins.

Had Ella a plan, kidnapping a prince would never have been part of it. She had never snatched a live body before. It was considerably more complicated. Truly, she'd only meant to ask a few questions. But when he'd passed out drunk after announcing he knew her secret—and that rumor of her activities had reached the palace—Ella had, admittedly, acted rashly. It was the only chance she would get. Likely ever.

Festival mask still in place, Finley helped drag the prince from the borrowed cart, haul him upstairs, and tie him to a spindly chair. They stared at him for a long moment, then each other, the bucket of wash-water they planned to pour over the prince's head resting between them on the worn wooden floor of her attic room.

"He doesn't deserve this," Ella said.

"Unlikely," said Finn. "Look at him."

They did. He looked like a wealthy courtier who'd passed out drunk in the stable after hours of bemoaning the state of his existence. Ella picked up the bucket and splashed it onto a man who was the only son of a monarch.

The prince sputtered awake and immediately attempted to spring from the chair. The chair came with him, tightening the rope and yanking both prince and chair back to the floor where the assembly wobbled dangerously before finding its center. His glare shot toward Ella.

"Good evening, again," she said.

"Why was he crying earlier?" Finley asked Ella.

"Why were you crying earlier?" Ella asked the prince.

He appeared momentarily caught off guard, then flicked his head, lukewarm water droplets splattering a threadbare rug and the plank floor, but only really succeeded in plastering the strands of his dark hair to his temples. "My... my valet."

Ella's brow rose, then she immediately felt rude and tried to nod in an empathetic manner instead.

His face hardened at the implication. "He died."

Finley's head tilted, his shoulder inclining toward Ella as he studied the prince. "That must have been hard for you, pressing your own suits and whatnot."

"It was devastating!" the prince thundered.

Ella and Finley exchanged a look.

The prince jerked futilely against the ropes. "Not the suits. Because I was *grieving him*."

"Oh," said Ella. "I see."

"It's not ..." His expression hardened further, accusatory gaze flicking between the pair. "What is wrong with the two of you?"

*So much*, Ella thought. *So, so much.*

Finley shook his head, likely aware precisely how it made the feather jutting from his mask dance. "All that money. All those looks. Wasted on a prince." He straightened his jacket. "Well, I think you've got this sot well in hand. Best I go before the lady of the house finds me out."

Ella nodded. The Spinster was the last person they needed involved. "Thank you, my friend."

Ella followed Finn to the door, then secured it behind him, slipping the key into her pocket as she listened to his footfalls melt into the noise from the streets below. Something sounded behind her, too close, too soft.

Before Ella could turn, a strong hand locked about her middle and another over her mouth, and she was yanked hard against a very tall, very angry prince.

"Not a word," he murmured into her ear, "or one of us will be very, *very* disappointed."

Ella's curse was muffled against his palm. He was pressed so close that she could feel when his wide mouth slid into a smile. Her arms were trapped, his feet positioned too cleverly. His fingers splayed across her entire middle, and he had far more muscle than she could outmaneuver alone, at least in her current position.

Voice low, he said, "Tell me you understand."

She nodded.

"Now, I'm going to—"

There was a heavy metallic *thunk* before the prince hit the ground. Ella spun to find Henry standing over the body, short-handled coal shovel at the ready. "Sorry, miss." He glanced at his foot where it lay beside the prince, bandages unfurled. "I'm afraid it fell off again."

"It's no problem." Ella waved a hand. "We'll get more

dressing and fasten it back. Perhaps I'll try additional pins this time."

The prince, Ella kicked in the leg. "I believed you were drunk."

His eyes had not come off the corpse that was Henry, though it remained to be seen whether he had noticed the foot. His hand was pressed to the side of his skull. "Who said I wasn't?"

"But not daft."

Gaze traveling over Henry, the prince murmured, "Well, that remains to be seen, doesn't it?"

Henry attempted a lopsided bow. "Apologies, Highness, but... well, men of quality do not grab hold of a miss."

The prince blinked. "Are you having me on?"

"You did grab me," Ella said. Without the gag, Silas managed the properly indignant look he'd tried for earlier. Ella shrugged. "So, what is your intention? Do you aim to fight us, or are you willing to answer our questions then be free to go?"

"No third option?"

"Best not trifle with her, Highness," Henry put in. He still held the shovel, but it came across nothing like a threat and everything like the advice of someone more experienced in matters such as people who were a great deal more dangerous than they looked.

Ella could appreciate that.

The prince sat up, scrutinizing Henry as he asked, "Have we met?"

Then, evidently realizing the hand he'd placed on the floor rested beside a mangled, sock-covered foot not currently attached to its body, the prince jerked back, half-swallowing a yelp of distress before he winced and palmed his head again.

Henry and Ella shared a guilty glance.

"This is Henry," Ella said, forgoing proper introductions, given the circumstance.

Henry slid the shovel behind his back.

"Henry," the prince repeated. His focus shifted to Ella. "And you're looking for Harold."

Ella nodded. She held forward a hand to help him off the ground.

Silas took it, coming to stand before her, his fingers wrapping softly around hers, his gaze too intent on her face. His presence was entirely overwhelming. "And you are—" he started.

"Desperate," she breathed.

"Ellenora," Henry put in, unhelpfully, from behind the prince. "She's the one who necromancered me."

"Ella," the prince said. "The witch."

She snatched her hand from his. "I am not a witch."

His mouth tilted in the wry smile of a man who knew he was well-worth looking at. "Well, you're not a necromancer without a High Cinder who bestowed the title to oversee your work, and I happen to know there's not a titled High Cinder in the kingdom at the moment. That means you're practicing illegally."

"And you intend to turn me in?"

He crossed his arms over his wide chest, the move flashing a good deal of flesh below that muscled neck since he wore no cravat. "No."

"In that case ..." Ella brushed a lock of hair back from her face. "Put down the shovel, Henry. Let's see what he has to say first."

⁂

SITTING ATOP A SHORT, padded stool in the center of Ella's tiny attic room, Prince Silas looked more like a man playing at tea with his nieces than a prince of the realm, assuming said nieces were a badger and two field mice. He was as yet unaware of the lizard behind the trunk.

"I will not pretend I am not somewhat terrified by your little collection here, but it does provide evidence that you truly can do..." The prince gestured uncertainly at the room of undead beings. "This."

Magnus eased closer with practiced menace. The badger really was having too much fun. Ella was going to have to have a talk with him. And with Henry, who was too honest by half. Boundaries were important when one was hiding from the law. To the prince, she said, "Why would you need evidence? You said you were not planning to turn me in."

"Indeed, that is not my plan, but while we are on the subject, that friend of yours at the very least deserves to be hauled before the magistrate. How could you possibly convince someone with even a modicum of virtue to help you drag the crown prince's body to an attic prison and tie him to a chair?"

"I told him you owe me money."

He looked at her for a very long moment.

"He takes financial obligations seriously."

"He seemed to be taking a great deal of delight in the ordeal."

The way he said *he* made clear the word implied *you both*. Ella pressed down the corners of her mouth and lifted her shoulders. "What sort of person would take delight in distressing a member of the aristocracy?"

His gaze was level. He leaned forward before abruptly straightening when the badger twitched his snout. Prince Silas cleared his throat. "Putting that aside for the moment, you said you were looking for Harold. Tell me why you need him and what it has to do with his dead cousin."

"Harold has something of mine. Something I need very badly. Or, to be more precise, he knows where it is. Henry was merely caught up in my search. It's not that complicated."

The prince waited, then said, "Try to uncomplicate it more. For me."

"My father was Emeri Morgrave. Harold was his scribe."

"Ah." His long, blunt fingers tapped against his long, muscled thigh. Ella should not have gotten his trousers wet.

Regrettable, truly. "Because your father was High Cinder, you—"

"I need that title."

He placed his cup on the small rickety table. "This is not merely about a title. Emeri only had one heir, and yet here you are, taking residence in an entirely inadequate lair above a fashionable inn." Where anyone might see her. His chin tilted. "Explain it to me."

"Lady Locke," she said, uneasy that he knew more about her father than she had expected and preferred.

His nod was slow. "I've been introduced to her daughters, I believe. They're—"

"Yes, very beautiful."

He ran a hand over his mouth, and Ella could not quite make out the manner in which his lips had shifted. She crossed her arms.

He lifted the teacup again, but only brushed his thumb absently over the rim. "You have heard, perhaps, that the king intends to announce your father's successor. It's my understanding that Lord Morgrave had already chosen his replacement and the title will be appointed by the end of the month." His blue eyes met hers. He did not add, *the replacement is not you.*

Ella gave him her gaze. She knew a thing or two about his father as well. And Ella understood, without a doubt, whom her father's documents named as the next High Cinder and whom he meant to keep from the post. "The king intends to lie."

The prince considered Ella for another overlong moment. He returned the cup to the table, then his hand slid over the dirty, damp fabric covering his thigh, coming to rest at his knee. "Very well, I will give you what information I can. In trade." When she did not respond, he explained, "I will help you find Harold so that you may prove your case, and, in exchange, you will do something for me."

"Find him? So, you don't even know where he is."

"I know better than you, clearly."

"What do you mean *clearly*? What idea could you possibly have about what I know?"

"Well, you've abducted me just to ask his whereabouts, haven't you? After you dug up his cousin, I might add. Apologies, Henry."

Henry gave a little nod.

Ella shifted. "Henry was run down by a carriage and placed in his cousin's grave, seemingly without a single investigation by the crown. And while we are on the subject, why are you the one protecting Harold instead the king's guard?"

"I can't tell you that."

"Can't?"

"Won't. It's nothing that will help you find your documents, in any case. If Harold decides to meet with you and risk placing himself at further risk, that's his decision, but as far as I'm concerned, any business between Harold and me remains outside the scope of my bargain with you."

Ella sat heavily onto the lid of her trunk. "And what could I, a mere maid at a fashionable inn, possibly be able to do for a prince?"

He shifted on the tiny stool. "My valet."

"The dead one?"

He stared at her.

Ella stood. "You can't just bring people back."

The prince graciously did not look at Henry. Or Magnus. Or Fritz or Cybil. Saints, she really needed to stop bringing people back.

He said, "*I* can't bring them back."

But Ella could. She gestured toward the detached foot on the floor. "It doesn't really work that well, does it?" To Henry, she said, "Sorry, Henry."

Henry gave another nod.

"I don't need him to return for good. I'm not asking to keep the man so he might press my coat. I just want... I just need more time. One more hour. A few minutes. I didn't get to..."

Prince Silas shook his head. "I understand that you cannot undo what's been done, that his fate has been decided. I only need a chance to speak with him again."

A hollow feeling spread through Ella. And even though she had no intention of resurrecting the man, the desperation in Silas's tone was unsparing. "He truly means that much to you?"

"I cannot explain how important this is." His eyes, still red-rimmed from crying, or perhaps the wash-water, met hers. "You are the only one who can help. I need you, Miss Morgrave."

Fingers twisting into knots along with her nerves, Ella paced the small space, trying to sort out a way to convince him she could not do it without revealing why. It was not lost on her that the prince of the kingdom was in her bedroom, its shabby little bed on full display, the tattered curtain hanging over the single small round window, and a dead man sitting on an empty crate watching the entire scene play out. The fact was, Ella wasn't the only necromancer who could bring back his valet. She was simply the only one he believed he could convince to do it illegally, without the express approval of a High Cinder and beneath the nose of the king. Still, as much as Silas already knew, Ella could not tell him the truth. She could not tell *anyone* the truth. "It's not a good idea. You don't understand the risks, and I cannot in good conscience agree, nor in moral or legal obligation. I just can't."

"Well, you don't have a choice, do you?"

Ella froze in her pacing to stare at the prince.

He said, "You need to find Harold."

"It's not worth—"

"And if you don't do as I say," he interrupted, "then I'll be forced to report your activities. To my father."

## CHAPTER 5

Ella spent a shameful few minutes vigorously insulting the prince. Then a few more refusing to believe the truth: she was done for, blackmailed into doing something they would both regret by the man she'd only just kidnapped.

"Give it up, Miss Morgrave," he said finally. "You have no ground to stand on. You're clever enough to recognize how the matter stands. If you were not, you would not be so angry."

Silas was right. Ella had nothing. He had the ear of the king and pull in society. He had all the advantages that had allowed the Lockes to prevail, and more.

But Silas could bring her to Harold. With Harold's information, Ella could reverse not only her fortune but the Lockes' as well.

"Fine," she said. "But I keep your boots."

"My..." He blinked, then glanced down at his feet.

"You heard me. Give over your boots, or you can drag me to the palace right now to tell your father and all his courtiers what I've done. It will be interesting to hear your explanation when he asks how you encountered me, but I'm sure you've worked something out."

Silas eyed her for what felt like ages, both of them knowing Ella had no real choice. She was angry; she couldn't help it. Silas represented everything that had gone wrong. He was going to regret having ever made the bargain, and that made her angry too.

His dark hair had begun to dry in spiky clumps, and his extravagant wardrobe was in shambles. It did nothing to make him less appealing. Gaze on her, he reached down, tugging off one shiny black boot and then the other, settling each neatly on the uneven floor. The entire situation felt impossible, and she could not quite fathom how she had come to exist in such a state of affairs.

She crossed the space anyway, picked up the boots, and pointed Prince Silas, barefoot, toward the door. "Use the back stairs. I'm sure you can find your way to the stable."

Silas's expression spoke volumes. Mostly gothic fiction, if Ella had to guess. When he stepped over the threshold, he turned, his words a vow. "I will send for you soon."

Ella closed the door, knowing full well it could just as easily be a handful of guards who showed up to carry her to a cell. If not soon, then certainly after Silas realized what he'd agreed to.

"Good day, Miss Morgrave," he said through the wood.

Ella leaned against the door. Even should she find a way to back out, there would be no defense for what she had already done, particularly when the king didn't tolerate embarrassments. Not a great deal would be more embarrassing for the king than his drunken heir being captured from a horse stall mid-sob, carted away by his dead High Cinder's unseemly daughter and a tavern performer in a feathered mask. The idea made Ella feel a bit better, at least.

Truly, if Finley and his friends didn't take the ordeal to the stage, it would be a missed opportunity.

AFTER A SCANT FEW HOURS' sleep, Ella sat tightening the last bandage over Henry's shoulder. She gave it a gentle pat. "There. Hopefully that will last until we can work up something better. Remember, no singing or overloud activities. Be careful of even tripping if you can, anything the Spinster might hear. She has no goodwill for illegal goings-on under her roof, and I'm afraid she would not treat any of us kindly if you were discovered." No prince was going to save them, that was for certain. Ella did not want to even consider what would happen should one of her undead be caught, but she would have no allies in the matter.

Henry nodded. "Thank you, miss."

"Magnus will keep you company, and I've two books there by the bed."

Hair tied back in a tidy knot, Ella drew up the hood of her cloak. It was Sunday, so the inn was closed for breakfast, as every respectable member of society was attending service. And Ella, disreputable and debarred, would be ransacking her father's estate.

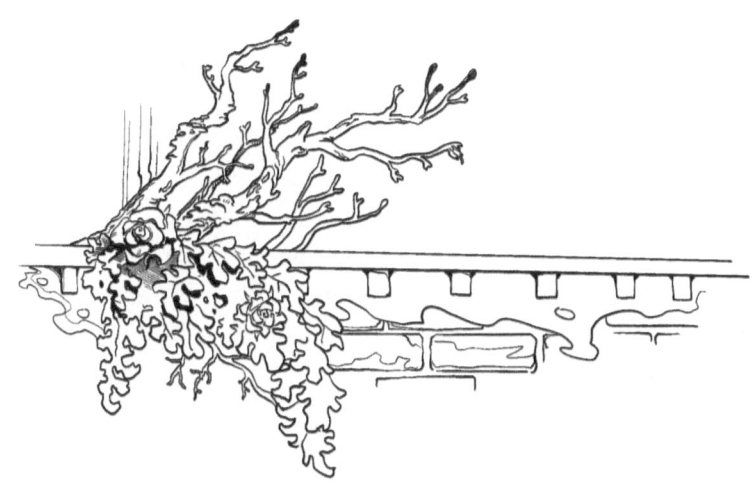

MORGRAVE HOUSE WAS a substantial three-story affair with deep-cut corner blocks and fashionable wrought-iron balconies over every window. Ella could not be certain which of the staff might be loyal to the Lockes, since most of the household had been tossed out along with Ella the moment her father was gone. So she approached the manor not from the road, but from the grounds behind the house, past her father's favorite garden—his affinity had not been for flora like Ella's, which had made her talent feel even more special. At least, it had before things had gone so wrong.

Ella used the thick vines, cut stone, and decorative railings to scale the wall and enter the level that housed the bedchambers. It was not easily done, but she managed with no more than a few scratches and a decent-sized tear in her skirt. She would have to remember to replenish her stock of thread.

Wedging a foot into the last rail, Ella leaned forward to peer into the window of her youngest stepsister's room. The awful hag had painted it blue. There were so many lovely shades of blue—celestial blue, imperial blue, arctic, and azure. Colors like the sky or the sea, even the forget-me-nots the queen favored for all her gowns. It was not one of those. It was repulsive. Worse, the new decorations were garish, trimmed in all the wrong shades of yellow and green, and discarded silks in the same sort of shades were scattered over the floor. They were not merely squandering her father's capital; they were going about it in the gaudiest ways possible.

Ella slid open the window latch. The only sounds came from deep within the house, so she climbed through and carefully crossed the room, only pausing to tip over a bottle of Lena's favorite perfume.

At the entrance, she listened until the halls were silent, then eased open the door to cross to her own bedroom.

The door was locked. Ella did not have the key, but she did possess a skeleton key that she had paid dearly for. Once inside, she drew a deep breath and leaned her back against the wall beside the closed door. It was terribly difficult to stand inside her father's house and not feel his absence like a weight on her very being. It was like drowning, like she could not draw enough breath beneath the burden of it. She missed him every moment, but there, in the places he had walked, she could nearly feel his hand in hers or hear his voice echoing through the corridor, and Ella could not find a safe place to lock the loss away. What they had done to him was monstrous.

To know her own room, the space she'd felt safest since she was a girl, was in possession of the people Ella hated most was a whole other torture—a torment she leaned into when she needed the rage to get something done. She thought very hard for a moment about what she was going to do to the Lockes once she had possession of the will.

Then Ella straightened, taking in the space with as much cold detachment as she could muster. Lady Locke had ordered the room boxed up the day Ella had been thrown out, but having no actual use for the space, the staff had left several crates and trunks stacked in a corner. Ella's personal effects were gone, all her beautiful gowns and jewelry rifled through by Lena and Lora before the rest were sold, but some of the furnishings and decorations remained. She crossed to the stack of crates, picking through the paintings and framed mirrors in search of one small enough to carry. Finding easily transportable items was becoming more difficult each time, and she wished she had brought a larger satchel or an extra belt. She found a novel she suspected Henry might enjoy but had to leave the ones on medicine and floriculture atop the stack to prevent a member of the staff noticing the pile had been disturbed.

She could not risk staying long, but as Ella turned for one last glance at the room, she was reminded that each time might be her last. It never became easier to walk away. She breathed, "I love you, Papa," then, holding her spoils against her body so they could not make a sound, returned to Lena's room. The space was still empty, the window still open, but from her place at the door, a pale silver strip of silk behind a crack in the wardrobe doors caught Ella's eye. She froze, a sick feeling settling in the pit of her gut. No part of her wanted it to be what she suspected it was.

As she crossed the space, her stomach sank impossibly further. She eased open the wardrobe door. Her mother's best gown, the one she'd worn to her last ball, was stuffed carelessly in with a half-dozen others, its shoulder torn. The sound that rose from Ella could not be helped. It was agony and grief and a vow rolled into one. She hated the Lockes for what they had done, but she hated even more that she had any hand in how things had turned out.

From down the hallway, sounds rose in return. Ella had been heard. She would be caught.

She momentarily lost the ability to care. She yanked the gown free, beads bouncing off the extravagant new rug to ping across the floor. Ella would rather tear the dress to shreds and set the house aflame than let a Locke touch anything that had belonged to her mother ever again. Fists clenched on the rich fabric, chest heaving, Ella felt the magic inside her becoming as volatile as her emotions. The footfalls in the hall were just outside the door.

Ella tried to take hold of her senses. Wadding the gown into a ball, she rushed toward the window. The wardrobe was open behind her, ribbons and lace trailing as she flung herself through the window and onto the balcony rail. Shouts rang out from the bedroom. If she made it off the property, she could not come back again. Morgrave House would be lost to her, just like everything else.

Halfway down the trellis, Ella jumped. Her boots landed in the soft green earth beneath the sitting room window as a footman at the edge of the house caught sight of her. The man had known her since she was a girl. He had not approved of his mistress's acts.

He had known too much to be sacked with the rest of the household.

The footman tipped his head toward the garden shed, giving Ella the moment she needed to hide. Despite her fierce desire to fight, the magic still wild and roiling within her and Lady Locke's treasured garden right there begging to be unleashed, Ella hunkered down just inside the shed. The lawn trembled beneath her magic. By the following day, even the winter roses would be in full bloom.

The footman shouted toward the front of the house that the intruder was running around the edge of the opposite walk, and the house staff followed his direction. When their voices grew distant, Ella slipped through the foliage and off the manor grounds for what would have to be the final time.

※

BY THE TIME Ella made it to the hazel tree at the farthest reaches of the estate, she'd begun to cry. Crying was a problem. Crying created new difficulties that she did not have the time or ability to solve, and not just the crushing pain in her chest. Grief was too strong; it triggered her magic. It was how everything had gone so horribly wrong in the first place. She wiped furiously at her face, willing the tears to stop.

"Oh, my darling," said the sweetest, kindest voice to ever exist.

Ella choked on a breath, hurriedly brushing her sleeve over her eyes and knocking hair loose to cover her cheek.

The voice cooed. "What is it, darling? What has gone wrong?"

"Nothing," Ella chirped. "It's only the chrysanthemums. You know how they make my nose water and I was just in the garden..."

Ella's words trailed off as a gentle hand pressed to the side of her face, and she had to swallow down a new wave of misery. "Hello, Mama."

"And what is this?" she asked.

Though Ella could not lift her gaze, she was sure her mother had seen the torn dress tucked beneath her cloak.

"We decided you would not go back there, my darling girl. What has made you so unhappy that you continue to return?"

Ella hiccupped in a breath. She hadn't been a girl in a long time, but in the presence of her mother, the grief-stricken youth she had once been was all that was left. She felt hollowed out. "I've done something bad."

The hand on Ella's cheek shifted, lifting her chin.

Ella stared up at the face of a woman dead these six long years. She was still beautiful, somehow, at least in Ella's eyes, but Ella knew, soul deep, that her mother was so very tired. She was tied to a world that would not let her go, and it made Ella sick. Ella said, "It wasn't an accident, the bad thing. I thought if only I could find father's scribe, then I could fix this."

"Oh, Ella." She ran a thumb over Ella's cheek, wiping away the last of the tears.

Then she placed the salt-stained thumb to her pale lips, tasting, and Ella had to look away. "I can't put them back. I try and I try." Ella withdrew the wadded gown from inside her cloak, laying it over the bench to smooth the wrinkles. "And he was not even the scribe. He was a tinsmith in Harold's clothing." Now he was stuck with her, the same as the rest, and Ella was no closer to finding the will.

Her mother clicked her tongue. It was a dry, wrong sort of sound that filled Ella with remorse. "You must let this go, Ellenora. Your father is gone. It is time for you to move on. And when you do, perhaps we will move on with you."

The hollow feeling inside Ella only grew. She could not let it go. She had done too much too wrong, to the point she could no longer see a way out. She meant to stop the Lockes. To fulfill her father's last wish. Set things to rights. But she'd only gotten herself tangled in a bargain with the prince and would have to do it all again, to drag back his poor valet.

Ella sat on the bench, folding the gown into place as precisely as possible.

Her mother settled beside her, brushing a loose lock of Ella's hair back toward its knot with pale, fragile fingers. The leaves of the hazel tree rustled. Time seemed to be a thing made of dandelion fluff, a pappus on the breeze, and Ella's chest eased.

She glanced down at the circle to be certain she had not accidentally crossed. Twine and tethers to keep the dead in. Hazel wood to keep Ella out.

Her mother said, "Tell me about your friends at the inn. How is Grace? Has her mother found a position at a bakery yet? Has she perfected her gingerbread? And what of Finley? Does his sister send news from her travels?"

Grace was too thin because she insisted on giving half her meals to the family who lived in the alleyway behind the boarding house, her mother had not gained a new position anywhere, including any of the worst kitchens, and Finley had to keep sending his sister money because she'd trusted the wrong sort of man. Ella worried for them all. But she did not want to bring more troubles to her mother. She shifted to face her, taking her hands. "I will put things to rights, Mama. I promise. I just need more time."

Her mother squeezed Ella's hands, then her cloudy eyes trailed upward, toward the branches of the hazel tree that had grown twice the natural size. Desperation had given it life, and that life refused to recede. "I wish your father were here. And not merely to avoid this mess with the king." She was still for an eternity before her gaze came back to Ella's. "We should have told him. You should not be forced to bear this alone now."

Ella's voice was soft. "You know he could never have let you go."

Ella's mother smiled the saddest smile. "Perhaps, my girl,

letting go is just the thing." She stood, seeming drained from lingering too long from the tree. "I wish I could moor you with a touch, the way he always did. But I cannot. It is up to you to find something in the here and now to hold you."

## CHAPTER 6

The letter arrived early the next week, handed to Ella by the Spinster herself. Formidable, forty, and flinty to the core, the Spinster had no time for fools. In a crisp apron and a serviceable gown, her dark hair drawn up in a sleek knot, she stared Ella down. "What sort of mess are you in that a king's messenger is bringing fine-papered notes about?"

Ella dipped her head, resisting the urge to snatch the bright white paper from the Spinster's hand. "No mess, my lady. It's just a favor from a relative who works in the palace."

The Spinster's gray eyes narrowed. "Do you think old women are fools?"

Ella stood patiently, despite that her arms were loaded with three heavy baskets she'd been taking to the kitchens. "I think no women are fools, my lady. Just misled, sometimes, or perhaps under-read. Besides, I'm not certain what *old* has to do with you."

The Spinster snorted. "Old has nothing to do with years; it has to do with having lived." She held forward the letter. "I'd best not find you've been lying to me, Ellenora."

Ella glanced at the parchment, the burden she carried, then at the Spinster. The Spinster did not offer aid. Placing the baskets on the ground one by one, Ella emptied her hands, then reached forward, half-afraid the parchment would be snatched away at the last moment, half-afraid it would not and she'd open it only to find a summons.

As it was, neither happened. The note simply said, "Be ready at half eight."

Ella was ready at half eight, which had required trading a good deal of her chores among three different inn employees. She sat in the growing darkness outside the inn until half past nine. When the prince finally arrived, Ella was well on her way to annoyed. "You're late."

The prince did not respond, instead staring down at Henry's feet where he stood beside Ella.

Henry did a little bow in greeting. "Highness."

"Might as well call me Silas," said the prince.

Ella stood, then turned to Henry. "Go on up. Signal at the window so I know you've made it. Don't forget to lock the door."

He nodded. "Thank you, miss. Felt good to get some air."

She bit the inside of her lip, hating that she'd had to trap him inside, and watched as he disappeared into the shadows.

The prince sidled up to her. He was a fair bit taller than Ella, who was not especially short. He said, "Your tinsmith is wearing my boots."

"They are no longer your boots. You traded them for ill deeds." Ella's eyes stayed on the small round window at the top of the inn. "What did you think I meant to do with them?"

He studied the side of her face. "I don't know, sell them? Do you have any idea what craftsmanship like that costs?"

"I can't imagine," she said dryly. "But I'm certain the shopkeepers would know. And they would no doubt assume I had stolen them."

"No doubt," the prince repeated, even more dryly. His own face lifted toward the window. "What happens if they find him while we're gone?"

Henry flipped the curtain. Ella waved, then looked at the prince. "They would turn us both over to the king. The same as you."

In Silas's defense, he did attempt to hide his wince. But Ella knew exactly what she risked. She adjusted the hood of her cloak. "I think you should know, it doesn't always work the way it's meant to, even under the best of circumstances. It is both unwise and reckless to force me to try. We are likely to end up pilloried."

The prince bit the edge of his thumb.

She added, "Or worse." Because it would definitely be worse.

His blue eyes darted toward the rear of the tavern, then toward a few sketchy figures down the lane before coming back to Ella. "You're not backing out on me now, are you, Miss Morgrave?"

"I possess not only education but experience in the matter. You should take my warnings more seriously."

He sighed. "I'm told I should take a lot of things more seriously. Are you ready?"

"Where are we going?"

He appeared to ask the night sky for reprieve, but it only served to allow another view of his strong jaw and neck. Criminal, really, how attractive the man was. He said, "We are going to find Harold. Best we secure your paperwork before you go waking up any more dead."

"Oh," she said.

"What?"

"Well, I guess I didn't expect you to be astute."

He blinked. "What *did* you expect?"

"A profligate, mostly. Reckless and inconsiderate. A bit selfish and overindulgent."

He stared at her. "Finished or would you like to go another few rounds?"

She hummed. "I believe that's enough for now. Shall we go?"

The prince ran a palm over his face. "Let us, before I grow tempted to change my mind."

---

ELLA AND SILAS wound through the kingdom toward the river and a less tended area known for the more disreputable sorts of business. It was much closer to the inn than to the palace, and not just in regard to location. Each class welcomed their own and viewed the other with suspicion and disapproval, and while Ella had grown up on the fringe of high society, her position as Cinder meant far more for how she was treated by high society than it did by craftsmen and merchants. But Silas could only ever be a prince. It was well past nightfall, the streets lit by gaslamps beneath a cloud-covered sky and the alleyways pitched in shadow. Ella did not think he would drag her so far only to have her killed, but her remark about him being astute was beginning to feel optimistic.

"Do you suppose we should hire a carriage?"

He glanced back at her. "Are you tired, or are you frightened?"

"Merely sensible."

His teeth flashed in a grin. "You hide it well." When she did not return the smile, he gestured toward the end of the street. "It's just up the way. I like to be certain I'm not being followed."

"Who would be following you?" And how, she wondered, might it be related to his aiding Harold in hiding?

The prince did not answer, but as they approached the tall building he'd gestured toward, he walked closer to her side. The scent of bilge water and discarded fish hung in the heavy air, and the sounds of waterfront goings-on echoed off the block storefronts. Muffled voices, chaotic and boisterous, came from inside the building. A rich carriage rattled by, and Silas urged Ella farther from the street.

"You're not very good at evading questions," she said.

The prince paused to look down at her. "What do you mean? I've barely answered your questions at all."

Ella was forced to stop as well, because he'd paused right in front of her. "You're ignoring them. There's no skill in that."

His gaze tracked her face, as if searching for anything that might get them into trouble, though Ella was not the one who was recognizable. He reached up to tuck the edge of her hood closer to her face. "Why waste time misdirecting you? Perhaps I simply prefer efficiency."

"With respect, Highness, you've shown no real sign of it."

He tugged her closer. "Call me Silas. And don't start any fights you can't win."

"You haven't won."

He turned, grabbing hold of her hand, and drew her toward the door. "I would never assume as much. I meant once we're inside."

A man in a brown velvet tailcoat nodded at Silas before closing them into a modest entrance lit only by a pair of gaslamps. Down a narrow wood-paneled hall, the space opened into a gaming room, bright and loud and thick with smoke, people, and strong cologne. A tall pair of well-groomed men shouted a greeting, jostling into Silas and laughing at some joke Ella could not make out over the noise. It appeared she might be the least fashionably attired in the room. In the corner sat a man at a square piano, his upbeat tune barely audible across the lively gathering. The prince dragged Ella closer, one hand sliding over the small of her back, and led her through the crowd to a separate, smaller room. If he'd meant to practice any kind of covertness, he was doing an especially poor job of it. Half the crowd seemed to know him.

The door to the lounge closed behind them, shuttering the chaos of the game room and leaving only muffled noise and a handful of low conversations. The lights were dim, the paneling dark, and the furniture covered in a rich shade of red velvet. Silas directed Ella into one of the chairs while gesturing discreetly toward a server.

The prince slid into the chair beside Ella's, one elbow on the table as he leaned forward, casually scanning the room with his back toward the wall. A few dozen men sat scattered at various tables in close conversations, not seeming startled by the appearance of their prince, if they recognized him at all. A server placed two glasses of amber liquor on the table. Silas left the drinks untouched. Ella hadn't been the only woman in the establishment, but she was the only one wearing a heavy cloak.

She inched forward. "Is this a common haunt for you?"

"I've been here on occasion."

"What occasions, specifically?" She could not help but wonder whether the business with Harold was the first of its sort or if the prince was often involved in suspicious goings-on and palace intrigue. Perhaps it was a hobby of his, something to do when he grew bored with his usual entertainments. She dearly wished he wasn't so easy to look at. It was making it very difficult to stop.

"Why are you frowning?"

"I think you should tell me why we are here." Why, if Harold was in hiding, they'd gone to an establishment filled with witnesses. Why he cared so much about a scribe, and why it seemed everyone in the room was casting glances at them.

Silas watched her, then leaned very close as if he hadn't caught her words, his ear by her mouth. Like he meant to better hear. His skin was smooth, freshly shaved, his dark hair cut short in a clean line above his ear. He smelled like soap and a hint of something woodsy and warm. Several men across the room watched the exchange, meeting Ella's gaze over the prince's shoulder. Unprepared for the proximity, for the intense desire to draw in the scent and for so much of him all at once, and under the watchful gaze of some sort of society, high or otherwise, she wasn't sure, Ella found her words caught in her throat. Silas's face —the face that belonged not to a boy she'd once met but a grown man and a royal—tipped toward her, eyebrows drawn in confusion.

He was inches away. Warmth rose up Ella's neck, and she reached to tug the laces of her cloak free, but his hand covered hers, preventing her from removing even the hood. He did not move away. In fact, his other arm slid across the back of her chair, bringing him closer.

His voice was low, his eyes on hers. "You traverse graveyards in the night, kidnap men twice your size, and spend your days working inside a crowded inn but find a gaming den uncomfortable?"

"I do not traverse graveyards."

His gaze did not waver.

"You are not twice my size."

One of his dark eyebrows lifted.

She sighed. "I am not uncomfortable. It is only that the air is close and this cloak is warm."

He picked up one of the drinks and brought it toward her cheek. "Place this against your skin."

She took it from his hands, their fingers tangling overtop the cool glass. She would not let him toy with her like some nameless courtier, in front of strangers or not. "Why are you like this?"

His lips parted in a surprised laugh. "Like what? Kind? Thoughtful?"

"Presumptuous."

"Well, Miss Morgrave, if that isn't a fine bit of hypocrisy, coming from you." His voice was a low rumble that did nothing to cool Ella down. "Do you know what I think, Miss Morgrave? I think you're so prickly because you cannot tolerate the way you're drawn to me."

She scoffed. "Drawn to you? We've been in each other's presence only a matter of hours, everything considered. I barely know you."

"Don't you?" There was a new, playful hint to his tone. "It

seems you've made a great deal of judgment. I am feeling very known."

She did not like the practiced way his words rolled from his tongue, then was annoyed that she would even care. "I am not prickly."

He bit the edge of his lip. "A veritable hedgehog."

"If you're trying to win someone over, pointing out that they are spiny and solitary may not be the best tactic."

His attention slid down to where her fingers held the glass perilously close to her overheated neck, his lashes lowering before his gaze lifted again to hers. "Oh, I don't need to win you over. Only to wait you out."

Ella's face reddened.

Silas's grin widened.

Just before she could tell him precisely where she rated his character and precisely where she meant to jab her quills, the door to the gaming room swung open.

A stout man in a dark suit stepped in, his bright eyes scanning the room before landing on the prince. Silas sat up. The man made the sign widely known as a warning that the king's guard was near, and Silas was on his feet, a firm grip on Ella's elbow taking her with him.

The drink splashed over the rim of the glass, and Ella barely settled it on the table before he was dragging her from the room. They did not leave the way they'd come in, instead rushing through a back entrance and down a dark and narrow passage. Silas opened a tall door, pressing Ella in first, then closed it behind them. The room smelled of tobacco and parchment.

Silas crossed the dark space then peered out a window onto the street. "Change of plans," he said.

"There was a plan?"

He turned to her. "Tell me you can run."

"Where is Harold?" Ella hissed, mostly to the back of the prince's neck as he fought with the window latch.

Shouts rose from another part of the building, and Silas cursed, then shouldered hard into the window, knocking the sash loose. It swung open, and he climbed onto the sill and held a hand toward Ella.

She took it, fool that she was, and climbed past him through the frame before leaping down from a rather dangerous height. Flaking paint snagged her cloak, paving stones caught her feet, and Silas landed behind her, grabbing her elbow again as he towed her toward the street. He whistled, the sound loud and sharp, and an answering chirp came from the opposite alley. Dragged again—he really did not have the manners of a gentleman—Ella lifted her skirts to keep from tripping in their run. At the entrance to the alley, Silas hoisted her into a nondescript carriage and shoved in after.

With a snap and clatter, the carriage jolted into motion, fast enough to toss Ella into the wall. She grasped hold of the strap. "How much danger are we currently in?"

Silas did not look away from the window. "Less than if you get caught waking the dead. Possibly more embarrassing for you, given you'd be caught with a profligate prince and tavern bards would sing our shame. Personally, I wouldn't mind if they sang about something a bit closer to the truth for once."

"What about Harold?"

The prince slid back into the narrow seat, his thigh pressed against her skirts. He glanced out the window near Ella's grip on the strap, then out the rear window. "He was supposed to meet us about a quarter hour ago. He was to send a signal for us to find him in a private room at the gaming den. There were two men in the lounge who appeared familiar—the pair who insisted on leering at you. I'm not certain who they are, but I've seen them lingering about at other meeting locations. I suspect their presence scared him off."

An unpleasant sensation swam through Ella's gut. Silas had

known they might have been in danger, and instead of warning her, he'd put on a show. "What about the king's men? Were they there to find you or to find him?"

He blew out a breath. "I'm not certain."

"Who wants Harold dead?"

"I'm not certain."

"But you at least suspect someone. Elsewise you'd never have been going to so much trouble in order to secretly meet with him for the past weeks."

He looked at her.

"Henry," she explained.

He ran a hand over his face. "And they say the dead will keep your secrets."

"Necromancers don't say that." After no more than a sound of agreement as his reply, Ella pressed, "Who do you suspect?"

"I don't know, Miss Morgrave. Perhaps it is you."

"Me?"

He turned to face her, his body pressing harder against hers as the carriage kept its speed. "No one is looking for Harold more enthusiastically than you."

"Because I need information. Not because I want him dead."

His eyes stayed on her, relentless in their judgment.

"You believe someone wants him gone because he knows something. And that we, this person and I, cannot just happen to be searching for a scribe *who handles a great deal of text regarding investigations* at the same time?" She turned her face toward the front of the carriage. It was dark, only flickers from the occasional streetlamp passing through the close space. It was not the rich conveyance of a royal; it was one meant to go unrecognized. Also, it smelled a bit like roasted walnuts. "I've bad news for your theory, Highness. I've been trying to reach my father's scribe for months. Whatever he's witnessed in the time since my father's death, I could not say." Because aside from her single attempt to persuade the king, or perhaps because of it, Ella had not been allowed access to the palace.

"Silas."

She glanced at him. "What?"

"I asked you to call me Silas."

"I hardly think—"

He leaned nearer. "Do you argue with everyone at this rate or are you simply put off by princes?"

"I've not encountered any other princes to determine a rule on the matter."

"Well." He settled back against the seat once more. "I suppose we shall never know, as I'm not about to introduce you to any."

The carriage traveled a maze of darkened streets in the opposite direction from which they'd come.

"How did you find Harold?" Ella asked.

His mouth went tight, and Ella suspected he would not answer. Then he said, "Pembrook."

Ella nodded, swallowing down emotion at the mention of a fellow necromancer, not because she was especially fond of Lord Pembrook—and saints knew he would never have helped Ella locate the scribe—but because it dredged up memories of her father.

After a time, she asked, "What do you miss about him most?"

In the dim flash of a passing gaslamp, the prince's face turned toward her. "Who?"

"Your valet. What is it that you feel the loss of most keenly?"

He shifted, adjusting the hem of his jacket. "I suppose our talks. He knew a great many things about a great many subjects. He was quick-witted, honest to a fault, and an excellent advisor. I was proud to call him my friend."

Ella turned to stare out the night-darkened window, throat tight. She knew many in the king's employ had not treated his son kindly. In the palace, among courtiers, trust was hard to find. "I'm sorry that was taken from you."

"And what of you?" he asked after a moment, then almost

immediately followed with, "Forgive me, I should not have asked. Not when so much else was taken with him."

"His hands." The remark was made without hesitation, and the prince's attention on Ella was so intense that she could feel it, even in the darkness. "He was a very busy man, always absorbed in his work, but he had strong, sure hands. When we toiled side by side, or when I was younger, when mother was alive and we played, he never hesitated to place a reassuring pat on my shoulder. To guide me when I was struggling, to offer solace, his touch was always there. Anytime I was sad, he laid his hand over mine, and it helped." Her shoulder lifted in a tiny shrug. "There was so much comfort in it. I never expected that was what I would miss most, but the loss of it is something I feel at every turn. It was different with my mother, but... There is a hollowness in me, an emptiness where their very existence used to be present."

The prince was quiet as the carriage rattled on, finally making its way in the direction of the inn. His own hand rested on his thigh, very close to Ella's hands in her lap, the length of their legs touching in the narrow seat.

In the darkness, Silas's fingers moved to curl over hers, then he settled their hands together without a glance or word.

Ella tried not to think about life before her father's death, when she'd lived at the palace, learning the craft under his guidance alongside the others, the way Pembrook and the older lords had dismissed her despite her greater skill. She worked very hard not to let the scenes replay in her mind of Lord Locke specifically, how he had introduced the widowed Emeri to his sister, and, when that hadn't worked, had maneuvered and manipulated the king to pressure a match. She could no more touch the memories of what had been done to her father, and of what she had done herself, than she could hold her palm on a hob. Her throat thick with rage and guilt, Ella tried not to think at all, just focused on the weight of the prince's hand in hers.

It felt like a long while before Silas let go and cleared his throat. "Well, it seems you've destroyed my speculation regarding Harold, we've missed our chance to meet with him tonight, and neither of us is a bit closer to getting what we want."

As the carriage slowed a few streets from the inn, Ella asked, "So, what is next?"

He met her gaze. "I will send a message for Harold so I can discover when we might attempt a new meet. Meanwhile, we will arrange for you to wake my valet."

## CHAPTER 7

Ella was dropped from the unmarked carriage two blocks from the inn and given detailed instructions from the prince on how not to be followed. It was not advice she took terribly seriously, given that the advisor in question had just gotten them chased by kingdom guards. She was not overly concerned with being followed by the king's guard in any case, because if the king had wanted Ella, Lady Locke would have told him exactly where to look. It did not mean Ella had no concerns at all.

Time felt as if it was slipping away, and the prince's confirmation that his father meant to name a new High Cinder by the end of the month had not helped. Of course, Ella had known it was coming. The king would have business in which he would need the services of her kind. And she had known the king would lie, would replace his Cinder with whomever he deemed fit, despite that her father had trained the other Cinders and had chosen Ella over them all. There was a reason he'd expressly written it all out in his will.

It had not been because she was his daughter, nor was it simply out of love. In fact, if Ella's father had loved her more, he might have never recommended her for the post.

It did not bode well that the prince had heard rumor of a witch practicing necromancy near the taverns and inns, but not much could be done about rumors without spreading worse ones herself. Tempting as it was to start a bit of hearsay about the king's son, it would only bring more attention their way. Because, somehow, Ella and the prince had become a *they*. If Ella's younger self could see her grown self, she would dunk her in a bucket of cold water and common sense.

As Ella approached the rear entrance to the inn, Cybil and Fritz shot into Ella's path, chattering wildly and waving their arms. She crouched nearer to make out their gestures in the dark, terrified because she had left Henry and Magnus alone. "What is it?"

Motioning her to follow, the mice darted through the shadowed alley, bounding over crates and around buckets to lead her toward the back of the tavern. Cybil turned, coming up on her hind quarters to hold a mousy digit to her snout in a shushing motion, then leapt onto a wooden block before climbing the distance to a stack of crates below the window.

Ella leaned against the wall, listening for conversation inside.

"... this is the third time he hasn't shown. I cannot keep him on if he's not reliable. We need entertainment, or the crowd will turn rowdy."

It was the Spinster's voice, in a distant discussion with the man who helped manage the bar. Ella could not quite make out the man's response, but the Spinster said, "No. Book the entertainer from the north side. That tall one with the tights and the balancing acts. What's his name? Rory?"

Ella's stomach dropped. She shifted closer, trying to peer through the shutters into the room. Through the cloudy glass, she could only make out the forms of two people as they crossed into the storeroom, their conversation apparently at an end. Ella squatted beside Cybil. "Where is he?"

Cybil squeaked anxiously, gesturing in the direction of the shed where Finley usually slept while explaining that he had not been there recently. Fritz tugged on Ella's cloak. She lifted the mice toward the window, and Fritz ran inside.

"I'll find Grace," Ella said. "Maybe she'll know."

Cybil nodded then jumped onto the ledge.

Ella tugged her hood up once more, making her way toward the boarding house where Grace lived with her mother, two younger sisters, and a strict curfew. The tall brick building was in need of repair as badly as the streets around it, its door worn smooth near both knocker and lever. The footman immediately turned Ella away, and without a single coin to bribe the man, she stood in the shadows outside the building, staring up at the darkened window of Grace's room. Ella did not want to get her friend into trouble; they'd all had a hard enough time finding places to stay. But she was not certain how else to discover what had happened to Finley and if he understood he was about to be replaced. If he was safe.

"I told you to go home," a voice said into Ella's ear.

She shrieked, spinning to strike the assailant who'd crept up on her. He caught her hand inches from his face, his grip impossibly strong, and held very still as her racing heart caught its pace.

Ella stared, baffled, at the prince, whose carriage was nowhere in sight. "Are you following me after you just warned me not to be followed?"

His gaze flicked toward the darkened windows of the boarding house. "What are you doing here?"

She jerked her fist from his hand. "Looking for a friend."

"It's the middle of the night."

"What business is it of yours?"

"You've made it my business, Miss Morgrave. We had a deal."

She stepped nearer, considering giving the punch another whirl. "Don't you have somewhere to be? Great *prince things* to handle?"

"Ellenora?"

The hushed voice floated from the window three stories up.

Ella cursed, spinning and shoving the prince deeper into the shadows before taking a step toward the scant light. "Grace, it's me."

"What are you doing?" her friend hissed.

Ella winced. Her business was about to become the prince's, whether she liked it or not. "Finn missed his show."

In the dim moonlight, Grace's hand came up to cover her mouth. The slender form of one of her sisters stole into the space beside her, only to be elbowed back.

"You don't know where he is?"

"No." Grace tucked her dark hair behind her ear, leaning farther out the window. "Haven't seen him since this morning. He mentioned planning to add a shift, nothing about ducking out. Do you want me to get my coat and come help look?"

Ella waved away the offer. "You need rest before your own shift. I'm sure it's fine. He'll turn up." It was too late to save his position at the inn in any case, as the Spinster was bound to replace him. Finn would have to find new work, likely at an establishment nowhere near the inn. Ella felt sick. "Goodnight, love. Sorry I woke you."

"You're right; he will turn up. Go home." Grace blew a kiss then drew the window closed.

Then Grace's sister pressed her face and palms against the glass dramatically and Ella made the most ridiculous and gruesome expression she could manage in return. The girl fell back from the window for a moment, likely in a fit of giggles.

Ella gave her a playful wave then turned and bumped hard into the prince. She jerked back, swatting at his chest. "Stop doing that."

"Finley is missing?"

"Finley is none of your concern." Finley was going to be very angry that Ella had let the prince learn his name if said prince ever connected that Finley was the masked man who'd helped drag him to the inn.

Prince Silas peered down at her. "Why are *you* like this?"

"Normal? Maybe because I'm not used to getting everything I want and because I respect other people's personal space." She brushed past him.

He followed. "Miss Morgrave." When she did not stop, he grabbed her elbow, which spun her around. "Ella."

Her gaze narrowed.

He let go. "I need to know that you're safe." He took a step back, shaking his head. "If your friend has gone missing, then you should not return to the inn."

Ella crossed her arms. "You do realize people leave all the time? Perhaps not in your circles, but here, it's a hard life. They have to make do however they can."

"He's left like this before?"

"No, but he's a grown man. Perhaps he had a chance at a better opportunity. For all we know, he's off performing for the king at one of those fancy society balls you're so fond of." Or, more likely, he had once again gone to rescue his sister from the man who refused to leave her alone.

All emotion seemed to drain from Silas's face.

Ella shook her head. "I have to go, Highness. It's hours before cockcrow, and some of us must labor for our living."

The heels of her worn shoes padded against the paving stones as she strode in the direction of the inn. At her back, the prince said, "Call me Silas."

Ella drew her cloak tighter.

---

TWO DAYS LATER, another message arrived. Finley had not returned, and with each day, Grace and Ella grew both more concerned and more convinced he'd gone to save his sister again, but in his absence, they'd taken up his inn chores, and that left little time to inquire past the locations of his usual pursuits. Though Ella had sent word to every inn and tavern she could think of, it was clear the note she received was from none of them.

Ella was tired, her nails, black from the fire, and fingers, red from the wash, pressed against the fine white paper. Basket leaned against her hip, she tore the sealed fold open with a thumb. *Tonight. Half eight. Dress accordingly.*

She muttered *accordingly* and resisted the urge to toss the note into the hearth. Good paper was scarce, and, unable to return to Morgrave House, she wasn't certain she could source more, so she tucked it into the pocket of her apron.

At half nine, Ella settled on a step out back of the inn in borrowed boots, listening to the horses nicker and sigh in the stable and George coo in the eaves. A band of travelers had come, overfilling the rooms, and their groom was already snoring soundly where he'd opted to sleep in the stall. From the sound of things, the rest of the group were drinking loudly in the tavern.

The prince arrived at ten.

Ella looked up at him. "Are you ever on time?"

"Perhaps you underestimate how complicated it is for a prince to escape."

"Past *your* guards? I doubt it." She lifted an eyebrow. "Besides, would they not think you were merely out carousing?"

The breath he released was long-suffering. "Are you ready or would you like to quarrel for a bit longer?"

Ella stood, brushing off the rear of her simple wool dress. "I've been ready. That was my point. Where are we off to tonight?"

He took a step backward, ducking under a low beam. "How are your riding skills?"

Ella had not ridden since witnessing a horrible accident in which a necromancer in training had brought back a horse and was dragged screaming over a steep ridge. She sometimes still woke in the night with the sound echoing in her ears, her heart pounding, shift soaked with sweat. She said, "Perfectly acceptable."

Two fine black geldings waited tied in front of an establishment a block away from the inn, out of sight of the few men lingering street-side near the tavern. Considering Silas had been chased earlier in the week, it was unlikely that he was suffering from delusions that he was being followed, but a prince was surely too recognizable for his schemes to do much good. Ella pinned her skirt, and he handed her up onto one of the horses. His palm lingered for a moment over her leg, where surely he could feel that beneath the layers of fabric Ella's muscles trembled. His gaze rose to hers. Ella stared back. The gelding did not dance beneath her, not even a single step, though it was clear the animal had ample energy. Fingers curled tightly over the reins, she nudged the beast forward.

The prince adjusted the sword at his hip and climbed atop his own mount. They rode in silence past the shops, north toward the palace on a less traveled route, far from the elegant row houses or sprawling estates where a royal might be recognized. The parks and squares would not be deserted during the season, despite the late hour, but few were out on the lanes Silas chose.

A great wall surrounded the palace, and as they mirrored its winding path from a good distance away, the prince threw more covert glances over the surrounding properties than an unconcerned man might. Eventually he led them into a copse of trees, stopping to tie the horses in the center where it opened to the night sky.

"Is this a park?" Ella stood too close to the prince, but she could not seem to help it, given that he was the only thing she might place between herself and the beasts. Her skirt smelled like horse, her palms like leather. Previously she'd had to crawl through a window. She was going to have to start wearing gloves and an apron on her outings with the prince. And possibly carry a weapon.

"It belongs to an elderly lord who is in the country for the season. He uses it to hunt, I believe."

"And why are we here?"

The prince tipped his head toward an ancient stone building near the palace wall. "We need to slip unnoticed into there."

It was a tomb, the stones carved with skeletons and palm fronds and deep-etched letters. Ella's voice dipped. "How many bodies are inside?"

"I—" He turned to look at her. "Will you be able to wake just the one?"

She stared back at him. "Do you honestly not understand how any of this works? Yet still plan to go through with it? Despite my warnings?"

His lips pressed tight. "Yes. All of those."

"You should change your mind."

"Perhaps, but I won't."

Ella should change her mind as well. She said, "If you turn me in to the king for refusing, you would have no one to wake your dead."

His head tilted meaningfully; they both knew he'd soon have whoever the king appointed in her father's place, or any necromancer to whom the new High Cinder granted license to practice. But he only said, "Come."

Glancing far too often at the road and the trees, Silas led Ella into the tomb. The door closed, shutting them in darkness broken only by sparse moonlight through the vents. The prince lit several lamps, and Ella moved through the space, her finger tracing over the names carved in stone. "Is this his family?"

"Yes. Blackthorn was with me since I was a boy. His father was gifted lands in service to the king, but Blackthorn wasn't ready to retire. He stayed on, my advisor and confidant, often acting on my behalf when the restrictions of my title tied my hands, and then..."

And then he was dead. Ella pressed furiously down on the memory of the emotion she'd heard in the prince's voice in the carriage only nights before. She had a job to do, and emotion had no place near it. "When did it happen?"

"Two days before I found you."

Ella turned to argue that she had, in fact, found him, but he was so close behind her that her shoulder bumped against his chest before she'd made a full turn. "Must you always stand so near?"

He studied her face for a long moment. "Evidently."

Ella took Fritz and Cybil from her satchel and the prince did step back—in alarm.

"You brought *the mice*? The *dead* mice? To a resurrection."

Fritz presented Silas with a gesture that was universally offensive.

Silas blinked.

Ella curved her palm around Fritz, giving him a warning glance as she set the pair on the ground. She reached back into her bag to retrieve the hazel tree branch, then handed it over. The mice held it reverently at each end.

"Is this—" The prince's gaze traveled from the mice to the twine Ella was pulling from the satchel. He ran a hand over his chest. "There's no need for a show. I am not my father."

Ella froze.

"You are welcome to use your"—his hand rolled ineffectively as he finished—"natural ability."

"Natural ability?" Her fingers closed around the twine into a fist. She placed the fist on her hip so as not to be tempted to swing it at him. "That is the problem with people like you. You have no idea how many years it takes to develop a skill. You think everything is put on just for you, that craftsmen are performing a task anyone with the right tools could manage— that the magic just hops into us fully formed and suddenly we are the most brilliant at whatever task the king assigns, that we do not have to choose a trade and work and work and work to develop our craft. Do you have any idea how long a body has to be *bad* at something before they can be great at it? No, I suspect not. Because you wouldn't know about proficiency, would you?

What's a prince to learn but to shout at someone else until you get your way?"

"I don't have to shout. Getting my way without shouting is one of my most highly honed skills."

She glared at him.

He flicked one of his fancy jacket buttons. "The truth is, I generally pay someone proficient to do what I cannot. It is the most efficient and effective method to get things done well, particularly for one as myself who cannot possibly know *everything*. And, though I've admitted to knowing nearly nothing of your profession, often those I hire do put on a show for me as part of the bargain." He stepped forward, studying her again. "Yet, somehow, I am not finding your services to feel like much of a bargain."

"Telling that you would need my services at all."

"That's a weighty charge when you yourself dug up a tinsmith just to ask him questions."

Ella slammed the satchel onto the vault. "Perhaps I would not have had to if your father were an honest man."

"He is not merely a man. He's a king. To govern means to make decisions, and the kingdom needs a High Cinder."

The sound that came out of Ella was embarrassing, but she did not call it back.

"I do not wish to fight with you, Ellenora."

She picked the satchel up again, wrapping it over her shoulder as if she might leave. She probably couldn't. She definitely should. She said, "I will remind you that I was blackmailed into doing this, that it remains a terrible idea, and that I have not given you leave to use my given name. Now, open the tomb."

He leaned forward. "I'll remind you that I'm used to getting my way."

His voice was low, challenging, and she narrowed her gaze, suddenly suspicious. "Is there some reason you're delaying?"

Silas straightened, stepped cautiously around the mice holding the branch, then unbuttoned his jacket before laying it over an ornate pillar. He slid the heavy lid aside to reveal the head and shoulders of the body inside the vault, and Ella came closer. The prince's valet had close-cut white hair and a thin face with high cheekbones. He was perhaps five and sixty and looked in a shape that ought to have had him happily living out his final decades. He was fresher than Henry had been by at least a few days, and Ella wondered exactly how he had died. Given the way the prince had wept for the man, mid-exhumation was likely not the best time to ask.

"Step back a bit," she told him. "I'll need to create a boundary to keep him safe."

Silas did as she asked, his attention on her so thoroughly that she suspected he must have been avoiding looking at the valet. They were just bodies until they were not. Until they were someone who had been loved.

Heartsick, Ella waited a moment before she began the song. Then, slowly, as she threaded the thin braided twine between her fingers, her voice grew stronger, ringing through the tomb, sounding sweeter inside the chamber than it ever could at a midnight grave doused in rain. The prince appeared mesmerized, as still as the surrounding statues as she leaned over the corpse, smearing ash from the man's forehead to the base of his throat. She was not self-conscious, nor did she care what he thought of her work, because at this part, at least, Ella was a master.

Her voice rose, and Cybil and Fritz lifted the hazel branch. Ella took it, chanting the words that would draw the man back, whether it was wise or not. The tip of the branch traced through the dust on the stone, marking a circle around the rope. The circle closed. The warmth spread through her.

From his place outside the proceedings, the prince seemed to hold his breath, his shoulders rigid, fingers slack.

Ella forced her focus to remain on the body; she could not forget and become distracted. It was not wise to practice in front of anyone unfamiliar with the process; she could only hope that her audience did not attempt to interfere. The man's throat began to glow, then flare, the light tracing outward before fading once more. The prince stepped back.

Ella spoke the binding word.

The man sucked in a gasping breath. Silas lurched forward, and Ella's hand shot up to stop him. She said, "I need you to stand very, very still."

The body attempted to open its mouth. Ella reached over the circles with her branch, knocking his chin prop out of place. "Good evening, Mister Blackthorn."

Blackthorn's head turned on its stone pillow. His bright gaze slid toward Ella, then, slowly, took in his prince. To the prince, he said, "What in the name of the crown are you wearing?"

Ella looked sidelong at Silas in his waist coat and trousers.

He brushed a hand over the front of his waist coat. "We were digging up graves. I thought it was appropriate."

Blackthorn scoffed. His hands had been folded over his chest, his own suit pristine. He had, perhaps, not registered the bit about digging up graves.

"Mister Blackthorn," Ella said carefully. "Do you mind if we speak with you for a tick?"

"I'm at your service, miss. Though I fear we are late."

"Late?"

"For tea with the king."

Ella's grip tightened on the hazel branch.

The prince did not have the look of a man relieved that his valet had returned from the dead. "Blackthorn, we won't be having tea with the king."

"Tea with the king," Blackthorn said again. "We only need to..." He seemed to take in the ceiling of the tomb. "Has someone died, Highness?"

Ella cleared her throat carefully as Fritz climbed onto the lid of the tomb. "Do you remember what you did last, Mister Blackthorn? Before waking up here?"

"Tea with the king," Blackthorn said. "The same as every day."

Silas came closer, his boots stopping against the edge of the ring. "We do not have tea with the king, Blackthorn. You help me dress, advise me on the day's events, and in the evenings we play chess."

Blackthorn again gave the prince a once-over. "I would never have dressed you in that."

Silas stared at his valet for a very long time. The look he slid toward Ella asked, *what is wrong with him?*

Ella shook her head. "Blackthorn, please stay still for a moment. The prince and I need to speak privately, and I would not want you injured should you try to sit up. Can you do that for me?"

He gave what Ella took to be a nod of assent, and Fritz peered into the tomb as Ella and the prince stepped back.

Across the chamber, she whispered, "How did it happen? Was he hit on the head? A fever? Had he been sick and a physician gave him some sort of remedy just beforehand?"

"No. We found him in his bed. Lying just like that."

When Silas gestured toward the tomb, where the valet should have been lying in the standard burial repose, they both startled, because the tomb sat empty. Fritz, standing atop it, pointed toward the pillar, where Blackthorn was refolding the prince's jacket.

"Mustn't dally," Blackthorn said. "Tea with the king."

"How bad is this?" the prince asked low into Ella's ear.

"I'm not certain. But it has nothing to do with bringing him back. He had to have been like that before. Was there nothing strange? Something noted during the preservation process, perhaps?"

"No."

"You should speak with the undertaker."

"I can't just speak with the undertaker."

"*Now* you care about protocol?" She flung a hand toward the vault and the undead valet. Silas's jaw tightened, reminding Ella that everything he had done had not just been in secret; he was also trying to keep a man safe from pursuers. She said, "Well, I can't speak to the undertaker. I'm not even allowed in the palace."

Blackthorn perfected the collar of the jacket, seemingly untroubled by the argument, the mice, and the tomb.

Silas sighed, his breath shifting Ella's hair and tickling her neck. "Put him back. We'll wake him again when we can figure this out."

Ella felt suddenly sick. A muffled crack sounded from the hazel branch in her grip.

Silas's hand came to her waist. "Ellenora?"

She shook her head, then stepped away from him, crossing the chamber to the valet. "Mister Blackthorn, we need to talk."

BLACKTHORN HAD NOT GONE BACK to his tomb. In fact, Ella was not certain he ever would. Not because she'd asked him nicely and he'd refused, but because Ella could not get the resurrection process to reverse.

"You said you're a necromancer," the prince hissed.

"I am." She threw her hands skyward, the hazel wand pointing wildly. "He's back, isn't he?"

"We need him *back*. To the…" Silas gestured toward the vault and, possibly, the hereafter. "They're not supposed to be left like this. The resurrection procedure is minutes long, hours at most."

"This is not a palace investigation, Highness. There is no procedure. And I told you, it doesn't always go the way it should."

He stared at her for a painfully long time. "Is this why you've a tinsmith and half a dozen rodents living in your room?"

"Badgers are mammals. And lizards are reptiles."

"There's a lizard?" He pressed his fingers to the bridge of his nose and closed his eyes. When he looked at her again, it was with resolve. "How do we undo it?"

"I need my father's work. I told you that."

"You said you needed his title."

"Well, I lied. I *want* the property he left me because it's my home and because I need coin to do extravagant things such as eat. I *require* his title because I made him a promise and because I cannot practice legally without it unless the person your father appoints gives me license to do so, which is guaranteed to never happen given the potential candidates. And I am, quite frankly, *desperate* for his books. It is a problem, because I cannot operate properly without them and there are many concerns that need addressed in that regard. His life's work is recorded in a dozen journals, along with all my instructions, and I don't have access to any of it because your father won't let me have my father's possessions, despite that they remain, unquestionably, bequeathed to and meant for me alone. So. In summary, if I cannot locate my father's will, none of this"—she gestured toward the undead valet picking horsehair from the prince's neatly folded jacket while a pair of undead mice rummaged the tomb—"will ever be remedied."

Silas rocked back. "You knew this would happen, that he wouldn't go back. And you did it anyway?"

Ella's jaw clenched, and Cybil and Fritz abandoned their exploration, bounding across the space to climb her skirt, headed toward the satchel. "You left me no choice."

He gaped at her.

"Blackmail. Do you not remember? *Do this for me or I will turn you over to the king.*"

"Do you think I would have gone ahead with it? That I would have still wanted this if I had known?" His tone was incredulous.

"No," Ella said. "Likely not. You would have simply waited until your father named a new High Cinder. And any chance I had to find Harold would be gone. Which meant I truly did have only this as an option. You cannot fathom how badly I need those documents."

Silas cursed. "Oh, I'm beginning to fathom. I am fathoming to depths I have never fathomed before, Miss Morgrave." He tugged at the knot in his cravat. "What are we supposed to do with him now?"

"He's your valet," Ella said. "Take him home."

"I cannot keep a dead man in the palace!"

"Highness," Blackthorn chided. "A prince does not speak in such a tone."

Silas glared at Ella. "He's going home with you. He can stay in your room with Henry and the lizard and that minacious badger until we sort this out."

"I hardly think—" Ella started, before Blackthorn cut in with, "But we'll be late for tea."

The pained expression that crossed Silas's face was not one of grief. "Blackthorn, grab your things."

They were striding from the tomb and across the moonlit clearing toward the trees, Ella and the much taller but recently exhumed Blackthorn trying to keep up with the prince's furious pace, when a rather distant bird call sounded. They kept on toward the trees. The prince, still in his shirtsleeves, jacket folded precisely over his arm, told Ella, "Blackthorn will take your horse. You'll take mine."

"And you intend to walk? We're miles from the inn."

"I'm not certain what else you'd have me do, Miss Morgrave,

given that the saddles are built for one. I'll get you both safely back to the inn and then..." His words fell off as the bird call sounded again, this time nearer.

The prince's steps faltered, his ears perked toward the road. He must have heard something more, because he turned to Blackthorn, making a gesture only the valet seemed to understand.

"And then tea, after?" Blackthorn asked.

Silas winced. The moment they reached the opening in the copse, he took hold of Ella, as if to throw her on the horse. But before he lifted her, the crack of a branch came from within the surrounding trees. Too close. The prince whistled, Blackthorn kicked his mount to speed, and Silas grabbed Ella about the waist and dragged her onto the horse with him.

Cybil and Fritz were inside Ella's satchel. Stuck in front of the prince as he kicked the gelding into a run, she had no time to adjust. She wrapped her arms around Silas with the satchel between and clung to him for all she was worth. Trees rushed by, branches tugging at her hair and dress, and the prince leaned forward, his hand molded to her bottom the only thing keeping her from being bounced off to, if not her death, at least serious injury.

She chanced a look past the prince's shoulder but could only make out shapes moving in the distance. Men on horseback, possibly the king's guard, possibly not. A limb caught at her arm, another her shoulder, and Ella ducked away from the onslaught, burying her face into the prince's chest.

When they broke through the trees, Ella watched the shadowed woods for sign of pursuit, but no one appeared.

They had escaped, again. The prince kept on, cutting a jagged path toward the kingdom's center. It could not be a coincidence that he had also been pursued when they'd attempted to meet Harold, especially given that Henry had been buried in his cousin's clothes. Whoever wanted her father's scribe wanted him badly, and no one seemed to know how to find him save the prince.

Ella wondered if it was the only reason Silas was being hounded, or if there was something more.

They finally slowed, and Silas straightened, his posture loosening. Ella drew back, meeting his gaze from where she sat awkwardly in his lap. He was still holding her bottom; it couldn't be helped. It was not the first time Ella had been close to the prince, and he'd never had hold of her bottom before, but looking into his deep blue eyes, she could not help but recall the memory of their first encounter, despite having spent a great deal of time burying it. Silas was no longer that boy. And, unlike her, he would not have been plagued with thoughts of their meeting.

Silas would not remember.

"Miss Morgrave," he said softly. "You astound me."

"Oh?"

His gaze did not track the undead mouse making its way up her shoulder. "I can honestly say that, in all my years, I have never met anyone else like you."

Her fingers remained fisted into the material of his shirt. "Resourceful and full of pluck?"

The horse came to a stop, and the prince's hand slid slowly down the curve of her thigh, his gaze locked with hers and his fingers firm in their grip with only two thin layers of cloth between them. If he let go, she would surely fall. If he didn't, she might say something she would come to regret.

Instead, she tried, "Perhaps you should tell me why so many men are chasing you."

He said, "Perhaps they are chasing you."

"I am not so difficult to find, Highness."

"Silas," the prince said. He had not taken his eyes off her. Or his hands.

The mouse tugged a lock of Ella's hair. Then Blackthorn

cleared his throat, the sound very dry and very wrong, and all the melty feelings inside Ella went cold.

She'd done it again, woken a man and been unable to send him back. Ella slid from the horse, and though Silas did not seem eager to let her go, he stepped down beside her. Ella did not let the men see her face until she gathered her composure, instead adjusting her clothes and checking Cybil and Fritz were unharmed. When she climbed back onto the horse, it was facing the proper direction, the mice secure in her satchel.

Silas had resumed his jacket, his attention on her despite that he appeared busy with other tasks. He kept pace with the horses in their walk back to the inn, and, in the small hours, the group finally arrived. He had a private conversation with Blackthorn before he began to walk away without so much as a farewell.

"You're not worried about our safety here?" Ella called to his back.

The prince turned, his mouth shifting in a manner that made Ella suspect he was working up to a lie.

She crossed her arms. "Don't bother. I was only checking if those men watching from the corner are yours. I do hope they're more skilled than your usual guard."

He released a breath without even a glance at the dark-clothed figures in the shadow of the neighboring shop. "Good night, Miss Morgrave." He gave her a small bow, then tipped two fingers to his temple for his valet. "Rest well, Blackthorn. I shall return in a few days."

Blackthorn murmured, "But, tea..." and Ella took hold of his hand.

"What could possibly be more urgent than this?" she again called to the prince.

"Nothing," he answered. "Which is why I'll be busy handling what I can for the both of us. Perhaps you could practice patience while I'm gone."

## CHAPTER 8

Ella introduced Henry to the prince's valet, organized a makeshift cot for him in corner of her small room, and promised to find the pair some sort of cushions and a few diversions as soon as she was able. Magnus eyed their new lodger with distrust, starting around the third time Blackthorn reminded Ella they were late for tea.

Ella was left with about four hours of sleep before her work at the inn. The morning went terribly, overall, and it was not even a Tuesday. She wasn't in the best of tempers when she came out for a new bucket of wash-water and caught sight of the prince's guards lingering near the rear of the stable. Her eyes narrowed on the figures. One glanced up, then the pair shifted out of view. Ella picked up the hem of her skirt and strode through the stable to cut the men off at a side entrance. They startled, one stepping back, the other putting a palm to the hilt of his sword. They were not in the uniform of a guard, but their clothes were a bit too pristine to be convincing if they meant to portray locals.

"You," Ella said to the older one, who couldn't have been more than six and twenty. "What's your name?"

The man gave her a cold shoulder. "Clear off, miss. We've nothing for you."

"He already admitted why you're here." Ella took in the man's all-too-familiar copper hair. "I've seen you before. At the market."

He shrugged.

"You looked at me."

"That a crime? You're looking at me right now, and when I've already asked you nice-like to make off."

"Looking isn't a crime, no, but suppose the king doesn't know exactly what you're about loitering outside the Spinster's inn. Might that be, oh, I don't know, operating outside of his orders?" The second man shifted uneasily. The copper-haired one didn't even flinch. Ella stared up at him. "So how'd you end up here?"

His mouth twisted in a wry smile. "Keeping the wrong sort of friends, I guess."

"And what about him?" Ella tilted her chin toward the second, lankier man.

"He's just got a talent for standing around and holding his tongue." His gaze lifted toward the inn. "Best be getting back, miss."

Ella had no sooner crossed her arms than a voice shouted, "Ellenora!" out the back of the inn. The man flashed his teeth. Ella narrowed her gaze at him one last time for good measure before turning to go.

If Finley were there, he could discover precisely who the men were, their usual duties, and how close they were to the prince. She missed Finn dreadfully.

The duties that occupied most of Ella's days were carrying, scrubbing, and staying out of the way while also needing to be several places at once, so later that morning, when one of the servers shot from the front room to interrupt Ella at her task because a patron had requested her to serve, she was immediately uneasy. She placed the last piece of wood onto the fire, then stood, dusting off her hands.

Grace gave her a look. "Your stepmother has never been off schedule."

Ella hoped very much that it was not because she'd left evidence of her trespass into Morgrave House. "It certainly cannot be good, whatever she's here for. How do I look?"

Grace gestured toward her cheek. "Smudge of ash, straggly hair. Otherwise, like an overworked maid at an understaffed inn."

Ella gave a grateful grin, wiped the side of her face with a cloth, then dampened her palms to smooth back stray hairs as she bumped her bottom against the door to press into the main room. The late morning crowd was in full swing, chaotic laughter and chatter filling the room. It was festival season, and soon the kingdom would be buzzing with fresh gossip about what they'd seen at this event and that ball. Events Ella and her friends would not be invited to attend, except as labor, to serve or sell or entertain.

At a table by the far wall sat Lady Locke. Ella had never seen her stepmother out alone; she was always accompanied by a lady's maid at least.

"Ellenora," Lady Locke said when she approached. Her gaze trailed over Ella's soiled apron and scuffed shoes with a truly impressive display of disdain. "Honestly. Would it not be preferable to give up this farce and simply do as I ask?"

"You must know that it would not. Why are you here? Has something happened? Are Lena and Lora unwell?" Had Lady Locke's horrible brother fallen into a pit never to be seen again?

Lady Locke flicked a small piece of lint from the cloth covering the table, making Ella wait. "The girls are fine. I have left them to practice piano forte with their new tutor, the best in the kingdom, as a matter of fact. They could not come along, as I have private business this afternoon." Her light eyes rose to meet Ella's. "With the king."

The dread that sank in Ella's gut was far worse than being caught at Morgrave House, and the threads of the most grievous possible outcomes unspooled in a dozen directions at once in her mind. It could not land on one outcome, though the sharpest were that Ella was too late, that Lord Locke had already won. "What business could you possibly have with the king?"

Lady Locke's lips twisted in something of a smile. "That is certainly none of your concern, not as a scullery maid."

And yet she had made a point to be certain Ella knew it, had gone very much out of her way to do so. Ella bit down every single question that wanted to spill from her tongue. She asked, as coolly as she could manage, "You're here to eat, then?"

"Tea," Lady Locke said. "As I'm sure the king will offer me refreshments." She leaned forward, tapping a clean fingernail on the tabletop. "Our meeting is certain to last quite a while."

---

Lady Locke's threat settled heavily on Ella, the dread wanting to drag her down and the fear wanting to leap from her heart. All afternoon, she had to fight the intense desire to storm into the castle on her stepmother's heels and demand to see the king. But Ella had already tried that. King Julian would not hear her case unless she had proof.

And Lady Locke would not attempt to persuade the king of whatever she was about with threats. She would coax and flatter and lure. If a Locke was good at anything, it was pretending. After all, Lord Locke had convinced the king he was capable of the very magic King Julian most desired.

Surely Lady Locke only meant to request permanent ownership of the manor, had concocted some scheme that required a legal ruling, or forged new documentation. But any contact Lady Locke had with the king presented a danger to Ella. If the king and Lady Locke shared what they knew...

"Ellenora!" the Spinster shouted, and soon the time Ella

might have devoted to a plan was spent taking inventory of the cellar instead. It was difficult to plot an effective rebellion when one had root vegetables to tally.

Hours later, worry nagging her in regard to the king, and Finley, and the valet currently hiding in her room, Ella set the crate of pickled cabbage she was carrying on a wooden block to pop into the shed for a handful of dried peas. The dead did not eat, but they loved to chew, and Cybil and Fritz could not be trusted to grab a few peas on their own without causing some sort of disturbance. Cybil in particular possessed an anxious sort of restlessness and seemed to fare better when given a task, and sorting or peeling or counting did well.

When Ella reached for the satchel, a bit of color on the floor caught her eye. She opened the shed door wider to let in light, then leaned down to pick up a scrap of dark velvet. It appeared torn, the edges frayed in a violent pattern. It was far too fine to be discarded in a shed, and not a shade Finley had ever worn. Ella glanced through the space. Nothing seemed out of place, but she had an uneasy feeling about what the scrap of fabric might mean.

Ella crossed to the curtain, pulling it down for more light. She kicked through the straw where Finn slept, searching for a clue they might have missed. Before, they'd been looking for a full-grown man. Ella hadn't suspected anything nefarious—she'd been worried for his safety in an entirely different manner, even when the prince had told her that she should not return to the inn.

Ella froze in her shuffling of the straw at the sight of a scrap of paper. Bending down, she reached through the stalks to pick it up. Her stomach dropped before she even held it to the light, then she did, and she was running, through the inn, up the stairs, and to her attic room.

When she burst into the room, Henry and Blackthorn startled up from their game. "Miss," both said, watching as she rummaged through the stack of books to find one of the prince's notes.

She held one of his messages near the window to examine it, the scrap she'd found beside it.

The paper was identical.

Ella cursed.

Henry and Blackthorn came to stand behind her.

"Blackthorn, who uses the same writing paper as the prince? Is it shared among all courtiers or used exclusively by those of royal office?"

Blackthorn took the scrap of paper to inspect it. "It depends. I suppose a good deal of courtiers and staff might have access to it, given that the prince and his sort are surrounded by so many. Or one might reuse it. There are any number of reasons one might receive a message on such paper."

"Don't say *invitation to tea with the king*," Henry whispered.

"Invitations," Blackthorn said. "Such as to tea."

Henry leaned forward. Ella waited. When Blackthorn did not bring the statement to a conclusion with his usual refrain, Ella, Henry, and the badger released a breath.

"Miss Morgrave," Blackthorn said gravely. "I'm afraid we need to leave now or we'll be late."

Ella pressed her lips together.

He finished, "For tea with the king."

Ella patted his hand. "Very good, Blackthorn. Thank you for letting me know. I'm certain if you prepare, the prince will be here soon."

"Oh," Blackthorn said.

Ella froze at his tone. "What is it?"

"Well, it's only that the prince isn't invited." Voice dropping, Blackthorn explained, "The prince must never go."

Behind him, Magnus clucked at the ominous statement.

"To be sure," Henry breathed in agreement. "To be sure."

## CHAPTER 9

Ella spent two days trying to decide whether she should attempt sending a message to the prince to inform him of Blackthorn's warning or whether she should murder him for even the potential of his involvement in Finley's disappearance. She could not report the crime because she had no real proof that a crime had even been committed. Finn might simply have ducked out after a scuffle or gone into hiding like Harold. But the thought made Ella sick, because Harold was in real trouble. Henry had already been killed by someone pursuing the scribe. And Ella had been relegated to a scullery maid; it was not as if she could ask old palace associates for help. No kingdom official would get involved in the search for a missing tavern singer, even if there weren't a potential connection to the crown prince. But there was that potential.

Tempting as the idea of murder was, festival season had kicked off, and the inn had flooded with patrons excitedly chattering about the picnic and games on the green. Ella had no time for messages or murder. She had to hope that Finn would be all right. Besides that sending a message to anyone at the palace risked discovery by the king, more so to a prince whose mail would be scrutinized, Ella could not be certain who was truly behind Finn's disappearance. Only that it was someone with access to fine garments and finer paper, that perhaps he'd been taken against his will, and that evidently it had been done without anyone who knew him being aware, which did not seem a chance encounter by a tavern patron.

Awake before dawn to place clean wrap on Henry's shoulder and leg—the instability of the ankle was beginning to affect his knee—to settle Blackthorn with a bit of mending since he could not be talked into relaxing with a book during the work day, and to take Magnus out for exercise while Ella climbed up to the stable rafters to bring seeds for George to pick through, Ella had barely accomplished her chores when a party of seventeen called for extra help in the breakfast room. Shortly after, a group of rowdy boys who'd gotten hold of a crate of fireworks ran through the crowd out front in their attempt to escape the group of equally rowdy men responsible for the festivities' explosions, stirring up the patrons, who began to place bets on the outcome. There was a treacle accident in the kitchen, an escaped horse incident outside the stable, and three good dishes broken before noon.

By the time evening came, Ella had been doused in ale, soup, and mop-water, was sticky in several places and smudged with ash in several others, and was in no mood for anyone in any sort of good humor.

Particularly not the fabled Prince Charming.

When Silas appeared, it was suddenly from behind a line of linens as Ella rushed to get through the wash. He was grinning, dressed in gray trousers, with an embroidered vest and blue tailcoat, freshly shaved, and, aside from the waterfall knot of his cravat, looked for all the world like a man still in possession of a valet.

"Miss Morgrave," he said, dropping into a dashing bow.

She gave him a level stare, having not entirely removed *murder* off her list of options.

He seemed to take in her attitude, or perhaps her attire, then cleared his throat, hat in hand. "Did you not get my message?"

Ella dropped the bundle of cloth she'd been carrying into a large woven basket. "What message?"

"To be ready at half seven."

She dried her hands on her apron. "It's half eight, at least."

"Yes. Well. I wasn't able to get away when I meant. Perhaps you can make haste for the both of us." When she made no move to comply, he asked, "Is something amiss, Miss Morgrave?"

Ella took two steps toward him. "Aside from you showing up at whatever hour you like as if I do not have tasks to complete, as if I am not doing so at this very moment right before your eyes, to demand I flit off with you on some escapade in which we are inevitably chased by the king's guard to who knows what end while not accomplishing the very thing we've gone to do, time and again? Aside from that?"

His nod was slow. "Yes, aside from that."

"Where is Finn?"

He seemed thrown by her question, then determinedly dusted off the rim of his hat. If he stuck around much longer, his entire wardrobe was likely to be ruined. "That is something I'm having looked into, of course."

"Having looked into by the king's own guard? Like the ones loitering about the inn?"

"Those men are my friends, Miss Morgrave. They can be trusted." At her look, he said, "In any case, our first order of business is finding Harold, because without him, you cannot locate your father's documents and fix Blackthorn."

"You mean hide what you have done. Rectify the problem you caused and would be entangled in should we be caught—that's where your concern lies. The man you so desperately wept over and now leave abandoned in a stranger's room without word for days on end."

His mouth opened slightly before he apparently thought better of his reply.

Ella did not give him a lecture about his choice of the word *fix*, or provide another explanation about how Blackthorn repeating concerns about tea could have nothing to do with bringing him back, or even broach the subject of Blackthorn's warnings having taken an ominous turn. But she did poke him in the chest. "The first order of business has changed. Tell me what happened to Finley and do it now."

The prince's expression shifted, but not to one of guilt. The evasion felt like the clearest indication yet that he knew more than he had let on. Ella pressed harder. "If you utter one word of denial, you will come to regret it. That much I promise you." His brow lowered dangerously, and she said, "I have evidence against you."

"You are the only one present who has committed a crime."

She pushed the finger against his chest, giving him a look that said she already knew the entire truth. She, in fact, did not.

His hand came up slowly to wrap around her finger, which he firmly guided away from his chest. "I am not afraid of you, Miss Morgrave."

"Aren't you?"

A small huff of air came out of him that was not a laugh. "I do not know what you think—"

She stepped closer, her finger still in his grip. "Don't say you weren't warned."

With her other hand, Ella shoved Silas. He stumbled back, over a conveniently positioned Magnus, and splashed seat-first into the wash bin. Magnus made a happy little badger noise, and Ella gave him a shooing gesture. "Get back inside before anyone sees you. It's too crowded today."

The prince shoved up from the bin, sputtering, and when Magnus turned to flash his teeth in what might have been a grin, Ella nearly chuckled, feeling the weight in her chest ease for the first time in days. Shoving a prince into a wash bin was exactly what she'd needed.

It was a relief, at least, until the prince stalked toward her. She took a step back but bumped into the low wall.

Silas placed his palms on the rail on either side of her, slowly caging her in. "Miss Morgrave, I have tolerated quite a lot from you. More, perhaps, than from any single other being on the face of this earth. And I need you to understand"—he stopped for a moment and his jaw ticked as, doubtlessly, the water that had soaked through his trousers began to trickle into his boots—"I need you to understand that my forbearance is over."

Ella pressed her lips.

"Tell me you understand."

Her voice was breathier than she intended, though, to be fair, he had not given her much room to expand her chest. "What precisely are you threatening, Your Highness? Do you propose to discipline me? That I'm only lacking a firm hand?"

His eyes went dark.

Then the window to the attic swung open, and Henry stuck out his head. "Shall I bring the coal shovel, miss?"

Silas's eyes closed for a very long moment. Ella stole the time to study his face in the light that bled from the back of the inn. His skin was smooth, lashes long and impossibly dark, his every angle sharp and defined. A complete waste of unreasonable attractiveness on a man who might gain the hand of any woman he desired simply due to his title. He even smelled good.

When Silas sighed, the loose tendrils of hair that had fallen from Ella's knot tickled the bare skin of her neck. She had not realized she'd tilted her head toward him until his eyes opened and locked with hers. Ella wondered, for one dark moment, what might happen if she pushed him past his limit.

"Is that you, Highness?" Blackthorn called from beside Henry. "It appears your trousers are soaked through. That's entirely inappropriate dress, even for lurking behind an inn." Disgust was evident in the man's tone, and he and Henry launched into an overloud discussion about the prince's many etiquettical shortcomings.

Before Silas had even managed a protest, a burly, bearded man stepped out of the back entrance of the inn carrying a large crate. He was one of the bar hands, built like a bear, and he immediately stilled at the scene. "Everything all right, Ella?"

Silas removed one of his hands from the rail, relaxing his posture but keeping his face hidden from view.

Ella stepped out of the cage Silas had made around her and waved. "All is well. Just helping out a poor, sad sap who's only a danger to himself."

The bar hand waited a moment longer, but when Ella smiled, he gave her a nod. "Call if you need anything. I'll be keeping an eye out."

Ella suspected that somewhere in the shadows, Silas's guard watched, too. Once the man was out of earshot, Ella turned to Silas, arms crossed. "Upstairs. We have a few things to discuss."

---

Safely locked inside her room, Ella said, "I'll ask you again. Where is Finn?"

The prince had lost a bit of his swagger, but whether it was owing to being surrounded by judgmental undead or having wet trousers was anyone's guess. "I do not know. Truly." When Henry, Ella, and a hostile badger advanced on him, Silas lifted his hands. "He is alive. That much, I know."

Fury rose in Ella. If she had known Finley had been taken, she would have done... *something*. Anything. She still hadn't quite figured that out. But she would not have let it go unchallenged. "You lied to me."

"I didn't lie. The moment I discovered he was gone, I told you to leave the inn. I said you weren't safe here. And when you refused, I set the guard on watch. You may not want to admit it, but you know all of that to be true."

"You think merely keeping information from me somehow absolves you? It was deception through and through."

"What was I to tell you? That I suspected some*one* of some*thing*? The moment he went missing, we both understood it could mean he was taken."

Ella's teeth clenched, because she had suspected no such thing. She'd been worried, yes, but she had not thought him stolen away. And more the fool her, because Harold and Henry had been tied up in something truly dangerous. Bad things did happen, all the time. But not to Finley. "Who would come for a tavern performer? And why?"

Silas's jaw ticked, as if Ella were the one in the wrong. She wasn't, she did not take well to unfounded accusations, and she had half a mind to tell him exactly what she thought of his ticking jaw and perhaps a few things more.

At her expression, he said, "It is not as if he kept his business quiet."

"What is that supposed to mean? He's an entertainer. His business is entertaining large gatherings of people. Of course everyone knows who he is." She gestured a bit wildly. It couldn't be helped.

Silas gave Ella a look. "His side business—gathering information. How do you think I found you? Word got out that you were looking for the prince."

Ella's hands dropped. "Are you saying it was my fault? That because I asked him to look for—Wait. Wait, wait, wait. *You* found *me*? You mean to say that all along..." She recalled his scene on the stable floor, the drunken slurring, the weeping. How he'd suddenly, silently, been behind her against her attic door. "Found. Because you were looking for me."

"You came to the palace, confronted my father. I suspected you could be urged to help."

Desperate enough to be blackmailed, he meant. Had she another water trough, Ella would have shoved him back into it. And possibly held him under. "Henry," she said, "get me the coal shovel."

"Miss," Henry asked, entirely ignoring her request. "What's happened to your friend?"

"If I had to guess, he was briefly in the custody of the king's guard," Silas said.

His words were level, and they sent a cold spike of fear straight through to Ella's core. "But you do not have to guess. You're the king's son. You can walk right in and ask."

Silas drew a slow breath. "Only if he were taken on the order of kingdom business. And only if he were indeed being held."

Ella pressed the palm of her hand hard against the bridge of her nose. "Wait. Just... If he's not being held at the castle and he was not taken on kingdom business, then what would the guard have to do with any of this? And what do you mean by *briefly* in custody?"

Silas leaned against her narrow table; it slid a little beneath his weight, and he straightened awkwardly. "I think he may have escaped."

Ella's hand fell to the base of her throat. "And he would not chance coming back here because..."

"Because they would know where to find him."

Ella was still for a long moment. Then she calmly asked Henry for the shovel. Again, he refused.

Silas came forward, hands outstretched as if gentling a horse.

Ella's nerves were anything but frantic. She strode toward him. "You knew what you were drawing us into this entire time. You heard Finley was looking for you, and you showed up at those stables and told your men to wait outside. You baited us."

"Ellenora—"

Her finger shot forward. "Don't. I have not given you leave. You played us, pretending to be out of your senses, passing out the moment Finn arrived, then miraculously jumping to your feet the moment he was gone." She poked his chest. "You had me followed. Posted your guard outside the inn. Kept track of me. Tell me now, Highness, was it for me, or was it for Finn?"

"I do not appreciate being poked in the chest."

Her fingers curled into his shirt, as if she might draw him down to her level. But she did not pull. Not yet.

"It was only for you. I needed you." Silas gestured helplessly in Blackthorn's direction, as if it were explanation enough. "I did not realize your friends might be endangered."

Ella's hand went slack.

Silas did not back away. "You were the one who involved Finley. You did not have to bring him, to—Saints, how was I to guess you would cart me back to the inn?—to entangle him so thoroughly. At the time, I believed you only had him searching for word of my actions. I thought to meet you alone."

He was right. She could not argue her fault in it, at least. Her voice was low. "I did involve him. I did ask him to drag you back here. All of it." Her eyes met his. "Because of Harold."

"Harold," the prince repeated. "Whom we are scheduled to meet by the river at tonight's festival gathering."

Her heart picked up pace at the words, then she remembered the state of herself. "I don't have time to prepare for a society event."

"It's the pleasure gardens; it's dark. No one will pay you notice."

She gave him a glower, but Cybil took to shouting and gesturing from where she had climbed to the top of the broken coatrack.

"Oh," said Ella. "Oh, of course." She rushed in Cybil's direction. "I could kiss you!"

Cybil made a face of disgust, and Ella laughed as she rounded the narrow privacy screen.

When her slippers flipped from behind the panel, the prince asked, "What's happening? What's changed your mood?" in a way that made clear he was not entirely certain that she had not been communicating with a dead mouse.

"Entertainers," Ella said. The prince did not reply, so Ella peeked her head around the screen. "Finley's friends. That's where he would go to find aid. The place he would hide." She smiled at Cybil. "Quite brilliant, really." Ella dipped back behind the screen and shucked off her skirt. "A quarter hour, that's all I need."

## CHAPTER 10

There had been a short but trying argument wherein Henry and Blackthorn had demanded to go along to the pleasure gardens. Henry because he wanted desperately to see his cousin and have an evening out of the attic room. Blackthorn because he could not tolerate the idea of anyone seeing his charge in damp, dirty trousers and did not trust Silas to keep them hidden away on his own.

Magnus and the others were made to stay at the inn, but Henry had asserted he would make the attempt on his own once Ella had departed. "What can we do?" Ella had asked the prince. "It is not as if we can tie him to a chair." It was true—if Henry wanted badly enough to leave the attic, even Ella could not stop him for long—but guilt weighed heavily on her because she had forced Henry into his current situation with no way to put him back. Silas had, of course, not agreed, but he was well-outnumbered and they were short on time. And because Henry won his argument, Blackthorn won as well. In his current state, the valet could not be left alone.

So it was that Henry, Blackthorn, and Prince Silas stood waiting for Ella near the back of the stable in cloaks Silas that had procured from his poorly disguised guard. They had fashioned masks out of what ribbon and material scraps they could find in Ella's room, and they looked more like a fit with street vendors and ragpickers than gentlemen on promenade.

When Ella finally joined the trio, it did not appear as if they'd been enjoying easy conversation or that Silas had softened his stance on the others coming along. Ella said, "I convinced Grace to stay late and finish the chores for me. There's just one catch."

The prince looked wary, but before he managed a response, a spindly girl popped up beside him, startling all three men and causing Silas to shift a step backward. "Who's this?" the girl asked, the question clearly meant for Ella, not the men the girl scrutinized.

"This is Silas," Ella said. "And these two are Mister Blackthorn and Mister Hicks. Gentlemen, this is Alice. She's Grace's sister and will be coming along with us for the night."

They gave the girl cautious nods, as if she might be about to strike them with her walking stick or to swing it around and break some priceless vase. "Miss," they said with varying degrees of regard.

Alice's dark eyes scanned Blackthorn's put-together suit and what pale skin showed beneath his mask with much more suspicion than she gave the others. She sent Ella a questioning glance.

"They are my friends," Ella said. Then, in warning, "And they are not the sort of men who would even think of tugging on a young woman's braids."

The men appeared to take in the advice with the gravity with which it was given, and Alice nodded firmly. "Very well. Let us be off." Alice strode forward, wooden cane sounding softly against the stones as she went. The girl was no fool, but she also wasn't an informer. Whatever Ella was up to, Alice would play along.

Henry stopped beside Ella, his eyes on the cane. "Miss?"

"Yes," Ella said as they watched Alice, the thin walking stick less sturdy and shorter than a man Henry's size might need. "I'm sorry I did not think of it myself. It's brilliant. In fact, we'll get started on it tonight. If the pleasure gardens have anything, it's a beautiful selection of trees."

※

THE PLEASURE GARDENS WERE A WONDER. High hedges created a maze that felt isolated, despite that the gardens were located in the center of a kingdom and drew a crowd of thousands. The prince paid passage, and they were taken in a small boat across a shallow waterway, where the real world floated away as they stepped into one that was breathtaking and ethereal. A constellation of colored lamps hung from trees that were tied with ribbons, and flowers drifted past in thin channels of water that made a maze of their own. Alice had worked at the gardens with Grace and their mother years before, and likely the prince and Blackthorn had seen such spectacles often enough to become jaded, but Ella and Henry paused to admire the scene while the others melted into the shadows.

There were simply too many features to take in. Within the maze waited temples, grottoes, and lodges, separated by lawns, cascades, and groves, and in the center of it all was a massive rotunda, beneath which played an orchestra. Music filled the night, echoing from the singers and players at porticoes and colonnades. Every structure was adorned with pillars, statues, and great paintings and murals that stretched along walls. Somewhere beyond the hedge, acrobats performed beneath arches, and merchants displayed their most festive wares, all illuminated by the glittering lamps.

Henry breathed out a happy sigh.

"How's the leg?" Ella asked. "We can get a cart."

"No, miss. I'd like to walk for now."

He held forward his arm and Ella took it gently. She wanted very much to go straight to the entertainers, to search out Finley's friends. But the prince had said Harold was to meet them near a private box, and Ella could not risk missing the meet again, not when her stepmother had been granted audience with the king and might be scheming against Ella even as they promenaded.

On their way to the box, a passing merchant nearly tumbled a stack of overloaded crates, and half a dozen apples from the top crate rolled across the ground. Alice rushed to help, and, likely to avoid notice, the prince stepped farther into the booth to browse while Alice and the merchant chatted.

Blackthorn seemed less troubled overall, perhaps because it was far too late in the day for tea, perhaps because his charge had somewhat returned to him. Ella felt a bit of the tension ease from herself as well, as they were at last close to finding Harold and to discovering what had happened to Finn, and it was difficult to brood overmuch among such a great deal meant to inspire awe.

Then a voice, high and loud and entirely uncouth, cut through the crowd. "Ellenora! Ellenora, is that you?"

Ella cringed, wishing she, too, had worn a mask. The prince's gaze shot toward Ella where he stood, head bowed over a display, and Blackthorn eased into the shadows of the hedge. Ella let go of Henry's arm and turned to face her stepsister. "Lena."

Lena snorted a laugh. "Do not let Mother hear you address me so coldly."

Ella glanced at the milling figures. "Is Lady Locke here?"

Lena waved a gloved hand that was weighed down with bulky jeweled rings—surely newly purchased, along with the elaborately embroidered dress and matching jewel-trimmed bodice. "Oh, you know Mother. She's surrounded by a flock of lords."

Fishing for a wealthy heir for Lora, no doubt. Certainly, she had not been focused on Lena, or she would have told her lady's maid those cheeks were too pink and the curls too tight for the current season's fashion. The lady's maid in question stood quietly back, already overloaded with parcels, and by the way the woman held her shoulders, Ella could guess the makeup missteps had not been an accident.

"And who is this?" Lena asked, scrutinizing the tall, cloaked man that was Henry.

Ella hoped the shadows and colored light were enough to disguise the pallor of Henry's skin beneath the mask. "He works with me at the inn." It was all Ella said, because thinking he was a commoner would be enough to douse Lena's interest.

"Well, where's the one who likes to sing and flirt?" Her bright eyes scanned the crowd. Inn staff might be beneath her notice, but Lena did enjoy the attentions of a handsome entertainer who appreciated tips.

"Finley isn't here."

Her bottom lip pushed out, then she grabbed Ella's arm. "Come, I need someone to help carry purchases and fetch me cake. Perhaps Mother will even allow you into our box."

Ella stood firm, tugging her arm free, but when Lena reached for her again, more aggressively than any society lady might get away with, the pair bumped into Henry. Henry's leg fell off at the knee. Lena glanced down, releasing a squeal of disgust, despite that Ella moved to shield him with her skirts. Then Lena opened her mouth to no doubt make disastrous scene. The last thing they needed was to draw notice. Ella lurched forward to grab hold of her stepsister, but a smooth voice froze Lena in place and stole the brewing attention of the crowd.

"Miss Locke, isn't it?"

Color draining from her face, expression slack, Lena only nodded.

Mask gone, Silas gave Lena a lazy grin. "I thought so." He stepped closer, cloak tossed back to reveal his fine clothes, though not the still-damp seat of his trousers. He did not so much as glance at Ella. "Prince Silas. We met at the harvest ball last year, I believe. Do you recall?"

As Lena gracelessly recovered, dipping into a low curtsy, Ella eased away. She gave Henry her shoulder, and Alice grabbed the booted foot. With the help of the cloak and a great deal of luck, any onlookers might not realize Henry was falling apart. They shuffled around to the side of the building where Ella could attempt to reattach the leg in the cover of darkness and settled Henry on the ground.

"Sorry, miss."

Ella glanced up from frantically winding fabric, her stomach sick. "You have nothing to apologize for, Henry. I did this to you, all of this."

"No," he said, patting Ella's hand. "Not that. I'm sorry that your family is awful."

Alice hooted a laugh, then covered her mouth, evidently remembering they were aiming to avoid attention. Beyond the building came the sound of Lena's tittering. It was over the top, even for her. Alice darted to the edge of the wall to peek at the scene surely being made.

"Is that too tight?" Ella whispered, using pins from her hair to ensure the bandages stayed in place.

"Feels right. Thank you, miss."

She bit her lip. "Perhaps a bit of smocking on the material would help. We'll work on that when we get home."

"Blackthorn and I can work on it tomorrow, miss. You've too much to do already."

Ella looked at him, begging the disappointment and guilt welling in her to stay safely beneath drowning levels.

"That man speaking to your horrible stepsister is rather good at playing fools," Alice said.

Ella sighed, pushing to stand. Didn't she know it.

Alice glanced over her shoulder to give Ella an eyebrow wiggle. "He's much more handsome without the mask. Sort of looks like that man you had with you the other night in the alley."

"Alice—"

Alice shrugged, turning her gaze back to the scene. "But he sure wasn't putting you on like that."

Ella reached forward to give Henry a hand, and once he was

upright and had checked the stability of his boot, the pair crept closer to watch with Alice.

"Certainly effective," muttered Ella as Silas leaned near Lena as if whispering conspiratorially. A crowd of ladies had gathered around the pair, but the gentlemen lingered farther back. Silas was the sort of specimen that other men didn't stand too near, lest they be compared in wealth, height, looks, or anything, really. Lena certainly didn't bother with giving him space.

Alice giggled. "Look at her. You'd think she'd just won the derby."

Ella put a hand on Alice's shoulder. "Let's not be uncharitable."

Alice gave a little wave to Blackthorn. "Mother says it is our duty to remain loudly uncharitable against those who take pleasure in being cruel."

"Well, your mother has always been wise," Ella said, watching as Blackthorn, in turn, made a very slight dip of his chin, which evidently signaled the prince, because he made a great show of departing Lena and the gathered crowd.

Silas tossed a coin to the merchant and strode toward the hedge maze, head high, as Blackthorn turned to discreetly follow. The entire audience watched the prince go. His attendance would be common knowledge before the hour was through. It seemed impossible that the Lockes had become so entrenched in Ella's life that they managed to thwart every plan she ever made. Even those they were unaware of.

"That's our cue," whispered Alice. She took Ella's hand and dragged her forward with a grin. "This is about the most fun I've had at the gardens since the year the acrobat's feathers caught fire." To Henry, she clarified, "No one was hurt, but it was quite the show when the streamers lit."

"Indeed," said Henry.

"I think I would like to walk the tightrope," Alice told him. "I'll have to use my hands though, and it's been slow going since

Mother says a body in a skirt shouldn't practice upside downs in public."

Henry concurred, keeping step with the girl as they entered the hedge maze, and, shadows closing around them, the figures moving in the distance faded to no more than dark shapes. Alice strode on as if she knew precisely where the group was headed, and perhaps she did, because as they passed a narrow alcove, Silas and Blackthorn stepped onto the path, the prince's mask and cape resumed.

"Is this the reason you are always late?" Ella asked Silas, voice low.

The group shifted to walk through a narrower section, and Ella somehow ended up on his arm. He said, "Something of the sort."

Ella kept her gaze forward. "Thank you for that. You handled the situation quite smoothly."

He made a little self-deprecating sound in his throat. "Well practiced, I suppose."

"At fending off beautiful ladies?"

He chuckled. "I do seem exceptional at that of late."

The path crossed a thin channel of water, its surface shimmering in the silver light that slipped through the greenery, broken only by dark stepping stones. Silas crossed after Blackthorn and Henry, turning to face Ella as he held her hand to steady her way. "That's twice you've referred to your sisters as beauties," he said.

Ella paused to look up at him, the moonlight through a gap in the ivy lighting her face. From his place in the shadows, he watched with too much intent. "What are you getting at?"

The prince wet his lips, then shook his head softly. "Only musing on what it must be like to have siblings."

"I wouldn't know." Having crossed the stream, she tried to brush past him, but he kept hold of her hand, tucking it back into the crook of his arm. Ella said, "They are not my sisters. They are the daughters of the woman my father married. I never knew them before my father was wed. I barely know them now. The only thing they feel for me is ownership, and the only thing I feel toward them is impolite to say."

"Even the time you spent as a family? Before your father died?"

"They have never been anything but horrid."

Silas hummed. "Well, I do not suppose I would like that."

Ella's step faltered. She was not certain precisely what he meant, but she found she did not relish the feeling that came over her at the prince thinking of her stepsisters at all, that they could so much as touch one more thing that had been—however briefly, however strangely—hers. She picked up her skirt so that Silas might only think she'd caught the hem on something, not that he'd managed to unsettle her. Because surely unsettling her had been his aim.

They rounded the last corner toward the box near their meeting spot with Harold, and the group passed a lawn with a small monument stone that bore the name of an ancient general's horse. Silas drew Ella wide.

"What?" he asked at her expression. "I do not intend to take chances. No idea which direction they bury a horse."

"Don't tell me you believe ghost pox is real. The graveminders only fabricated those stories to keep people from disturbing the grounds. And they certainly didn't include lore about animals."

He paused to stare down at her. "What about Lord Devlin? That rash..." He gestured toward his neck and face.

Ella shook her head. "You can't be serious. The man is allergic to chamomile. Keeps adding it to his tea."

Silas blinked. "Did no one tell him that?"

"I did. He did not believe me. Thinks he needs it for his nerves. 'What would a necromancer know about medicine,' he said." When Silas was quiet, Ella added, "I did not give up at that, it should be noted, even though I might have. Indeed, I explained that necromancers knew a great deal about death, and that was the likely end he would come to if he didn't stop rummaging around in chamomile patches."

Silas paused before the box, his thumb brushing over her hand where it rested on his arm. "He chose ghost pox instead."

Instead of listening to a necromancer. Instead of valuing her word. "He did. So I told his wife."

Silas's expression changed. Lord Devlin's rashes remained, despite his more sensible wife being aware of the cause—and the risk. She hadn't stopped him. And without other family, Lady Devlin was set to inherit. "Saints," he breathed. "No wonder the kingdom keeps a Cinder on retainer." He turned to look at her as the others found their seats. "Miss Morgrave, exactly how many such crimes had your father uncovered?"

"That, Highness, is privileged information." Ella climbed the steps to the box. If he pressed the matter, her stony silence would have to be answer enough. There were some secrets Ella meant to take to her own grave.

---

THE PRINCE HAD PURCHASED a lavish spread of ham, bread, cheeses, custards, and tarts, and several glasses scattered the table, half-empty of their port and champaign. The others had left the box to examine the surrounding trees, debating which woods were best suited for cane-making as Ella and Silas waited for the strike of midnight when Harold was meant to appear.

A few globe lamps hung from the trees, and every half hour, fireworks lit the dark pool across the path, marking the time, but the box was otherwise shadowed. Music floated in from far away, and in the distance, Alice argued loudly, "Oak is for old men. He needs something more versatile."

Ella pressed her lips.

Silas picked a berry from atop a custard, considering it for a long moment before placing it into his mouth. "What about Lord Kuhn?"

Ella took a sip from her glass, avoiding his gaze by keeping hers as distant as possible. "Oh, that's the pox. But he didn't catch it in any graveyard."

The silence stretched, and she could feel Silas's eyes on her. She wasn't certain what had possessed her to provoke him so thoroughly earlier, but it was becoming more and more difficult to keep a wall between them, particularly when he reached over, brushing grime from Ella's cheek. She'd only had time to splash her face and arms before they'd left, and her hair had been slowly falling from its place since she'd used the pins on Henry's bandages. She likely looked a mess. Worse, his touch was making her feel things that she could not want to feel. It must have been the garden. Dreadful how romantic a lamp-lit night alone could be.

She swept the loose hair into a knot and pushed it behind her neck. "Perhaps I should hide in the shrubbery lest someone sees the state of me."

His voice was low. "Miss Morgrave, why must you find friction with everything I do? It is rather vexing."

"I don't know what you mean." She reached for a square of cake, knowing precisely what he meant. But it was not as if she could say *your father's favor is the single greatest threat to me and also my only chance to restore my family name and my life.*

He leaned back into the wicker chair. "You've been this way since we met. I can only assume you've had it out for me all along."

"You staged our meeting and pretended to be drunk the entire time, so I won't be taking criticism on my conduct from you."

A soft laugh escaped him. "Fair enough." His gaze lingered on hers. "But that was not the first time we met."

Ella stilled, the delicate cake crumbling beneath her fingers.

"Do you not remember?"

She wet her lower lip, uncertain how to reply. Of course she remembered. It was not as if she was fool enough to waylay a man she wasn't at least a little convinced wouldn't turn her over to the guards. She had known at the very least that Silas was not the sort to physically harm her. It would be better to hold her tongue, to never admit to such a thing, but she could not seem to help herself; she turned to him. "You recognized me from the start?"

"Do you think I could forget?"

"And you said nothing?"

His brow raised. "You tied my hands to my boots and sat on me. And if I recall correctly"—he tapped a finger to his lips, his eyes glittering beneath his mask—"ah, yes, there was a gag in my mouth that prevented me from speaking at all."

Well, she supposed she couldn't argue with that. Their introduction hours later hadn't gone much better, though his hand had lingered in hers a bit long for strangers. She returned the cake to its plate, brushing the crumbs from her lap.

"That night was memorable, to be sure." The prince leaned closer, his smooth words spoken so low they dared her to lean in. "But it's not as if I could forget the first time I laid eyes on you. As if I'd ever seen such a thing. A slip of a girl, skirts flying, running full tilt across the palace wall." He made a self-deprecating noise. "I'd been reading the heroic novels Blackthorn had sneaked to me, and I thought to come rescue you. But when I leapt into the fray, you all but attacked me. You weren't running from anything at all, but chasing a creature, a... what was it?"

"A weasel," she said weakly.

A smile tugged at the corner of his lips. "A weasel. When I finally convinced you to let me join you, we chased that poor thing through half the palace before it gave in." His gaze traced her face. "How fast you were. How fearless. Your cheeks were flush and your hair was wild. I will never forget the absolute triumph in your expression when you held the beast in your hands, your fingers laced so carefully around it in a grip like iron. We'd fallen to the stones of the courtyard, gasping for breath, and I said, 'lady, I vow I am at your mercy.' Then you looked at me, really looked at me, and you said..."

"... I said call me Ella," she breathed, only just remembering.

"Ella." His word was barely a whisper. "As if I had earned it."

It sent a shiver over her skin. And a thousand memories of a lovesick girl. A girl who knew nothing but hope and happiness and safety, whose dreams were so very large and whose heart was so very soft. Which made her angry. "Then your father's advisor grabbed you by the scruff of your neck and dragged you away. Never to see that untamed girl again."

"I saw you again, though you only offered furtive glances and the cut." The prince's gaze drew distant. He was likely remembering the fury in the guards after having lost their charge for half the day. That they had called Ella a dirty Cinder in front of a crowd. That they had said a man of his station had no business near such filth and he had embarrassed the entire kingdom running after her for all to see. That the king would be mocked, and the courtiers would whisper.

Ella remembered. Ella knew they had said far worse. "I heard they punished you. A month in confinement."

His expression slid into one of practiced playful ease. "You were keeping track of me, were you?"

She did not answer. They both understood exactly what she meant. Back then, he'd only gotten the cane, but they weren't children any longer. Tangling with a Cinder would come to no good. Not for the prince and not for Ella.

"They certainly did try to hem us in." He slid back into his seat, but the move only served to brush his leg against hers. He did not draw it away. "It seems neither of us were ever very good at following rules, Miss Morgrave."

As she turned to look at him, fireworks burst overhead, sparkling on the dark water and marking the hour of twelve.

## CHAPTER 11

Harold appeared at precisely midnight, stepping out from the shadows of the tree line. In the flash of fireworks, he was visible one moment and gone the next. He looked so much like Henry, except that Harold was very much alive—movements wary and quick, skin flush with color. His suit was dark brown in the style of a tradesman or craftsman, and he wore a dark cap and dark boots.

Silas shifted, as if to stand, but Ella was already on her feet. Heart in her throat, she rushed toward the stairs, eager enough to have finally found her father's scribe that she might have leapt over the railing to reach their meeting place in the cover of the trees faster had she been alone.

It was fortunate she had not jumped down and given herself away, because as she rushed to the bottom of the few short steps out of the box, a figure strode through the break in the hedge. Ella's steps froze. She dared not glance back at the prince. "Lady Locke."

"Ellenora."

Lady Locke kept coming, and it seemed as if the trail of figures behind her would never stop its parade through the hedge. Lora. Lena. Their lady's maids. Two footmen. A courtier of unknown station and a half-dozen lords and ladies in fancy dress.

Ella took a step forward. "This is a private box."

Lady Locke's rebuke was overloud. "Ella, darling. Such dreadful manners. Do at least try to behave in the presence of company."

Ella hoped the prince had slipped away unseen. She hoped Henry and Blackthorn stayed safely in the trees. She hoped, very much, that a tree might topple, pinning down Lady Locke and ending Ella's torment—then she immediately and fervently rescinded that hope in fear her emotions were too high and the magic might catch. Every Cinder had magic, but Ella's affinity for flora was unreasonably strong, and right in the middle of a lush garden full of witnesses was the worst sort of place to lose control. If anyone, Cinder or no, possessed magic they couldn't control, they were a danger. A threat. And threats were not tolerated.

"You are not welcome here." Ella made certain her voice was clear, tone firm. The Lockes might push aside propriety, but the attending courtiers never would, in front of a prince at least. Oh, how she hoped the scene was not playing out in front of the prince. But she could not allow herself even a glance at anything that might give them away.

Lady Locke's smile was a thing made of too many teeth. "Step aside, Ellenora. We have not come on the invite of a scullery maid." Her gaze slid past Ella's shoulder, then she dropped into a dramatic curtsy. "Highness."

The prince's slow steps sounded behind Ella as he made his way down the stairs. "You're mistaken, Lady Locke. I've sent no further invitation."

He did not slide a hand around Ella's waist to claim her, but he might as well have. Lora and one of the courtiers gasped.

Lena could not seem to help the denial that burst from her. "But *why*?"

Silas stiffened. "I do not take your meaning, Miss Locke."

She made a small sound of distress. "Why would you want Ella? Is she your maid?"

A hushed murmur came from one of the courtiers, making note of the prince's recent loss of his valet.

"Perhaps her conversation intrigues me. Perhaps I like it when she sings," the prince told Lena coolly. "Whyever and whoever, it is no business of yours."

Lady Locke shifted in front of Lena. "Indeed, Highness, it is only that we are here on king's business."

Coldness sank in Ella's gut.

Silas shifted forward, all politeness gone from his tone. "State your business, then."

Lady Locke showed no fear, only dipped her chin in a manner that felt patronizing. "I dined with your father just last night and he informed me that he was concerned..." Her gaze traveled meaningfully toward Ella, then back. "That he was not certain how you had been spending your time of late."

Unclear was whether the remark was a threat—that she might tell the king about an assignation at the pleasure garden for all to witness—or something more. Clearer was that none of what was happening could be good. "You have no place here," Ella told her. "Go. Before it's too late."

Lady Locke's grin was so tight she'd surely drawn blood. "You misunderstand, Ellenora."

Muffled footfalls were the only warning before the uniformed guards marched through the break in the hedges, forming up on either side as the courtiers moved aside. Ella met her stepmother's gaze for only an instant, but it was enough to gain the understanding she'd missed. Lady Locke had discovered they were in the box and had sent for the king.

Ella fell into a deep curtsy, head down to hide her face. Her gaze darted toward the tree line, but neither Harold nor Henry and the others were anywhere to be seen.

King Julian's approach was not slow, his boots stopping only a half-dozen feet in front of Ella. Ella did not look up, but she knew what she would see. Julian always gave the opposite impression of Silas's mother and her ethereal beauty. He was in all ways substantial, thickly built, with dark hair, olive skin, a trimmed beard, and a severe manner. Upon his shoulders would be a festival cloak—lighter than those used at ceremony and edged with fine jewels. His gaze would be condemnatory, based on Ella's experience.

Beside her, Silas said, "Majesty."

The king grumbled, "You did not tell me you had a box tonight. Had to hear it from the rabble."

Lora made a small, choked sound. Not unexpected, given that she'd likely never been as disrespected, never mind that it was the sort of insult the king delivered regularly.

"I did not realize you would have interest in a private box, given that you've the royal box and all its accouterments and that you told me you would not be attending," Silas said reasonably.

"Watch your tongue. You know why I'm here." King Julian's boot shifted on the gravel path, pointing toward Ella. Silence ensued.

Silas said, "Get up, Miss Morgrave."

"I'd rather not," Ella said to the ground.

"Morgrave, is it?"

The king's question held so many insinuations that Ella could not sort them all out. But if any of them meant he was about to discuss her attempt at claiming her father's title, she really did not want to do it in front of the Lockes.

She stood. "Majesty. Pleasure to see you again."

King Julian snorted. Lady Locke's gaze was sharp, tracking every detail of their interaction. Lady Locke had never shown much interest in her husband's vocation, only his title and proximity to the king. She would not understand the sentiments flinging between her dead husband's daughter and her sovereign.

Ella dipped, bending the knee only slightly in her attempt at escape. "If you'll excuse me, Your Majesty, it is not my place to be here, so I'll just—"

"Try it," the king said.

Ella went still. There was a decent chance she might cast up her accounts. Alice's little face peered through the hedges, the girl having evidently sneaked around back of the guard to watch the goings-on. Ella wished she could shoo her back to the others, especially given Blackthorn's fixation with having tea with the king. If he walked out of the trees to join the group, they were finished. Ella could make no indication in any direction, though, because Julian had not taken his attention from her.

"You have one chance to offer explanation of your presence here, Miss Morgrave. Best to make it good."

Sweat dampened the skin beneath her bodice. She was absolutely going to retch. Perhaps it was for the best. He could hardly expect a reply if she was casting up her accounts. But Ella was frozen. Her mouth didn't open, and no excuses came.

"She's here to sing."

Ella's gaze snapped to Silas at his words. It felt like such a betrayal, even if she understood he would have no idea why. It took all of her self-control not to stomp on his foot and drive an elbow into his ribs. She fought an intense desire to run for the trees; there was no chance she was faster than the gathered guards.

The king's reply was sharp. "I did not ask you. I asked her."

"You're attempting to terrorize her when she was invited here as my guest."

"Your guest," Julian said darkly.

Silas gave a weary sigh. "You know I grow bored with the courtiers and their games. You said to find new pursuits, and I have."

The king's neck was turning a slightly violent shade below his collar. Patience had never been the man's strong suit.

Silas seemed unconcerned. "I found a wonderful bard performing at the local taverns. You know they have the best sort of entertainers—quick-witted and able to take charge of a crowd—and he was so well-suited that I fully intended to bring him on staff. Went by Finn, do you know of him? No? Well, it is of no consequence now, I suppose, since before I was able to even write up a formal offer, he disappeared."

Ella was so focused on the king's response to the mention of Finley and on whatever fool scheme Silas was unspooling that she did not notice Lady Locke's rapt attention of the same until the woman shifted nearer. All of them seemed to be maneuvering, and it was impossible to guess to what end. Ella was definitely going to retch.

"Get to the point," King Julian snapped.

"The point," Silas said smoothly, "is that Miss Morgrave is going to serve as Finley's replacement. At least, until I can locate the man and win him back. With all due respect to Miss Morgrave, she simply does not have the same talent with crowds. Even now, looking for all the world as if she wished to be anywhere else."

Ella's tongue felt thick. He didn't understand that singing would bring her magic to the surface. They were absolutely surrounded by grass, and she could not allow her magic to slip, even a tick. Losing control in front of the king, letting him see the depth of her power, would spell her end. She had dropped the reins on it the day her mother had died, and she had never quite regained her grip. Silas would not cease his ridiculous chatter. Was she fevered? She might be fevered. Perhaps she would simply black out and someone could tell her the next day or so how things had gone.

Julian's gaze was narrowed on his son. Societal favor was a balancing act. It would be risky to challenge the prince so publicly without any real indication he'd done wrong. The king would not wish to be seen as cruel or, worse, melodramatic. They were in a pleasure garden, after all. Even if Ella and Silas's meeting were an assignation, society would not necessarily deem it a crime. Ella was not, strictly speaking, a *practicing* necromancer as far as they knew. And it was not as if Silas had taken her to court on his arm. It might only be considered an embarrassment.

It could all turn out fine. Even if they'd missed their chance with Harold, it could still end reasonably well. Couldn't it?

Lady Locke demanded, "Sing."

"No." The word came from Ella without her intent and with far too much resolve. Her gaze shot to the king. *Never show your hand*, her father had always warned her. But Ella already had.

Julian had not missed it. "Yes," he drawled. "Do."

"I ..." Ella stepped backward, bumping into the prince. Silas steadied her with a hand on her lower back. "I can't."

"Because my son is lying."

"No." Ella swallowed. She thought she might die. Could a person die of dread? She could die of dread. That might be best. But what if someone tried to bring her back? It would probably be the new High Cinder named in Ella's place. That would be worse.

"Miss Morgrave," the king warned.

She swallowed again, harder. It was barely audible, but Lady Locke made a sound of disgust. "I couldn't possibly," said Ella. "I've nothing prepared."

Julian moved closer, tucking a finger beneath Ella's chin. His dark eyes watched hers, daring her to disobey. "Sing to me the piece you prepared for my son."

She was definitely going to die. Probably by hanging after a long-drawn-out trial. "Wouldn't you prefer to listen to the performers in the rotunda?" she tried.

"I would prefer you do as I command the first time I command it."

Ella nodded slowly. The king dropped his hand. To the gathered courtiers, he gestured toward the box. "Come, let us hear what treasure my clever boy has found among the commoners."

In the hedges, Alice's eyes narrowed at the remark. Ella made a furtive shooing motion.

Silas's hand was still on Ella's back. He seemed to be

attempting to communicate something, but she could not gather what because it took all of her being to force her feet onto each step. Her hands trembled, her emotions wanting to claw past her stays. She might as well be climbing the gallows.

Silas came from behind her, joining his father on the chairs, Lady Locke and the courtiers taking whatever spots they could around the box. Lora and Lena were nearly shoved off the edge of the platform by the other courtiers while Lady Locke deftly maneuvered nearer the king by use of her fan and wide skirts. Julian popped a piece of ham into his mouth, then turned his palm upward, as if giving Ella the floor.

Would that she could sink into it. Would that they were not surrounded by trees.

Ella closed her eyes and drew a long, steadying breath. If what followed brought her end, she might as well sing the most devastating melody she knew. She began softly. As her voice rose, the garden fell strangely quiet, as if the swell of her song drowned out the rest of the festivities, and perhaps it had. It was hard to tell with magic. Her audience seemed to have gone still, through there was no way of knowing whether they were captivated or bored. They were courtiers, after all.

Ella could not look, could not be tempted to think of anything aside from keeping the magic in check.

Focusing very hard on the words, she did not allow herself to wish, to want, or to grieve. She curled her fingers into her palms to keep the magic from unfurling. She could not let its ember catch. The refrain was haunting and hypnotic, and Ella drew back slightly, not wanting her voice to carry too far into the trees where the others waited, not wanting a bit of it to escape. The song ended on a long, lonely note. When the sound faded to nothing and the distant echoes of the garden returned, Ella opened her eyes.

The onlookers were silent, staring in a manner that made Ella feel as if she'd made a terrible mistake. Except she hadn't, she knew, because Lady Locke's anger was scored across her features, no sign of glee or triumph to be found.

Silas's gaze was on Ella as well, but he appeared more stunned than anything else. She tried not to look at him overlong, in fear of unlocking even a single emotion. Their surroundings appeared mostly unchanged. If anyone noticed the grass rose a bit taller around Ella's feet, that the vines surrounding the box had somehow bloomed, they did not let on.

One of the courtiers lifted their gloved hands and softly applauded. It seemed to bring the rest awake.

King Julian nodded. "I see." He set his glass of port on the small table. "Well done, Silas. Miss Morgrave will come on staff." He gave Ella a speculative glance. "In fact, set her up for the grand fête. We will give her talent its due."

Ella swayed. "What?"

"You're hired, Miss Morgrave. I hope you'll wear something more suited for a royal affair."

Two of the courtiers laughed. Lady Locke had gone an unhealthy shade of violet.

"I am not a singer." Ella's protest fell short, because no one was listening. She wanted to make them listen, make them hear. But what would she say? That she was a Cinder instead? She was not. She had not been granted the title, and with Lady Locke in attendance, she could not even bring it up. She was lucky to have come through with her life.

She was lucky the king didn't know about her magic.

The couriers chatted excitedly about the coming festivities, and Ella's frantic gaze shot to the prince. Silas did not appear concerned in the least. In fact, his gaze was on the hedges beyond Ella.

Ella turned just as the figure of Harold slipped out of view.

## CHAPTER 12

Heart in her throat, Ella edged away, hissing a plea to keep an eye on Henry toward Alice where she hid in the brush, then she slipped through the break in the hedges without looking back. The king had made his point. Silas had been subdued. The prince would not be able to come after Ella, but she did not need him.

Not if she had Harold.

Figures moved over the dark paths, but the hedge grew too thick for a grown man to climb through. He would have to stick to one of the paths. Skirts lifted, Ella ran toward the path she would have chosen if she meant to escape unseen. She passed a pair of servers and two women in full feathered masks, no one bothering to glance back. It was just the sort of night that running through hedge mazes wasn't cause for concern.

A dark shape turned the next corner, its steps hurried, and Ella pushed faster, nearly careening into a juggler as she rounded the hedge. She called, "Wait!" and the man she pursued glanced back, his step speeding. Beyond them was the canal, a wide waterway that separated the gardens from the kingdom. He slowed to navigate a low gate, and Ella did not. She drew her skirts tight and swung over the gate at full speed, heedless of the fabric that snagged on the iron.

Ella caught the man, grabbing hold of his coat. "Stop, please!"

He half turned, yanking his coat out of her hands. "Miss, I don't have time for games."

She reached for him again. "Harold."

He really looked at her then and seemed to recognize something in her face.

Ella nodded, gasping for breath. "Ellenora Morgrave, Emeri's daughter."

His dark eyes flitted away to scan their surroundings.

"I'm not here on behalf of anyone but myself." Her and everyone who counted on her. Her and a collection of the undead who could not be laid to rest. "I have no intention of allowing harm to come to you. I only need a moment."

He stepped backward, toward the shadows that would disappear him as quickly as plunging into the dark water. "Miss, I can't."

Ella stepped forward with him, her fingers clawing into his coat of their own accord. Horror crossed his face, and she shook her head. "Harold, please. You don't understand. I only need my father's binder. He left it to me, but I can't find the will or the records of his work. I can't find the binder, and I have to have it. You understand his work, what's at stake. You have to know what that means."

The tension drawing Harold away seemed to ease, if only a little. "You mean, you don't know?"

"Know what?"

His expression collapsed. "They didn't tell you?"

Ella's fingers tightened. "Tell me what?"

He placed his hands on her arms, as if to steady her. "The documents were in his satchel. He'd loaded it with the binder and anything else that would fit. He said it all needed to be copied, to be certain it was protected, and that we would work on it when he next saw me. But the fire... and it was with him.

Gone. Every word of it, burned. There wasn't a single possession spared." His voice changed, as if recalling the scene—a scene that Ella had never been allowed to witness. "Nothing but ash."

Ella's entire being plunged, as if she had leapt from the tower into the canal. The world fell into an abyss, and there was no climbing out. She had thought things could get no worse.

She had doomed everyone she loved.

She breathed, "How?" How could there be nothing, not one single trace? How could a man's entire life be reduced to ash?

How could anything so unthinkable be true?

Harold only said, "It's what they do." Then he took hold of her hand and dragged it free of his jacket. "I have to go, miss. Or they'll be after me, too." His head dipped, leveling their gazes. "Stay clear of it, do you hear? It's an awful mess, and no one's coming out clean. I don't care what your father told you to do. Don't attend it. The kingdom can sort itself out. Stay away from the magic they're fooling with and keep yourself safe."

*Gone.* All of it gone. For months, she'd chased a single man, searching high and low with the certainty she only needed one thing. Only the writings her father had hidden.

It was over. She stumbled backward, and Harold said, "Tell the prince not to cross the rose and king." Then he disappeared into the shadows.

---

ELLA RETURNED TO THE MAZE, fighting through thick brush that snagged her dress and scraped her skin to reach the trees behind the box without being seen by the king and his courtiers. In the dim light, Alice found Ella, a finger held to the girl's mouth, as evidently Ella's approach had been too noisy, and Alice took Ella's hand to lead her to where Henry and Blackthorn waited, their backs against the trees and wary gazes pointed in the direction of the box.

Ella tried very hard not to think about fire, or about her

father's last message, but it was like trying not to taste a mouth filled with ash.

When the festivities were over, the box finally empty, and Silas gone with the rest, it was too late to search out the entertainers whom Finley might have gone to for help. Dreams of finding her friend and securing the documents her father had left her were lost. Ella was leaving with less than nothing, and she'd somehow managed to become more entangled with the king. A king whose principles shifted with the wind.

The night was warm and the air close, the cobblestone streets scattered with stragglers. Soon, it would rain. Morning chores would be slow, everything made wet and heavy. Alice clung to Ella's hand, her other on the weathered cane. The foursome walked home in silence, broken only by Blackthorn voicing his concern regarding Silas, and tea, and the king. Harold's warning echoed in Ella's mind, but she was not yet ready to think about such things, or for plotting or revenge.

The walk was not terribly far, but the group had the weary, bedraggled manner of one that had trekked from kingdoms away.

Once they left Alice at the boarding house and finally climbed the stairs to the attic room, the weight of silence was as heavy as Ella's mood. Cybil and Fritz watched from a nest of soft grass and worn fabric as Ella and Henry adjusted the crates they'd used to raise his bed. When Henry settled onto the cushions to remove his boots, his makeshift cane slid to the floor. Ella knelt to pick it up.

Her fingers slid over the smooth bark. It smelled slightly sweet, an old injury scarred over and the break at the end somehow... alive.

Her gaze rose to Henry. His expression was soft, understanding. Kinder than Ella deserved.

The song had reached him in the trees. The magic had brought growth to the branch they'd chosen as his cane. She had not even known she'd let it free. Her control was getting worse.

Ella stood. "I have to go out. Please..." Her throat was thick with unshed grief. "Lock the door behind me."

Then she was gone, wrapping a cloak about her shoulders as she slipped into the twilight beyond the inn.

---

BY THE TIME Ella reached the tree, the sky was tinted pink with dawn and the anger and grief inside of her had unwound into a tangled vine of whetted thorns in the pit of her being that wanted to unfurl into eternity.

She fell to the ground, her face planted in the tall grass covering the soft, dew-dampened earth, and screamed.

Ella was barely through her first good howl when approaching footfalls sounded. She shoved up in alarm, cloak sprawled around her, fingers tightening into the turf.

It was Silas, unnaturally pale in the dim light, arms poised as if he meant to fight some unseen foe. Evidently realizing the unseen foe was also un-present, he stared down at Ella. "What happened? Are you hurt?"

Voice strangled, she said, "You followed me. Here." To the place no one could ever discover. The place her deepest secrets lay buried.

He knelt close, slowing his words. "Are you injured? Ella, you screamed."

She was going to have to murder him. Wasn't she? Could she murder a prince? Could she murder *Silas*? There were better people to murder, surely. If she was going to pay for the crime, it should be someone better.

*Like the king.*

Silas studied her face. "What are you thinking?"

She shook her head. It wasn't safe to think such thoughts in proximity to the tree. But she saw past Silas's shoulder, and the bottom fell out of her determination.

"Your expression... Ella, what is it? Tell me what happened."

Behind him, a soft voice crooned, "Oh, Ellenora. What have you done?"

It was filled with disappointment that crushed Ella's chest.

Based on the expletive that shot from his mouth, Silas felt only fear. He spun, palm on the handle of his blade, only to find Ella's mother.

Undead. Dressed in white. Lurking in the predawn mist.

She wore the gown she'd been buried in, because Ella had never made her take it off, and it was worn, ragged and thin, not unlike the woman herself. New was an inky blotch that stained her left shoulder and part of her chest. Nothing else about Ella's mother had changed, merely the fading of her light, the darkening patches where the magic had seeped from her into the tree.

It did not make her less terrifying. Or less dangerous.

Ella scrambled to her feet, rushing to place herself between the prince and her mother.

"Ella," the prince commanded, "come away from there."

"She won't hurt me." She would hurt Silas, though. If he did not put down that sword.

Behind Ella, her mother was silent, not even bothering with the pretense of drawing breath. It was a very bad sign. "Silas." Ella held very still. "I need you to stay calm."

"I do not think I can do that," he said.

Which was reasonable, given that as Ella's mother prowled closer, the magic that tied her to the tree spread roots through the grass toward the prince.

It had to be said, no matter how much Ella did not want to say it. "Please understand that if those shadows touch you, it will begin the process of necrosis."

Silas's eyes fell closed in a resigned blink, as if to say, *this is what one gets for consorting with a necromancer*. "And how should I avoid those shadows, pray tell?"

"I'm working on that."

The remark did not seem to restore Silas's faith in the situation. Ella's mother stalked nearer, staying wide of Ella's reach. She did not remove her gaze from Silas, another very bad sign.

"Mama," Ella said, "I was able to see Alice today. Do you remember Alice? Grace's sister with the big eyes and the long hair. I told you about her the day I started work at the inn."

Ella's mother eyed Silas's sword. "Does he think he can use it?" The words were soft, spoken perhaps to herself.

Silas said, "I've trained with this sword since I was a boy."

Ella glanced at him in disbelief. "I'm uncertain what you think that thing will do against magic, but unless you have training in necromancy, I suggest you reserve further comment before you get yourself killed."

He lifted his free hand toward Ella in acquiescence but did not lower the sword. Ella took one step closer. Her mother matched the step, putting her nearer the prince. "She has a new dress," Ella continued. "It's lined with her practice embroidery, so there's a lumpy porcupine in a garden of mismatched flowers hidden beneath the skirt. I don't believe Alice has ever actually seen a porcupine, but the composition is quite charming."

Ella's mother sank low, the material of her skirt trailing in the grass as the dark shadows snaked nearer to Silas. Ella gestured for him to move behind her, keeping herself between the shadows and his feet.

"Mama," Ella said quietly. "Can you tell me about the spring you taught me to ride? I'm afraid I've forgotten the story, and Grace dearly wants to hear it. You know how she loves horses. Do you remember the dappled mare, the one I insisted we name Carrot?"

Ella's mother lunged. Silas grabbed hold of Ella as if to spin her out of the way, Ella jabbed an elbow to shove him off, and as they struggled, the earth disappeared from beneath their feet. It was silent, really, when the tree root drew itself through the soil and the figures standing over it fell into the cavity that remained. Mostly just the huff of air that escaped the crown prince as he hit the bottom of a pit intensely similar to a grave.

Not the target of the magic, Ella had been able to lay hold of the edge of the cavity, her fingers digging into the earth. There was no circle to protect the prince, no way to get him safely out of reach. "Silas," she warned as she tried to pull herself up, "stay away from the darkness."

"That's going to be a problem," he said.

Clasping a root, Ella turned to look over her shoulder and saw the thick black fingers of the tree's magic coiling toward him. Their eyes met. It did not offer comfort.

Silas's grip tightened on the sword.

"Put it down," Ella told him. "It will do you no good here."

Silas did not drop the sword.

"Put it down," she repeated. "And give me your hand."

As he made to move toward her, a thread of magic cracked between them. Ella pressed her boot against the earthen wall and swung sideways, hand outreached. Silas took hold of it.

Ella closed her eyes.

When she opened them again, his grip went momentarily slack, and she knew he had seen the flicker of magic inside of her. But the pit was filling with shadows. Ella could not let go.

She pulled Silas with her to the top, and they scrambled out of the pit side by side. On the soft, dewy grass waited Ella's mother, shadows crawling from her fingers and her expression having shifted to something that no longer resembled the woman Ella loved.

Ella rose to her feet, arms spread wide. "It's time to go back."

A shriek tore from the woman like the shearing of limbs in a storm. She rushed Ella, Ella spun to the side, and three more pits opened in the ground.

Silas was trapped, surrounded by graves, and Ella's mother had disappeared. Ella ran toward the prince, but the earth exploded before her as a massive root burst through the surface. Ella rolled away, her hands and knees hitting loose, rich soil. She looked up just as her mother rose from one of the graves, facing Silas, atop a root all her own.

Silas stepped back, but he had nowhere to go. The ground was in shambles.

Ella called out, and her mother turned toward the noise, wreathed in magic so strong Ella could feel it in her bones. Clear was that the woman had lost touch with whatever part of her remained.

She had lost sight of who her target was.

Magic shot toward Ella in a dark shadow, cracking like a whip, and Silas, the fool, leapt from his spot across a too-wide grave in an attempt to save Ella. He landed short, hitting the opposite wall of the pit with his chest, then clambered up near Ella's mother. He shouted, "Run!"

Ella did not waste time shouting back. Silas was about to meet an especially unpleasant end.

But he had provided her with a distraction.

When Ella rose behind her mother, close enough to touch, her mother spun.

Her expression changed. She screamed, "*She burned it all!*"

The sick hollowness inside Ella threatened to swallow her whole. All she could say was, "I know, Mama. I'm sorry."

Then she laid her hand on her mother's chest and followed her to the ground.

---

ELLA'S MOTHER, diaphanous in the strange hazy glow before dawn, lay in the soft grass. The dark shadows that had spilled from her were gone. The clearing was silent. Ella's hands trembled, and the air chilled her sweat-damp neck. She wanted to retch.

Silas approached, coming to stand behind her shoulder.

Ella said, "She's only sleeping." It wasn't entirely accurate, but the explanation would have to do.

Silas did not reply. Beyond them, empty of birdsong and chittering bugs, the tree seemed to glow in the lightening sky, silhouetted by the indistinct outline of Morgrave House far in the distance. The household would be waking soon, preparing for the day, serving their new mistress. It would be hers, now that the documents were gone.

Lady Locke would own the soil beneath their feet, the ground where they had buried Ella's mother.

Ella swallowed. "You've seen it now."

After a long moment, Silas said, "I cannot say I'm certain what I saw."

Ella pushed to her feet then turned to face him. His fine waistcoat was dark with soil, his jacket torn. She flexed her fingers, the memory of magic still burning her skin. "This. Why I could not let the land go. Why I could not sing. Why it was so important that I find my father's books."

"What is *this*, precisely?"

Ella gestured toward the tree, its every limb alive like the hum of a bee's wing, the edges of its leaves like the glow of a firefly. It was alive in a way the right words in the right tone and a lit hawthorn branch could ignite a person's soul. Alive in the way the creatures Ella had awoken were—a way that would not go back, no matter how she tried.

It could not hurt her as it might hurt Silas. It had ruined her nonetheless.

"Six years ago, my mother died. I am not so much older now, and I cannot use youth as an excuse. But something terrible happened, followed by more terrible things, and in my anguish, I was rash. Foolish. Incautious. I did not understand." She released a breath. "I wasn't merely angry and devastated—I was ill-experienced, not yet fully trained. There was no fault but my own. I suppose, at the time, no one truly grasped how deep my magic ran. How much of a danger it was. That night, I fell to my knees over her grave, the soil so freshly turned that the smell of it, the sound of it settling, the overwhelming sensations were all that existed for me, my entire world. And so I cried. I cried so much it just..." She ran a palm over her forearm, which was caked with dirt, the same as it was in her memory. "The hazel tree grew where I knelt. I had fallen asleep in the grass, right there, holding tight to the earth that covered her. By the time I woke the next morning, it was a sapling. And it kept growing. It won't stop. Nothing I do will stop it and nothing, no man or beast that I bring back will return to its resting place. I've tangled that grief so tightly into my magic that I cannot get it unwound."

"I did not tell anyone. I could not. I thought, with time, that I could sort it. I practiced, trained, learned to lay protections with the branch, learned to focus the power with song. It didn't matter."

Silas's entire being seemed to be holding in emotion, but his voice revealed little more than confoundment. "You... you grew a magic tree? Ella, this isn't necromancy. This is..." He stared at her. "Something else."

"Something worse."

The weight of her confession seemed to settle fully inside of Silas—or else the recalled gravity of the dark shadows that had reached for him through the grass. He stepped closer. "Perhaps you were not made to let things die." When she did not reply at his misguided attempt to comfort her, he said, "The enormity of your ability... Ella, you were made to bring them back."

"I can't. Don't you see? They cannot stay forever, and I don't know how to let them return." It was killing her, hollowing her out. And no one seemed to understand. Her body was still weak and trembling, her heart sick. The emptiness inside of her only grew. Every time it escaped, there was less of Ella left to restrain it. It was like a gateway was opened, but the magic only flowed one way. She could press life into creatures, into vegetation, but she could not draw it back out. And it was a part of her.

"All you need is your father's work. We will find it. You can end this."

The words hit like the pits that had formed in the earth beneath their feet, a sudden abyss that left her no place to stand.

Ella wanted to turn away, to crumple in on herself. To let it finally devour her.

She forced her shoulders back, her voice to steady. "Harold doesn't have the documents." Silas's expression changed, but before he could ask, Ella explained, "My father's work is gone. All of it. He took it with him that day. And now there is no proof of succession. The king will name a man who despises me to the position, a man with no morals, no respect for the craft, and I won't have a single recourse. I will never be able to lay those I woke to rest, the Lockes will hold our lands, including the land on which we stand, which you can imagine is a substantial problem given the tree, and I will never be able to atone for what I've done." She would be punished for it, that was certain. But things would never be set to rights. No one would get what they deserved except her, and what she deserved was the worst sort of justice.

Ella's true punishment would come not from the king, should he let her live long at all, but by knowing what was to come of the magic she'd called into the world. The consequences of one foolish act.

The prince's hand lifted, but Ella turned to go. She would accept no comfort. "It's over, Highness. There's nothing to be done."

As she walked slowly from the clearing, dawn fully broke, and Silas did not remind her to use his given name.

## CHAPTER 13

Ella lay awake in her narrow bed, staring at the aged rafters of the attic ceiling while Magnus picked at straws beneath the thin mattress. Blackthorn lay on his own makeshift cot, pretending to sleep despite that Ella had given him leave to burn as many candles as he wished. In the moonlight coming through the small window, Henry leaned against the wall, quietly trimming the new growth from the end of his cane.

It felt like punishment to keep them locked away. The risk of letting them out did not hold the same weight since their chance to return peacefully to the grave had been lost.

She did not want to think about what would happen when it all came to an end, but decisions would have to be made. Ella would give them the choice. They could all go into hiding together or take the risk of living out the time that remained there at the inn, with the knowledge of the outcome should they be caught. Ella would not let them turn themselves in, not when she understood how the king would deal with their situation, but she would give them what freedom she could. They were owed that much, at least.

Cybil combed through Ella's hair, gathering loose strands into a bundle. Ella would find the hair later, shaped into tiny dolls, which was a bit unsettling, even to someone who reanimated corpses. She supposed the mice would be happy no matter where the group stayed, as long as they were given license to roam.

In the morning, she would bring them together to decide. If she had to, Ella would say goodbye to Grace. She would go to the market before dawn and do her best to get a message to Finn and send her precious books to his friends to sell in case he needed coin. She would leave behind what little of her life was left. Anything to lessen their suffering.

"Miss," whispered Henry. "I've been thinking."

Ella turned her face toward him.

He said, "If the king's guard wanted your friend after he was looking for the prince, and Harold went into hiding after meeting the prince, and they're still hiding while no one is after you, then it seems that, perhaps, they must all know something we don't. Including your friend Finley. Elsewise, they'd not have risked stealing him away in the first place."

Cybil's combing stopped, and Magnus rolled out from beneath the bed.

"Henry," Ella said. "You are genius." Harold and Silas might not be willing to reveal details to Ella about why her father's scribe was being so thoroughly pursued and what it had to do with Finn, but Finley would. He could tell her precisely what the king's men had asked him. If she could only find him. He was out there, somewhere, she was sure of it. Finn wasn't just smart; he was clever. He could be cunning if need be, and he had connections to so very many people.

Ella meant to search for him as soon as morning dawned. And she knew exactly where to start.

"I'd like to go," said Henry.

"Go where?"

He gestured with the knife. "Wherever you've just decided."

Ella sat up. "Henry, do you understand what's happened to you? The magic that brought you back?"

"Yes, miss. As good as any, I suppose."

"If I can't—if there's not a way to return you to your rest, is there some place you'd like to go in the time we have left?"

Henry rested the cane in his lap. "You should know, miss, that I do not blame you for where things stand. You weren't the one who murdered me, after all."

Ella felt wretched despite his attempt at reassurance. Henry was too good a man for what he'd been caught up in. And Ella had only dragged him into more of the same.

He said, "I can see it weighs on you, my situation. And I don't want you to carry a burden that is not yours to bear. You've given me days that I would not have had otherwise, and I can't be angry at that, even if the circumstances are not ideal."

"I would go home," Blackthorn said from his place on the cot.

"To the palace?" Ella asked.

Blackthorn's eyes remained closed, but his voice was more serene than it had been in days. "No, not there, and not to the estate house. There's a cottage at the back of our property, away from the streets and the activity, where the staff only visits a few days a week. A small pond for fishing, perfect soil for a garden, and some of the worst bird chatter you've ever heard. I never stayed much when I was younger, but think I would enjoy the peace of it, now that my family is grown and gone."

Henry glanced at Ella. "We could take him for a visit, could we not?"

She bit her lip. "There would be risk. Anyone could come and go. And everyone there would know that Blackthorn is…"

Her words trailed off, and Blackthorn said, "It is not for the staff to question whether a man is dead or alive. It's for them to manage the household well. And the staff at Blackthorn estate is among the best in the business."

Ella stared at him. The speech had been so very lucid.

Then his eyes opened. "Shall we dress for tea now?"

Henry sighed.

"We have time, Blackthorn," Ella said. "We'll dress for tea in the morning."

---

In the end, Henry and Blackthorn chose not only to stick with Ella at the inn for what time they had left but also to help uncover how Finn's disappearance was connected to Harold and the prince. Armed with new resolve and a plan to spend the morning scouring the entertainment district for clues, Ella bartered her way out of the day's chores and the group set out with a warm and promising breeze at their back—at risk to Ella's position at the inn if the others were caught doing her tasks and at risk of being dragged in front of the king if Henry or Blackthorn were seen at all.

Festival week was never dull, but this was a day of picnics and games, with merchants lining the streets that bordered the park, entertainment and exhibition tents scattered across the grass, and ladies and gentlemen in their finest warm-weather attire.

It was early when they arrived, despite the break they'd taken to reattach Henry's leg after a misplaced step, and the colored canvas tents were cut by shadow and light, the lawn still damp with dew. By afternoon, blankets would litter the entire lawn, and the sellers would weave between revelers hawking trinkets, novelties, drinks, and cakes.

Ella scanned the row of merchants in search of anyone familiar. Alice and her mother had set up in a stall near the fountains, the former selling painted miniatures and the latter breads, but Ella would keep clear of it. Alice's mother, like Grace, was far too observant, and the masks Henry and Blackthorn wore would not be enough to hide their secret from any real scrutiny, particularly in full sun. Two more merchants delivered regularly at the inn, and several were patrons of the tavern.

Ella kept the men to the shadows as much as possible as

Cybil and Fritz scouted ahead of the group, on the lookout for Finley's friends and for the king's guards.

Sticking near cover, Ella followed the scents of the food carts, where entertainers might be spotted grabbing a hasty bite to eat before starting a long day with little to no rest. There was so much to take in that she missed when Blackthorn wandered off. Her heart skipped but the crowd parted to reveal him standing before a small canopy where a group was working to set up a puppet show.

Approaching carefully, Ella brushed Blackthorn's arm, wanting to draw him away without words. But her gaze caught on the puppets, smooth-faced dolls strung through the hands and knees. One was dressed in a tall crown, a thick patch of fur glued to his chin, his doll-chest padded beneath gold-trimmed robes. Another was pale and willowy, her fine blue gown gossamer-thin and her queen's crown studded with chips like paste jewels. Somewhere among the pile would be a matching prince, likely featuring a chiseled jaw and mouth like a rogue. The stage was painted as one of the palace rooms, thorn trees blooming red in the scene beyond the painted balcony and a crowned rose emblem chalked on the floor. A wooden table with crooked legs centered the stage, tiny porcelain cups stationed on its top spilling over onto the tiny tray.

"Blackthorn, come away," Ella whispered, taking his elbow to lead him back to the cover of shade.

His gaze lifted, dark and distant.

As if he were remembering.

Panic rose in Ella—a breakdown in the middle of a festival event by the prince's dead valet would not do. She tugged him with her, throwing Henry a warning glance.

But Henry's attention was on a tall figure in a dark cloak a half-dozen stalls away from where Henry stood. Ella lifted to her toes to see over the crowd. The man moved in a graceful, familiar way, and when he stepped around an approaching merchant, the cloak blew back at the hem to reveal long legs and glittering silk.

Ella rushed to Henry's side with Blackthorn in tow, then drew both men farther into the shade. "Stay here," she told Henry. "Keep an eye on Blackthorn. Do not let him wander off, and if you see a guard, go home. Cybil will come find me."

Henry nodded, and Ella gently squeezed his arm. Then she followed the man with the familiar stride.

Hurrying past the line of carts and stalls, Ella kept her cloak up and her head down. She wasn't certain who was after Finn, but the clues they'd left behind had not seemed especially friendly, given that both the fabric and the paper had been torn. If Henry's supposition had been right, that Finn was taken because he discovered what Harold had witnessed, well, Ella had no time to be the next on that list. She could only hope it was worth the risk.

The man headed toward a row of buildings. He glanced over his shoulder, and Ella turned her face away, as if looking toward the last of the vegetable stalls and a handful of flower sellers. His shoulders drew up, hands sliding into his pockets, and he dodged around a group of men arguing over a woven cage of hens before he disappeared through a narrow door.

Ella went in after.

---

THE ROOM WAS dark and quiet, the only light coming from outside. The light cut off as Ella was yanked forward and the door slammed behind her. An arm clamped around her chest and cold fingers over her mouth. Ella drew a breath through her nose, grabbed hold of the arm with both hands, then knocked the man's footing off and tossed him forward.

He hid the floor with an "*oof*" as Ella's arm swung backward from the move, knocking into what she realized was an umbrella stand. She fumbled one out, then swung it back to thwack the shutter. The shutter latch came loose, and the man stared up at Ella as light flooded in. She drew back the hood.

He groaned with a bit more feeling and clear recognition. "Ellenora."

Ella reached the umbrella forward. "Rory."

He sighed, then took hold of it, drawing himself to his feet. He looked down at her. Rory, it had to be noted, was taller than even the most royal of footmen. He asked, "How did you do that?"

"You left yourself open. You weren't scuffling with a man, slow and bulky. You need to lower your stance, protect your balance, and be prepared to shift when your opponent does but from a level or two below where you're used to. That was a terrible hold for someone my height." She tapped his chest with the end of the umbrella. "Worst of all, you underestimated your opponent."

He took the umbrella from her, sliding it back with the rest as he righted the stand.

When he straightened to restore the shutter, she asked, "Who were you running from?"

Rory glanced over his shoulder. "What makes you so sure it wasn't you?"

She waited.

He released another breath. "We shouldn't talk here. Let's—" Rory pointed toward a back room, and Ella followed as he turned to walk that direction.

The side room was small, stacked with documents and ledgers, and smelled a bit musty and sweet. Ella nudged a record aside, revealing a ledger of purchases including glass and common herbs. "Getting into accounting?"

Rory closed the record book, concealing the stack, then crossed to peer out a narrow window.

"Rory," Ella said.

At her tone, he turned to look at her.

"Who has you hiding?"

He ran a palm over his face. Rory was a dancer, had grown up performing theater and ballet, and had only taken to the tavern circuit after an injury. It was a world he did not fit effortlessly into on a good day, the crowd more rowdy than he was used to and the coin insufficient for regular food and rent. But he had never seemed fearful before.

His fingers flexed. "Would that I had any idea."

Ella stepped closer.

Rory shifted toward the window.

"Rory," Ella said softly. "I'm looking for Finn." He knew that already, as he'd been one of the first Ella had asked. But she let her tone imply she knew more, that Ella understood Rory was hiding something.

Something like a tremor ran over him, so mild it might have been missed. He shook his head.

"I'm afraid he's in trouble, Rory. And I'm afraid it's my fault."

"It isn't."

Ella's pulse ticked up. "Tell me what's happened. Has he contacted you? Do you know where he is?"

Rory's gaze flicked toward the door. "I have to go."

She reached forward, snatching hold of his wrist. "Please. Just tell me if he's safe. Tell me if it has anything to do with the palace."

Rory wet his lips, his eyes anywhere but on her. "I don't know if any of us are safe. Not when we can be snatched from our beds while we sleep." Then he shook his head, possibly realizing he'd revealed more than he should. "I can't talk about it. I truly have to go. A show today and events all week leading up to the ball." He finally gave her a glance. "I can't lose this position. It's the last chance I have."

Ella nodded, letting go of his wrist and stepping back.

"Stay safe, Ellenora. And I know, wherever Finn is, he'd tell you to stay away from any business at the palace."

Then he hurried out the door.

Two things became quickly clear: Finley's friends had no intention of speculating on his disappearance, and with so much walking, Henry's boot had no intention of staying attached.

So the group returned to the stable to dig through old bridles and girths for any usable parts that might be helpful in stabilizing Henry's shoulder and securing his leg. Blackthorn seemed to enjoy the challenge and was a skilled tailor. The pair had taken to each other well, particularly in their dislike of disorder, and they were looking forward to more outings now that Ella sat atop a crate, idly brushing Fritz. She had given up the hope of keeping them all safe until she might find a way to put it all to rights. That chance was gone. It all would soon come to an end, one way or another.

Magnus was asleep at Ella's feet, but his gentle snore suddenly broke and he snorted in the direction of the entrance.

Ella glanced up to find Silas watching her, leaning his back against the doorway in a sort of affected and stagy pose that reminded Ella painfully of Finn. He was dressed in a deep blue jacket with buckskin breeches that were surely going to send Blackthorn into a state of agitation the moment he saw them. They were doing something to Ella as it was.

It didn't help that she'd not been aware of, or prepared for, Silas's approach. George was the worst sort of guard bird. Honestly, not even a peep. She should have trained the dog that had been skulking around the stable.

Had someone other than Silas sneaked up on her, at least the slat wall provided a bit of cover for Henry and Blackthorn. As it was, the men called out their greetings from behind it without bothering to give the prince much notice, once Magnus's snort tipped them off.

Ella continued running the soft brush over Fritz, mostly because he tapped her hand every time she tried to stop. Silas eyed the process dubiously.

She said, "Mammals like grooming. Have you never had a pet?"

"I have not."

"Because you're a prince?"

"Because animals are dangerous." He shifted to lean on one shoulder, bringing him to face her more fully. "Like necromancers."

Ella did not reply.

One of his eyebrows lifted. "Look at me now, following you around. Next thing you know, I'll be wanting to brush your hair."

She placed the brush on the barrel top and stood, dusting off her apron. "Why are you here? Our bargain is settled."

He crossed his arms, the long fingers of one hand curling around the opposite elbow. Silas did not glance in the direction of Blackthorn when he said, "It's hardly settled." He pressed off the doorway, then paced closer as if surveying the riding tack on the walls. Like a predator circling prey. "Besides, I'll be taking you to the ball."

"I'm not going to the ball."

"You were ordered to go to the ball. I was ordered to bring you. Ergo…"

"He can't make me go to a ball."

Silas examined a bit ring. "He can. He's the king. And if you refuse, then our performance at the gardens will look like a lie."

"It was a lie."

He turned to look at her. Silas had seen the tree. He understood she was in trouble, but he couldn't possibly understand how much. His tooth sank into the edge of his lip, and he stepped closer. His look shifted into something that said she was definitely his prey. "Come to the ball."

"What are you doing?"

"What if I said I was trying to court you, Miss Morgrave?"

Ella choked. "That's—" He took another step. "Ridiculous."

"Perfect." He reached to tug a bit of straw from Ella's hair, then twirled it in his fingers. "As that seems to be just the sort of notion you prefer."

"You can't."

He made a deep rumbling sound in his chest that seemed to say he disagreed with her but possibly liked watching her say it.

"You are unbearably provoking."

"What a pair we make, then, as you arouse the strongest emotion in me as well."

Ella wanted to grab hold of his lapels and... well, she'd not quite decided. "You cannot make out like you're courting a necromancer at a grand fête in front of your father and the entire kingdom."

He tucked the piece of straw in his pocket, then patted a palm over it. "Well, then, we've time, don't we, because you will not be necromancer until a new High Cinder is named."

"No, we don't. There will be no ruse at the ball, there will be no singing, there will be nothing more except keeping your valet at ease until the entire thing comes crashing down." Her only remaining hope had been that Finley might have discovered who was behind Henry's murder, that the attempt on her father's scribe would lead her to evidence of some kind. But that hope was quashed because she couldn't find Finn.

Silas looked a bit offended. "You're just going to quit?"

Ella's shoulders drew back. "I'm not quitting. I lost. It's over. There's no way to recover from this, to do what needs done."

"Well, if that's the case, then obviously you've nothing more pressing planned for the night of the ball. Be ready by seven."

"I'm not—"

Silas dusted his palms together. "I'll send a carriage. You can come in through the South Gate—"

"Silas—"

His gaze slid to hers. "—with the other entertainers."

Ella stared at him. Fragile hope swelled in her chest even as Rory's warning to stay clear of the palace swam through her blood. She had been searching for Finn without success, she would likely be fired for skimping on her duties at the inn, she could do nothing for Henry and Blackthorn aside from trying to make them more comfortable until they were caught, and the situation with her mother was getting worse.

Everything felt futile. But Silas had given her one small possibility to grasp onto.

She clung to it for all she was worth. "I'll go."

"Excellent. When you depart the carriage, you'll enter—"

"I've been to the palace," Ella said. "I know where to go. But I will not pretend to be courted. I prefer we not even be seen near one another. The last thing we need is more attention from your father."

The edge of his lip shifted. Ella could not tell if it was a grimace or the start of a smile. It did not matter. She would finally have a real chance to find Finn and discover how his disappearance was tied to Harold.

"Very well," Silas said. "I will see you at the ball, Miss Morgrave." He gave a little bow on his way out the door. "Until then."

## CHAPTER 14

Ella stood at the edge of the street, staring at the royal carriage and its team of drivers. She had not expected more than the nondescript carriages that Silas had used before, certainly not one covered in ornaments and gold. Everyone within three blocks would have word of it before the evening was through. The Spinster would require an explanation. Grace's mouth would gape in shock.

If Ella looked backward, she would just be able to make out the shapes of Blackthorn and Henry at the attic window where they'd been watching to see her off.

It was no time for cowardice.

Cloak draped over her hair and shoulders, she crossed the cobblestones to where she would have to climb inside. The footman opened the door as she approached, his jacket as ornate as the carriage, the pair of guards standing near the rear adorned with epaulets and aiguillettes. The footman took Ella's hand, her fingertips raw from reworking beaded dress seams beneath the fine white gloves that Fritz had stolen from someone at the inn, possibly from the Spinster herself. Truly, there was little chance Ella wasn't soon to be let go.

She settled carefully into the plush seat, which had room

enough for the voluminous skirts of her mother's gown. The gown was silver, adorned with countless beads, and Blackthorn and Henry had spent hours helping Ella mend and fit while Fritz and Cybil rethreaded the tiny glass ornaments. They'd not had nearly enough time to prepare, and Ella half expected to leave a trail of baubles wherever she went.

The carriage began to move, and she leaned nearer the window, staring up as Blackthorn and Henry waved. A small gray mouse scampered across her shoulder to peer outside.

Ella gently tucked him back into her cloak. "You mustn't be seen. Please, do take care tonight, Fritz. You can't imagine the disruption your presence would cause." She ran a gloved fingertip over his head. "We don't want to lose you."

Cybil made a soft chirp and smoothed a lock of Ella's hair beneath the hood. Ella moved her into the pocket with Fritz.

The carriage approached the south gate, bypassing a vast crowd of palace staff, servers, and entertainers on foot and using conveyance. It circled the drive, coming to a stop near several other fine carriages, and Ella ran a hand over her cloak pocket to check Cybil and Fritz. "Here we are," she whispered.

The carriage door swung open, and the footman proffered a gloved hand. Ella took it, stepping down into a world in which she'd only ever existed on the periphery. She nodded her thanks to the footman, he released her hand, and Ella strode toward the palace doors.

The crowd was thick and noisy and as colorful as any she'd ever seen. Silks and spangles, feathers and ribbons, and the many accoutrements of a performer's trade. She scanned the throng in search of any sign of Finley. He was a man of many talents, and she had no idea how or with whom he might choose to hide. He would choose a costume with a mask, presumably, which meant she should be on the lookout for the way he moved.

"Step aside," a voice called, shuffling past with a group carrying large musical instruments.

Ella was bumped by a man protecting his cello, and with a

sudden, sickening sort of realization, Ella recalled that she was not attending merely in pursuit of her friend. She had come as an entertainer, the same as the rest. The king meant to force her to sing. The room grew suddenly stifling. Too many lamps and candles, too many bodies. She could not seem to find a quick route out and had forgotten precisely which direction she needed to go.

Her palms found her cloak pocket again, checking the state of Fritz and Cybil, but they'd moved to the pockets hidden in Ella's dress. She tugged the cloak loose, drawing it off her bare shoulders. It was becoming difficult to catch her breath. Navigating the crowd poorly, she moved toward a wall. Surely, she could leave. Push her way through the oncoming crowd and into the cool night air. She might wait until the evening had progressed, or she might run back to the safety of the inn.

Only a few eyes were on her, the rest busy about their own tasks. Then a man farther forward in the crowd glanced her way. He wore a green silk jacket and full mask. His eyes were dark, rimmed in thick lashes.

The breath seized in Ella's chest. It was Finley. Wasn't it? Or had she lost her senses? There were so many bodies in the crush, so many masks, it was difficult to tell. She took a step forward, but the crowd shifted and the man disappeared in a mass of feathers and glittering beads.

Ella rushed after him, dodging first an acrobat, then a juggler's rings, her gloved fingers gripped in a tight hold on her delicate skirt. "Excuse me," she pressed. "Pardon." Bumping into elbows and ducking beneath headdresses, Ella moved as swiftly as she might in the direction the man had gone.

She was beginning to draw notice, but she could not stop. If she could only find Finley, if she could—

"Ella." Finn darted in front of her from the crowd, his fingers bracing her shoulders and jerking her to a halt. An ornate gold mask hid everything but his eyes.

It was truly him. "Fi—"

"Hush." He glanced anxiously at the figures pressing past. "What are you doing?"

"I'm..." Ella's words deserted her. He was alive, seemingly unharmed. She swallowed hard. "I'm looking for you."

"You need to leave."

"What happened? Tell me who you're hiding from. Tell me you'll be safe."

His gaze returned to her. "You can't be here, Ellenora. You shouldn't be anywhere near the palace. Please, just go."

"This is my fault. I'm the reason you're tangled up in this. You have to tell me. Who took you and what does it have to do with the prince?" Ella had meant to ask about Harold, about how it tied to her father. She had not realized how much she needed to hear it wasn't Silas until the words had come out of her mouth.

Finn said, "It's nothing to do with him. Only his father."

She gripped the front of Finn's costume, suddenly terrified. "No. You can't. Whatever you're planning here, whatever you think it will accomplish, please don't."

He shook his head. "It isn't like that, Ellenora. I'm not fool enough to attempt to expose the king. I am only—" He glanced over his shoulder. "They were badgering me about poisonings and missing place staff, so when I got out, we did some looking into it. We're only trying to get proof. That's all. So we can have our lives back."

"It's too dangerous. You don't know what you're dealing with." Fritz ran across Ella's arm, clutching hold of the silky front of Finn's shirt then skittering beneath the folds of his short cape. Ella tugged Finn closer, demanding his attention return to her instead of the crowd. "Who's *we*? Is someone helping you?"

Finn only glanced back at her. "I can't talk now, but I will. I promise I will find you. And I'll collect my ten crowns." He pulled her hands from his shirt, then squeezed them before he let go.

Ella let him, because she finally had her answer. It was someone he did not want Ella to be seen by, someone close to the king. She hoped it did not get Finn killed. Ella stood in the crowded corridor, staring after her friend until she was jostled into movement by the other performers. When she finally arrived in the ballroom, it was not to the glittering lights and chaotic chatter she'd imagined but to a scene from her nightmares. It was not that the gigantic hall was not breathtaking—it was. But the grand fête's theme was some sort of floral celebration. The entire space was filled with live plants and flowers. Staggering numbers of them.

Where Ella was meant to sing.

An archway of blooms opened into a landscape of topiary, lush arrangements, and flowering vines. White drapes hung from the columns festooned with bouquets, and garlands were strung between windows and doors. Every surface florescent, every blossom a threat to Ella's safety should her magic escape.

And there were so many people. It felt as if half the kingdom were shoved into the ballroom.

Ella tried to hide her distress as she made her way across the space, weaving past groups in conversation, servers already refreshing the tables, and palace staff quietly sorting any mishaps before bigger issues could take root. The scents and sights were overwhelming. Champagne, roasted meats, exotic fruits, and confections. All variety of decorations hid amid giant blooms, everything from nymphs to stars. So many plants and petals. It was a wonder, but unlike the pleasure gardens, Ella could take no joy in it.

She walked past a fountain centered in front of the balcony doors and found her place near the pair of columns where a palace assistant had directed her. Straightening her skirts, Ella did her best to prepare. Everything felt a great deal like preparing for her end lately and, unfortunately, her position put the dais where the royal family would sit in her line of sight. Perhaps the king would not show.

Perhaps a torch would be knocked over and the entire ballroom would catch before he had a chance to attend.

As if the thought had summoned him, the doors beyond the dais swung open, and the royal procession began to parade in with King Julian at its head. The crowd turned to face them. Julian wore one of his finest robes, his dark hair pinned beneath the weight of a thick jeweled crown. On his arm was the queen, pale and slender and with eyes the blue of sapphires, a match to her gown. The gown's sheer overlay was embroidered with hundreds of forget-me-nots, the actual flowers woven into her hair.

The king and queen crossed to the dais, followed by the duke and duchess and a dozen advisors and officials, the entire party lining up before their prospective chairs. Silas was nowhere to be seen.

"Thank you all for joining us. Tonight is a celebration of new beginnings, and I vow you will not be left disappointed, for we have something very special planned before the clock strikes twelve." The king sent a playful grin to his wife, whose elegant lips curved up in return. As the excited murmurs began, Julian lifted a hand. "Let the festivities begin."

The orchestra took up their instruments once more, and soon the ballroom was filled with a grand melody. Fire flamed high in each corner of the ballroom, and as the crowd gasped, acrobats in costume unfurled sheer white strips of fabric like petals and tumbled gracefully over the floor. In the center of the room, dancers threw their arms wide, painted panels of delicate tissue falling into place like butterfly wings amid delighted gasps. Then thousands of petals dropped from fabric nets near the impossibly high ceiling.

It was a celebration, truly, and Ella would only have to survive through a single song.

High society swanned past, as if she were merely part of the decor. For one moment, the urge to escape out the balcony nearly overwhelmed her, but when Ella glanced toward the dais, the king's gaze was on her. She swallowed but did not avert her gaze. Finn had said he was involved. And when Silas had told his father that Ella was a replacement for the missing Finn, the king had insisted on her coming to the ball. It could be no coincidence. Julian finally looked away, joining in some jest from a nearby lord, and Ella scanned the room. In the expanse of flowers, the green silk of Finn's costume would be impossible to make out. He had chosen his disguise well. She tried not to think about the danger he might be in or how he would react should he see her perform. Ella's emotions needed to be bundled into the tightest possible space and locked in a vault, lest she be imprisoned herself.

The orchestra played on, and Ella watched and waited. Eventually the dancing was broken by short performances, and some of the guests milled about outside. Conversation rose and fell, the music changed, and her time grew continually near. Across the hall, the crowd parted, revealing a tall, dark-haired man in an especially fine coat. A prince, unquestionably, even if he'd not had the thin metal crown. But he did. And he wore it well.

Silas stood among a handful of courtiers, though it was clear it was they who surrounded him. There was something detached and disinterested in his posture, even as he laughed along with their jokes. But he shifted, profile coming into view, and Silas looked every bit the charming rogue the songs purported him to be. So much so that Ella nearly questioned her initial assessment of his mien.

As he took a sip from a delicate glass, his eyes scanned the room, roaming past Ella only to dart back and lock with hers. His lips seemed to part, just the slightest.

Ella felt it in her gut. She cleared her throat, fighting the urge to chastise herself, then gave a little wave. A tooth caught the edge of his lip playfully in response, and Ella had never been more grateful that she'd refused his plan that they pretend to court. She could not be trusted anywhere near the man, and Silas could not be trusted at all.

He lifted his glass very slightly toward her. The courtiers around him laughed at an animated story one told, but Silas did not look away from Ella. His gaze held no hint of the fear she had felt, as if nothing they were about was dangerous at all. Ella knew better, and yet she could not look away, even though every part of her screamed that she should.

A voice sounded in Ella's ear and she started, turning to find one of the assistants, informing Ella her performance was to begin and ensuring she was in position. As more candles were lit around where Ella was framed by the columns, the music reached its finale, and revelers moved to better witness the next spectacle.

The crowd shifted, and the familiar figure of Lady Locke came into view. She stood tall and haughty among a handful of courtiers and lords, her attention firmly on Ella while Lora and Lena chattered on nearby, possibly unaware of Ella's presence, despite that they'd been there to hear the king order it done. Ella had never figured out whether they were fully aware of the machinations of their mother, but it had not mattered when they were so busy with schemes of their own. Their uncle, however, had more than simply known. He'd been party to every horrible deed. They were the worst people Ella knew but had suffered for it the least.

Lady Locke lifted one cruel brow in what felt like a promise.

Ella's stomach dropped. Her mind began to spin unlikely tales. Perhaps Lady Locke had discovered Ella's magic was out of control. Perhaps she had put the king up to the floral-themed ball. But Lady Locke could not have won such sway over the king. Surely, Ella was mistaking the woman's act for something other than the mild provocation it was. Surely things had not progressed so far. Perhaps Lady Locke had only recognized the gown.

The assistant prodded Ella to begin.

Ella's hands began to sweat, her heart racing. She had not calculated the presence of the Lockes when she'd agreed.

Emotion was the worst thing that might happen when she sang, and if anyone sparked emotion within Ella, it was the woman who had destroyed her father's life.

One of the courtiers coughed.

Ella wet her lips, her gaze darting over the crowd. Behind her waited masses of lush vegetation, begging her magic to reach for it. Pressing her eyes closed, she tried very hard to breathe. Something small and light brushed the nape of her neck, then Cybil tugged gently on Ella's hair. Ella's eyes opened, finding Silas.

He stared back at her, steady and calm, all hints of playfulness gone from his expression.

Ella drew a slow breath. She began to sing, as if to Silas alone. He held her gaze, despite the gathered observers, and something in it vowed that she would be all right. That if she only held on, she could get through it.

It went well, truly, for the first minute or so. Then Ella drew a deeper breath and a small glass bead rolled off her mother's gown. Lady Locke *tsked*. In the otherwise quiet ballroom, the sound carried too much consequence. To a person who had not known Lady Locke so well, it may have only been commentary on the unfortunate loss of a precious bead. To Ella, it was loaded with all the words the woman had ever said, with all the weight of what she had done to Ella's family. It was a condemnation and a gloat. A threat of what was to come. When a person lived with someone unimaginably cruel, they learned the language of their tormentor.

Ella could not help when her gaze snapped to Lady Locke, but she wished she could have, with everything in her heart. Because beside her stepmother was a man who had not been there before, tall and broad and possibly the only being Ella hated more. Lord Locke, the lady's brother. They possessed the same sleek brown hair and bright eyes, the same striking features. The same expressions of condescension and contempt and surety they would win. But though it was hidden by a pristine white glove, only Lord Locke possessed a hand scarred by fire.

The hand flexed, as if in acknowledgment, or perhaps recollection, and Ella's emotions burst from their vault. Before she could even form a reaction, a plant vined its way toward the crowd. Her voice caught, the audience took notice of the fumble, and Ella clawed the magic back. She picked up the song again, louder, and swung the hem of her skirt wide to cover the vine. She could feel Cybil skittering down her spine before the mouse disappeared beneath the fabric of the dress. Ella lifted her voice again to cover the crunch of Cybil's teeth against the vine.

Lady Locke's brow had lowered, her eyes tracking movement that Ella knew better than to acknowledge. For his part, Lord Locke had never looked away. Lord Locke was a necromancer; he understood the song. And though his paltry magic could never do such a thing, he knew of Ella's affinity for flora, and should the vines burst through the crowd, he would know who was at fault. Ella would be put to trial.

A nearby courtier whispered into another's ear, two more shared puzzled glances, and Ella's heartbeat began to grow frantic. She was going to lose the last of her control; she could feel it. In front of what felt like half the kingdom.

In front of the king.

Behind the columns, violets bloomed, threatening to spill into view. Ella shifted forward, bringing the song to an early crescendo, and Cybil grabbed hold to climb the back of her skirt. A lily fell from its vase, the weight of its bloom suddenly throwing off its balance, and Lady Locke stepped forward. Her brother's long fingers wrapped about the fine silk of her sleeve, preventing her from interfering, giving Ella the chance to hang by her own rope.

Her voice cut off, her chest heaving in breath. The Lockes would do whatever it took to expose her. They wanted nothing more than to see her gone. They would leave not a single witness to their crimes.

Ella would not go down without a fight. She lifted her hands.

Behind Lord and Lady Locke, someone released a loud "*oof.*"

All gazes shot to Prince Silas, who had evidently knocked into Lena, spilling a full glass of port onto her pristine white gown.

The crowd fell silent. The ballroom felt suddenly of a murder scene, and Ella had not even had the chance to commit the murder she wanted.

Silas drew his shoulders back inelegantly, his voice overloud. "Oh, Miss Locke, how graceless and clumsy of me. Please, do let me find you some help." He slid a hand over Lena's back, for all appearances oblivious to her gaping mouth, then gestured drunkenly toward one of the wait staff, his shoulder perilously close to bumping into Lena's chest. "Could you aid the lady, chap? Look, here, I've made a mess of her gown. And port, too. Disaster, really, and what a gown. I do hope it comes off."

Lora, in an exceptionally fine dress, had gone a bit scarlet. Her hair had been done up in a constellation of jewels, not unlike a crown, that had surely cost the Morgrave estate a small fortune.

The prince bent as if to examine Lena's skirt at close range, and the crowd let out titters and gasps. Such a scene could affect a great many things, such as Lena's reputation, Lora's prospects for a titled match, or the king's displeasure at his drunken son ruining a good ball, and a handful of courtiers jumped to intervene. Lady Locke gave a baleful glare before joining the hullabaloo herself, just as Lora leaned in, snapping a harsh whisper at Lena, likely because Lena's hand was straying near the prince's tousled hair as if she meant to run her fingers through it. The onlookers shifted for a better view.

The hand holding the offending glass swung wide, somehow managing to dribble down the front of Lora's exquisite skirt as well. She made a horrible little sound, bitten off at the end by pure rage.

Lord Locke held Ella's gaze. Ella had never wanted a man to

fall down a long flight of stairs into a pack of rabid dogs more. A boring death would be too clean for him. He needed to suffer. Ella meant to put the man into at least seven graves.

A wave of indrawn breath swept the crowd as Silas tipped forward. Lena was dragged out of his way just in time, and a pair of lords grabbed and buttressed the prince. Silas was led away in the chaos, surreptitiously signaling a senior member of staff. Other gestures followed, then an attendant approached Lord Locke, forcing his attention away as the entire Locke family was ushered from the room. To repair what the prince had done.

Ella watched as the scene played out and the orchestra resumed. Then one of Silas's men—the copper-haired guard—took hold of Ella's elbow, speaking not a word as he steered her away as well.

---

The moment they reached the cool night air, Ella drew a shuddering breath. The guard who'd escorted her from the ball said nothing as Ella patted her pocket with a trembling hand to be certain Cybil was there. A heartbeat later Silas was at her side, taking her arm and dismissing the guard with a low-spoken order not to let them be followed. Then Silas guided her farther into the night, on a winding walkway sheltered by flowering trees. When they were a good distance away, he came to a stop, turning to face her.

"Are you well?"

She still felt a little sick but drew another breath, deeper, slower, more controlled.

Silas's palm slid over her bare arm, his touch steady. "What can I do? What do you need?"

Ella shook her head. He could do nothing. Nothing was to be done, not when the only mending would be to erase what had occurred years before. Ella was not certain where precisely such a thing would even start—with her father's death? His appointment of Lord Locke as a Cinder? Earlier still, to be sure, and yet nothing could have prevented the death of Ella's mother.

It was Ella who should have been stopped, so long ago. The Lockes might deserve an ill fate, but had Ella had clean hands, her choices would not now be so limited.

Silas's fingers pressed gently to her cheek, as if checking for fever.

A small helpless laugh choked out of her. "No, it's... I am out of danger, for the moment."

Silas's shoulders settled a fraction.

"Thank you for that." Ella gestured vaguely in the direction of the ballroom. "I can't imagine ..." Her words trailed off because she *could* imagine what might have happened if the magic hadn't been stopped, if she had faced her stepmother in front of the crowd and king. Being able to so thoroughly envision the possibilities was not helping. "Thank you," she repeated.

He gave a single nod. "I am sorry that I did not understand. I see now that I should have. I see why you felt so betrayed by my suggestion that you sing for the king."

"I had not realized you'd noticed."

His lips tilted in the smallest smile. "You do not hide your emotions well."

"Oh," she said, hating the heat that rose on her cheeks. She'd had quite a few emotions in his presence of late.

His gaze tracked her flush.

Music floated in from the ballroom, soft and sweet, the sounds and the crowd muffled by walls and by distance. The air was cooler, the night darker, and the prince stood very close.

He watched her. She watched right back.

"Dance with me," he whispered.

"I do not want to dance."

"I do not either." His hands slid over her waist. "Allow me an excuse to bring you near."

Ella shifted, closing the distance, and Silas's gaze trailed once more over her face. She felt it like a caress. She wanted to dislike him, very much, but she could not seem to manage. He did have a great number of flaws, the first being that he was the king's son, the second being his potential to get her into unimaginable depths of trouble. There were more, surely. She should make a list. Her fingertips played over the seam of his jacket. Ella was not certain when she had placed her hands on him.

He said, "I have a confession, Miss Morgrave."

"Another?" Her head tipped toward him, and his eyes, too blue and glinting with distant torchlight, flicked to her lips. Ella resisted the urge to bring him closer. "Is it that you do not want to stand unchaperoned in a nighttime courtyard?"

"No, I'm afraid I am quite enjoying that. This confession is far more consequential." One of his hands slid to her back, pressing gently, as if fighting the desire to pull her flush with his body.

"Tell me."

His voice dipped. "From the day we met, I have wanted to kiss you." His eyes traced her mouth, then rose once more, as if to gauge her reaction. "And the desire has only grown more dire with each passing day."

Ella's lips parted, heart picking up in her chest. She should not want to hear what he was saying, should not feel so gratified by the way he watched for her response, should not want his hands to slide farther over her back. It was disastrous, foolish, and she should, at the very least, shove him away. Carefully, she asked, "Dire?"

He nodded slowly, fingers pleading for purchase, gaze devouring. Silas was not a man on the fence. "I cannot drive it from my mind, so relentless the notion is. I've been thinking of kissing you for years, Ellenora. Do you know what that does to a person?"

Ella had a fairly good idea, yes.

His thumb slid over a rib. "You cannot imagine how pleased I was to be near you after all this time—how much the impulse has plagued me. To have you so close… to have my hands on you time and again…" Ella wet her lips. It was not intentional. Silas made a sound that was nearly a moan. "You have to know, I would give all the gold in the treasury to taste you right now."

Her skin tingled, every part of her urging her to lean into him. "The treasury gold does not belong to you."

His tooth sank into his bottom lip as his gaze tracked her mouth. "Fortunate, I suppose. Couldn't be trusted." The breath he let out brushed softly over her lips. He whispered, "So what would it take?"

Ella should flee. She should leave so fast and run so far that he could never find her. The last thing she should do was encourage him, to even flirt with what they were on the cusp of. She said, "I suppose you would have to convince me."

His eyes darkened.

Any possibility of a second thought on the matter was laid to waste with the first touch of his hand. It slid from her waist to the inside of her bare arm, gently dragging her nearer, and he leaned forward, head bowed to her ear. Lips hovering the narrowest margin over her skin, he said, "With pleasure."

Ella nearly collapsed against him, but Silas held firm, the provoking almost-touch of his lips trailing down to skim the line of her jaw, perilously close to brushing her flesh as he swept slowly over the line of her neck, across her bare shoulder, then lower, dipping toward the curve of her breast. His mouth had not even made contact and she was weak in the knees, heated everywhere else. If her thoughts were transparent, the heaving of her bodice likely said more. He was torturing her, teasing, and he would not kiss her until she gave him leave.

Ella should not.

At that moment, she could not recall ever wanting anything more.

"Silas," she breathed.

His head came up immediately. "Take care, Miss Morgrave. If any word besides *yes* escapes your lips, I swear it will do me in."

"Just kiss me already."

Ella rose to her toes, but Silas's hands snapped to her waist once more, nearly pulling her free of her slippers as he tugged her against him. Their lips met in a breathless rush, far less graceful than Ella might have dreamed—which she hadn't. Not that Ella hadn't dreamed it, only that her imaginings of Silas had been less about satiety and more along the lines of rebuffing him, leaving him to want her more than she wanted him.

Because even in her dreams, Ella understood wanting him would go badly.

His fingers tangled in her hair, and any misgivings fled. He tasted not of the drink he'd carried all night, but of the ripe, sweet fruit that had been on display. Ella clutched his vest in an attempt to drag him closer; she could not get enough of him, never mind that they were already pressed fully to one another. It was all a bit frantic, and when he hitched Ella higher up his body, her head fell back and she made a desperate sound. Silas's mouth slid over the exposed skin of her neck.

Laughter echoed down the path, light and carefree, and clearly coming closer. Ella froze. Silas lifted his head, breathless, his gaze flicking only momentarily toward the approaching noise before rising to her kiss-plumped lips.

They needed to leave. Or hide. Anything but be caught. But Silas hadn't moved, his attention still on her. She kept her voice low. "You need better guards." When he didn't reply, she asked, "Are you listening or thinking about kissing me again?"

"Of course I'm thinking about kissing you. I told you, I've been thinking of nothing *but* kissing you since we met. All the ways I can kiss you, all the places... I'm not sure I can stop thinking of it."

"The first time we met or the second?"

His grin was slow. His fingers pulsed where they held her off the ground. "Well, the second time my hand was up your skirt. I was probably thinking of something much worse. You might have been in trouble if not for that badger." Silas lowered her to the ground then took her hand.

"Where are we going?"

He glanced back at her as he drew her toward the shelter of the glasshouse. "I aim to make up for lost time."

Heat swam through Ella, and she clasped harder onto his hand, rushing to keep up as the path wound deeper into the greenery and nearer the glasshouse. It was a massive structure, tall and wide, the enormous windows dark with plants and vines. The entrance rose as high as the windows, elaborate stone gutters and channels ornamenting the towering arch.

Silas stepped over the threshold, grinning as he turned to tug her with him, but Ella paused to look back at the emblem in the stone they'd just crossed.

He came closer, letting go of her hand to slide his palm over the small of her back. His head bent, teeth grazing her bare shoulder. When she did not move, he asked, "What's amiss?"

Ella's attention did not stray from the symbols carved into the floor. "What is that?"

His fingers roamed idly over her back. "My father's family crest. The Rose and Crown."

"Not the rose and king?"

He chuckled quietly as he toyed with a loose strand of Ella's hair. "That's an old jest between my father and his friends. There used to be a strangely drawn falcon—" He paused. "How would you know that?"

He stepped forward, and it was Ella's first indication that she had moved away from him. In the distance, the voices grew nearer. Silas took hold of her once more, drawing her into the shadows of the glasshouse.

Ella stood, shaking her head, hand on her suddenly too-tight bodice. "I've made a mistake," she whispered. "Silas, I—" She glanced up as he peered warily out one of the tall windows.

He pulled her deeper into the garden, between vining trees, their blooms scented rich and sweet.

Her hands wrapped around his forearms where they supported her. He was merely trying to prevent their being discovered together; he had no idea the danger they might truly be in by what she was about to say. Ella could only be grateful for the darkness. "That night at the pleasure gardens, Harold asked me to give you a message. I was so upset, and your father was there, and then we left, and when I saw you next…"

"I followed you to the tree." Where everything had fallen apart.

Ella nodded, though in the slender strips of light, he might not have even seen. "Harold said to tell you not to cross the rose and king. I didn't warn you."

Silas went still.

Ella tugged his arms.

"It's… no, it's all right. That emblem is everywhere. It's just… it's all right, Ella."

It did not sound all right. It sounded as if Silas knew precisely what the warning meant. Details of the royal play in the market repeated in Ella's mind. The thorns of a rose wrapping the crown painted on the stage floor, the tea and rose petals spilled around it. Blackthorn, staring as if he'd just recalled some critical memory.

Blackthorn's warnings about the king.

"That's not all," Ella whispered.

In the darkness, Silas leaned closer, his thumb sliding over her skin. He meant to comfort her in the midst of her terrible confession.

"Blackthorn said—" She wet her lips, unable to easily speak what might be words against not just Silas's father but Ella's own king. "He said you must never have tea with the king."

Silas's touch stilled.

Ella waited.

In the darkness, his hand slid against her neck and into her hair, his thumb stroking once over her cheek, slow and light. It felt strangely forlorn, as if he believed it was the last time he would.

Ella's mouth opened, but before she could speak, one of the figures moving past the glasshouse hissed, "In here."

Ella froze. It was not the sort of tone that the earlier voices had held, light and playful. It had the sound of guards on the hunt.

Silas's hand fell to the crook of Ella's neck, as if to still her, despite that she hadn't moved. Desperate to ask who the men were, she eased forward. His palm warm on her bare skin, Ella listened as the footsteps of at least three men whispered through the glasshouse.

One passed a break in the foliage, becoming momentarily visible. The man looked familiar. Ella shifted her mouth toward Silas's ear, a dry leaf brushing against her shoulder. "At the risk of sounding treasonous, are those your father's men?"

"No, it isn't like that... it can't be..." His head shifted, his fingers sliding toward her shoulder. "I'll sort it, Ella. I just need more time."

"It doesn't appear they're going to give us more time."

"Me," he reminded her. "They're after me, not us."

The men came closer, as a group. They were pursuing the prince on palace grounds, the night of a ball with the king only a good, loud scream away. So many things were wrong with the situation that Ella could not quite sort them all out. Her voice was as low as a breath. "Do they intend to harm you?"

He was silent for a long moment before admitting, "Yes, I believe they do."

"In that case, I suppose if I'm caught, this might be considered an act in service to the kingdom. Perhaps I won't hang for it." Ella closed her palm around the nearest vine and drew in a slow breath. She reached for the magic.

It started small, the stinging nettle stretching into the path of the men, then something from the parsnip family that would cause a blistering rash. It would not thwart the men, but it would leave them marked for all to see. Ella would finally find out who was pursuing Silas, as long as what followed didn't end with her in a cell.

One of the guards swatted at his neck as another hissed out a curse. Ella released the vines.

There was a muffled, guttural quality to the sounds men made when they were attacked by plants. At first, their instinct always tended toward an assumption they'd merely knocked into a potted plant or tripped upon a shrubbery they had somehow not seen. Then came the harsher curses and growls as they could not seem to step free. But there was inevitably a moment when realization dawned and the sounds transformed into something other than those of well-trained guards.

For these men, the moment came when the orange trees descended from the hot walls. Ella felt Silas tense behind her and hoped very hard the men in the glasshouse did not become loud enough to alert the king's men on palace rounds. The vines had grown especially thick and strong, and Ella sent them to tangle about the legs of the men. Then, with new growth at the vine's base, she drew them back swift and sharp. Two of the three bodies slammed against the wall. The third man slashed and hacked, his reactions faster than Ella's magic. She would have to fight him more directly.

She stepped from the shadows.

Silas moved with her, his grip ready around the hilt of an excessively ornate ceremonial sword, his gaze tracking the movement of the vines with wary unease. "How are you doing that?"

"Even well-maintained trees have dead spots. They shed as they grow."

"But—"

"They're dead, the same as a creature."

"Then—"

Ella flexed her fingers. "While I appreciate that you've finally taken an interest in my craft, consider that now is perhaps not the best time to discuss it."

"Noted." Then, "I just... Is it puppetry or—"

"Silas."

"Right." He adjusted his grip on the sword. "Carry on."

The man fighting vines across the aisle finally took notice of Ella and the prince. His gaze flicked to Ella's hands then back to her face in a manner that made clear he suspected she was somehow responsible for his attack. Which was fair, given that Ella was the only practitioner of any sort of magic in the glasshouse. His stance shifted. He meant to rush her.

Silas stepped forward. "Me first."

The pair on the wall struggled noisily free and Ella pushed her magic into a sapling to bar the glasshouse door.

The men's blades had already been knocked loose; it was quick work to encase the weapons in thorns. They were decently sized men, likely stronger and more skilled than Ella, but at the very least they would be easier to manage unarmed. She strode toward them.

She heard Silas shout, "Ellenora, what are you doing?" between the clashing of swords, followed by a few grunts and thumps. She did not stop. She did not look back. Silas cursed.

Ella didn't like to get hit—it hurt—so when the first lunged toward her, she took hold of her skirts and rolled to the floor. As the second adjusted his attack, Ella swung a kick into the first man's knee, and her magic burst new shoots that tugged the vine that had attached to the man's jacket suddenly backward. He crumpled to the ground. Ella curled forward, her palm flat on the stones of the glasshouse floor. Her gaze rose to the second attacker. The man hesitated, then clearly recalled it was the wrong thing to do.

Beneath Ella's palm, the branch of a citrus tree sprouted vicious thorns.

He reached for her. She shoved to her knees. The bulk of her skirt caught beneath her legs, preventing further movement, and as the man closed the distance, Ella had no choice but to thrust the weapon forward.

An instant before they clashed, the man was knocked

entirely away. Silas, evidently at a full run, collided with the bulk of him, and the pair tumbled in a brutal scuffle across the plant-strewn floor. Yanking her skirt free, Ella pressed to her feet and rushed toward them just as Silas landed a solid elbow to the man's jaw. The man went limp.

The prince's chest heaved in a relieved breath, then he looked up at Ella with, at minimum, a shade of disbelief and disappointment. Probably owing to her lack of any real plan before taking action. It was certainly something she meant to work on. "Well," she breathed. "That went better than I expected."

⊙⊱⊰⊙

They stared down at the bodies, which were now wrapped in vines and gagged with their own cravats. The stone floor was strewn with tiny glass beads from Ella's gown. She surveyed the mess. "So, if your father's men find this, they won't take long to figure out it was us."

"Yes."

"What do we do?"

"Alibi. Back to the ballroom where witnesses can see us leave. The rumors will have less weight if we can muddy the waters."

He took her hand, dragging her toward the glasshouse door, then froze as he saw that she had barred it. His fingers squeezed hers gently. "You are terrifying. Do you know that?"

Ella closed her eyes, sending just enough magic to the base of the tree limb that it shifted away from the door. They exited the glasshouse in a sprint toward the ballroom, but before they could make the fatal mistake of bursting through the doors in view of a crowd, Silas tugged Ella into the shadowy cover of a balcony column. His skilled hands ran over her, tucking her hair back into place and straightening her dress. The fight had been surprisingly clean—the glasshouse was more stone than dirt—

but the only thing that had saved her dress was that the entire ordeal had been quick.

Ella received an apologetic glance before Silas licked his thumb and wiped what she could only assume was the crumbly loam from her cheek. By the time he finished, Ella's breathing had calmed and her magic was tamped down. She moved to sort Silas's jacket, but he jerked the cravat free, mussed his hair, and reached down to retrieve an abandoned glass, the contents of which he sprinkled over himself.

"Have you considered that you use that trick far too often?" Ella asked.

The grin he shot her was wicked. "It worked well enough on you."

"Your reputation did half the work for you, but I suspect you labored a great deal to earn it."

Silas hummed as he regarded her. He let out a slow breath, then leaned in and kissed her, thoroughly and unexpectedly. Ella melted against him, letting her hands curve around his chest. When he finally drew back, he whispered, "When this ball is over, I intend to fulfill my promise, Miss Morgrave. Count on it."

Ella's pulse kicked, but before she could reply, Silas spun her around and patted her backside as if to send her in the right direction. "I'll come in through a different entrance. Find somewhere safe to linger until I have time to send for your carriage. Lucian will escort you back to the inn."

"Lucian?" Ella asked toward the doorway.

"My guard." He moved behind her, closing any distance he'd made. "Don't pretend you have not already discovered his name." Then, as if he could not help it, Silas drew her back against him, tugged her chin around, and kissed her once more. His mouth was soft, and warm, and saints but she could die in it. He pulled away with a light growl. "Go," he chided. "Before you get us caught."

Ella could not bring herself to laugh, because the jest was too near the truth. Being near Silas made her want to do dangerous, foolish things.

---

Ella entered the ballroom to what she believed was no great notice. The celebration was in full swing, the revelers freer with their dancing and conversation. As rumpled as she might appear, Ella was not the only one who wore signs of an assignation, even if Ella's were the most streaked with green. No others had been doused in port, though, and Ella suspected Lora and Lena had already been driven back to the estate in the family carriage. Scanning the room for any sign of Finley, she wandered toward the fountain where couples stood on its edge, dancing carefully atop the narrow ledge and chasing the floating blossoms with the tips of their shoes. She took hold of a decoration stand and stepped onto the fountain ledge with the others, hoping for a glance at Finley before it was time for Lucian to retrieve her, and a few more beads dropped onto the floor.

A quiet sigh of relief escaped her, but when Ella glanced toward the dais, King Julian's eyes were on her. She felt the shock of it through her entire being, as if she'd been caught out for using the magic. But surely he could not know what she'd done, not so quickly. And if he had, he would have already ordered the guard to collect her. Perhaps he had only noticed that she and Silas had both been gone.

The music ended, and Julian stood. The crowd fell silent, angling for a better view but stilling even their fans in anticipation of his promised announcement. Ella resisted the urge to back away under the weight of the king's scrutiny. It could be no mistake.

When his gaze finally left her, it felt pointedly so. To the crowd, he said, "I have made a promise, and those I do not break. At the start of this evening, you were told the queen and I had something special in store. A revelation, if you will, one the likes of which our kingdom has not had in an age."

Gasps and titters chased through the onlookers, but not because of the king's speech. It was Silas, having performed his grand re-entrance while making certain one of his indecorous scenes could serve as an alibi. Ella could not quite make out what he'd done across the ballroom, only that several courtiers had lifted their skirts to scurry away and half a dozen others were chattering enthusiastically behind their fans. If nothing else, he had mussed hair and a missing cravat. But there was always something else.

King Julian did not entirely pull off his attempt at hiding his displeasure before he gestured grandly. "Here, you see, my son." As every eye in the room shifted toward Silas, the king's voice dipped. "The future of our kingdom. Heir to the throne."

Scattered chuckles broke out through the audience before being overwhelmed by applause.

Julian waved the praise away. "If one is to be a great king, he must first be a great man"—here he paused to grin playfully at the crowd, but it turned warm and genuine when he looked at his wife—"and thereupon a great husband. For no kingdom is complete without its queen."

Ella's gaze shot toward Silas just in time to see his expression change.

A sick sort of dread began to weigh in her stomach. Near the dais, one of the courtiers gasped.

"The lady has it correct," Julian said of the gasp, with a wink at his audience. "The kingdom has every reason to rejoice. Two great families will soon be brought together, and though the introductions will have to wait due to an incident earlier, owing, I suspect, to a bit of eager overexcitement"—his hand lifted, and he let the anticipation built—"my son is to wed."

Cheers and exclamations rose through the crowd. In their excitement, Ella was nearly knocked from the fountain. The color had drained from her face, she knew, and had anyone looked at her, the game might be given away.

But Silas did not look. He stared only at his father while his father stared back.

Beyond the king, perched on a chair too near Queen Amaya, sat Lady Locke. The expression on Lady Locke's face could not have been clearer. She leaned in, placing gentle fingers on the queen's wrist, and spoke low words that made the queen smile. When Locke straightened, her gaze hit Ella like a knife. Then she delivered a cut direct.

The weight of Ella's dread dragged her from the fountain, pulling her straight to the ground. Hands caught her, and she realized, distantly, that perhaps it was not the dread that had dragged her down at all. "Lucian."

The word was weak, but Silas's guard was not. He propped Ella against him in a gentle manner that may have appeared she'd only swooned from excitement, not that he'd tugged her from the fountain where she had been making a spectacle. He inclined his head briefly with a warning glance, then led her from the chaos of the ballroom.

When the night air hit Ella's skin, she came back to her senses, frantically searching her dress. Her pockets were empty. But Cybil hadn't gone with Fritz to follow Finn. Cybil must have slipped away with the prince.

## CHAPTER 15

Across the carriage from Ella and her slowly unraveling dress, Lucian said not a word as they rode through the cobbled streets, surely empty of revelers because of the ball. Not that Ella bothered lifting the shades to check. She was racked with emotions, none of them pleasant. She had lost well before the evening's events; she knew that. Her father's documents were gone, any chance of setting things right gone with them. The Lockes would own Morgrave House, the entire estate, and everything Ella held dear.

Her friends would never be returned to their graves.

Ella had thought things could not get worse. What a fool she, because she had not fathomed a Locke could be wed to the prince.

Such bleak rumination was perhaps why Ella had not immediately noticed the carriage had turned. Or the way that Lucian's gloved hand remained rested on the hilt of his sword. She sat forward on the seat, the buildings passing the narrow strip of visible window confirmation that the carriage was headed in the wrong direction. "Where are you taking me?"

"Don't make trouble, Miss Morgrave. You won't be harmed."

Ella stared at him, awareness sinking in that she had not a

single weapon for defense. Cybil and Fritz had gone, she was adorned in only silk and beads, and her pockets were empty of all but a few small clods of glasshouse dirt. She had nothing, and she did not entirely believe his assurance she would not be harmed. She said levelly, "The same cannot be guaranteed for you."

Lucian's mouth turned down. "This will be brief, then you will be returned to the inn. Make peace with it."

"You had orders to take me directly there. Does Silas know you're a traitor?"

The man's jaw ticked. "You are far too presumptuous, Miss Morgrave. He is your crown prince."

Ella took hold of the seat edge, surveying the guard's position to see if she might be able to kick him hard enough somewhere critical enough to gain time to leap out of the carriage. He would be too well trained. She would never make it. "Perhaps your surety of my ill-mannered behavior will be a comfort when you're locked in a cell questioning your decision to betray him."

Lucian's lips parted momentarily, as if he meant to reply, but he evidently restrained himself because they sealed shut when the carriage came to a stop. The narrow bit of window beneath the curtain revealed what appeared to be a castle wall. Ella clutched her skirts in preparation, but there was nowhere to run.

The carriage door swung open. Lucian gave Ella one final glance before stepping down. Then the carriage shifted as a hulking figure climbed inside.

Ella pressed back into her seat as King Julian settled into the seat opposite. They stared at each other.

Ella thought she might be sick. It would likely not help her case. "Majesty," she said weakly.

He did not reply. His hand shifted to his knee, where two big blunt fingers heavy with jewels and gold twirled a tiny, delicate flower. It was a cut forget-me-not from the queen's hair.

It was alive, touched by Ella's magic.

Ella went cold.

The king's mouth slid into a knowing line. He knew about her magic, and he'd made himself clear without a word. Ella really wished he'd give her some words already and have the whole thing finished, even if she suspected she would not like a single statement he made.

She asked, "What do you want?"

"You have been spending a great deal of time with my son. It has begun to gain notice."

"Our business has concluded, so you may discharge any concern on that account."

"Concluded," he repeated. His dark eyes roamed down to her smudged and torn skirt before they rose and pinned her to the seat.

It was quite a weight to bear the direct gaze of a king inside a dim, closed carriage. Ella held it, trying very hard not to think about the last thing her father had told her.

Julian shifted further back against the cushion, no hint of unease or agitation in his bearing. Though, he likely had such confrontations far more frequently than Ella. He said, "I would like for us to come to an understanding, Miss Morgrave."

"And you thought abduction best to gain my agreement?"

His mouth hardened.

Ella obediently snapped hers closed.

The forget-me-not spun between his fingertips, not idly. "I believe you are aware of such understandings between the crown and your father. I believe you are aware of far more than you let on."

An emotion rose in Ella's throat. She could not seem to swallow it. There was no way to guess if the king was aware how much Ella knew, and how much more she suspected.

The forget-me-not ceased its spin. Julian held it up, scrutinizing the bloom. He made a little hum of approval at the change her emotion had wrought.

She needed to take control of the conversation. Her words

were sharper than she intended when they came, but she did not relish being toyed with by a king. "Why her?"

He glanced at her curiously.

"Of all the potential brides in all the kingdoms. Why a Locke?"

"It was only a little fire, Miss Morgrave. Wives have done worse."

Ella shot forward. The forget-me-not shifted, and Ella had to stem her desire for violence by digging her fingers into the cloth of the seat. He was only testing her. He knew the truth about the Lockes as well as she, but he wanted to see what her anger could do. She said, "Make your proposal so that I might be done with this."

The king did not so much as flinch. "I would offer you the same arrangement that I had with your father."

"I have no interest in being buried for the crown's misdeeds." Ella's father had not, either, but it had not kept him out of their machinations. It had not kept him safe, not when they had needed lies from the dead and not when they buried those who spoke the truth.

"I do have alternatives."

Ella swallowed down her immediate response. She did not know why the king had suddenly changed his mind. Perhaps because of the forget-me-not or her display in the glasshouse. Perhaps something more. But it would come to no good that he had seen what Ella was capable of, what her power could do. "You would be a fool to trust a Locke."

"It has nothing to do with trust." *Decide*, his tone demanded.

Her breathing had gone shallow. The carriage felt too small. She could not outright deny him. He was the king, and her only way out. "What would I receive in exchange for this betrayal of my principles?"

King Julian placed the flower on the seat beside him, then folded his hands in his lap. He looked at Ella. "I cannot break my contract with your stepmother, but the Lockes will not care about Morgrave House once they've secured a title. You may keep it, along with the rest of your father's holdings, I will grant you the position of High Cinder, and all will be done."

It was everything she'd ever wanted, tied up with an elegant bow. All for the price of her dignity. "And Prince Silas? What about him?"

"Silas will keep his father's word."

He would marry Lora because she was the eldest. They would someday become king and queen—should Julian die. Voice cold, Ella tested the king right back. "You would have a Locke rule over the kingdom."

Julian's expression did not change. "Ellenora, such a statement does not reflect the astute reasoning of a High Cinder. You'll have to do better."

Ella felt sick. But she could not be certain whether he meant that Lora would never make it to her coronation, that some great ill would befall her well before she was to ascend to the throne, possibly before the pair even wed. Like Ella's father. Or if King Julian intended to go ahead with his darker plans. If Ella refused, the worst would happen in any case. He had made certain she understood that. Ella might want Lady Locke and her brother to suffer, but she was not sure she could wish the same fate upon the kingdom at the loss of their would-be queen. Because there remained a solid chance the Lockes would see to it that Lora reached the throne.

She could not even consider the outcome should Lord Locke find a way to make King Julian's true wish come to fruition.

As for the bargain, Ella understood precisely how the arrangement the king offered would work, that even with a title she would be powerless to oppose him. He would use Ella, or someone like her, to keep his reign alive. And yet she could not let anyone else become High Cinder. She had made a vow. She had to save her friends, her family, and honor her father's final wish. She had to stop him, and to do so, she needed the title more than anything else in the world.

Julian knew it.

Ella turned her face away from him. "Let me out."

After a long moment, the king nodded toward the footman standing watch outside. The door swung open.

Ella moved to exit the carriage, but Julian's warning stopped her. "You know you are too powerful to be let go."

Ella turned to face him, her grip tight on the door. He had left her for months to fend for herself or die in the streets. He did not mean she could not be left alone. He meant she could not be left to stand against him. Ella gave him her gaze one final time. "I have no authority. Only responsibility. And we both know you're not about to take that from me."

The king leaned forward, his face illuminated by the waning moon. "That is a sharp tongue you have, Miss Morgrave. Best you keep it sheathed." He leaned back with a dismissive wave of his hand. "I'll await your decision. Send word with Silas's guard."

❦

ELLA WALKED BACK to the inn from the palace, earning blistered heels and ruined slippers for her refusal to play along, sick that she'd let the king see how deep her magic ran. Lucian had followed her, wordless and by all indications unrepentant. By the time her dress was hung and her hair was down, Henry and Blackthorn had heard the entire tale—excluding Ella's suspicion about the promises Lord Locke had made to win favor with, and power over, the king.

Ella had watched Blackthorn's reaction at her mention of the king, but he seemed nothing more than concerned on Ella's behalf. Whatever had happened, his memory did not seem triggered by the king alone, even if it did seem as if men near the king were meeting unpleasant fates.

She climbed exhausted into bed and drew the covers over her head. When she woke, it was well past dawn and something small and soft was smacking her nose. Ella blinked. "Fritz."

The mouse wasted no time with greeting, gesturing wildly as Ella sat up. Finn had met with a man in fancy clothes who reeked of an apothecary. One scent in particular—sharp, bitter, and musky—made Fritz dislike and distrust the man. But Fritz had not followed the man, instead sticking with Finn who, after the ball, climbed into a trunk of supplies that Rory and his friends loaded onto a wagon. The wagon stopped and Finn was let out, then he walked to a building near the big clock that housed a great deal of other mice, as well as children, which Fritz also did not particularly care for, but the building did not smell of anything suspect and Finn had only seemed interested in getting some sleep.

"Excellent work, Fritz. Cybil was with me at the palace, but I think she followed Prince Silas. If she's not back soon, we'll have to search her out." She scratched the mouse's head. "Thank you. I know it was a risk. Now, it seems I haven't been discharged from my post yet, so the rest will have to wait."

She pulled on a dress, splashed her face, laced her boots, then hurried down to the kitchens.

As soon as she entered, Grace looked up from her work. "Ella! Where have you been? Ran straight out of eggs, the coal's not been carried, and no one scrubbed the floors. You've ruffled feathers I didn't even realize the Spinster had."

Ella brushed her hair from her face with a wrist, then settled her bucket onto the kitchen floor. "Sorry, Grace. Late night." She squeezed her friend's arm on her way past. "How are you?"

"You won't believe it. I hardly can myself."

Ella took up one of the dirty pails, but at the tone in Grace's voice, she paused, turning back to look at her friend, only just remembering someone might have seen the royal carriage that had taken her to the ball.

But Grace wiped her hands on her apron, cheeks flush with color, eyes bright. "It's Mother," she said. "Ella, she was offered a position in the palace kitchens." She rushed to close the distance, grabbing Ella into a hearty hug.

Filthy liquid sloshed out of the pail, and Ella set it down to return the hug. "That's incredible. I'm so happy for you, truly."

Grace pulled back to grin at her, eyes rimmed with red. "It's unbelievable. They just found her. A royal messenger came to the boarding house. Said some fancy courtier had sampled her bread at the pleasure gardens and insisted the palace bring her on." She laughed, brushing at her cheek. "Look at me, a mess. It's been waterworks all morning."

"Grace, I'm so pleased." Ella's voice was weak, but Grace did not seem to notice.

Her expression turned serious. "An unbelievable stroke of luck. I know I never let on, but things were dire. You could truly have no idea. After Alice was born, well, we didn't think Mother could find a good position again. It wasn't like she could take Alice along when she was small, not when she couldn't walk far or help carry things. Then years passed and positions only got harder to find." She squeezed Ella's hand. "But the messenger said she could bring Alice too. Said they'd find work for her in the scullery, peeling, scaling, small chores she could do from a stool. As long as she doesn't get underfoot. The latticed mats will be tricky, but she's getting so clever with that cane. Can you believe it, Ella?"

Ella could not. "Of course," she said, drawing Grace back into a hug. Into Grace's hair, she said, "You deserve it. More than anything, you all deserve a good turn."

"The messenger was adamant Mother wasn't to tell anyone, on account of the unusual circumstance. But I knew I could share it with you, given how your father worked at the palace himself when you were young. If anyone can keep a secret, it's you."

Ella nodded. Grace wasn't aware what role her father had filled at the palace, only that when he'd died, the woman he'd been married to had stolen Ella's home. Grace had found her outside the boarding house, having been turned away. She'd gotten Ella on at the inn, applying hard-earned leverage to persuade the Spinster, risking a position her family depended on in order to save a stranger. Ella had been at the inn long enough to stand on her own merit, and if she were to be fired, it would no longer reflect on Grace. But Ella had not forgotten.

She had always planned to pay her back, but she had assumed that chance was lost. Offering Grace's mother a position at the palace wasn't the king's doing. He did not work via inducement, only applied pressure. It could only have been Silas.

Silas, who was about to be wed to a Locke.

Silas, whose father was playing dangerous games with magic and who Ella needed very much not to be growing fond of.

THAT EVENING, Ella was carrying a crate from the stable through the edge of the courtyard when a figure stepped out of the shadows and into her path. It was the prince, dressed in a plain dark suit with none of his usual flash, his hair freshly washed but his jaw in need of a shave.

"You shouldn't be here, Your Highness."

"Don't call me that." When she turned away, he moved to stand in front of her, giving her no choice but to look at him. "Ella."

Whatever emotion was on her face, Ella could not have said. She could not even decipher those inside her heart. But it was too sharp to be anywhere near peace or patience. The last thing Ella could allow herself to be in that moment was soft. "You shouldn't be here."

Silas's voice was even. "I won't marry her."

She slammed the crate on a bench beside the low wall. "You think I'm angry over your engagement?" He must not have discovered what Lucian and his father had done, and the very idea of it, the fact that she could not just tell him, could not trust that he would truly understand, made her irrationally angry. She jerked the soiled rag from where it had been draped over her shoulder, then slapped it into the crate. "It is not up to you. Your father is king. He made a proclamation. You must do as he says, the same as the rest of us."

Silas's jaw went tight. He did not step out of her way.

She untied her apron, yanking it off before wadding it into a ball to shove into the crate as well. "If you want me to believe it, then tell me how you intend to prevent the marriage." He did not respond, and Ella said, "See? You have no plan because there is no way to stop what's been done."

"It will never happen. The Lockes are intolerable." His fingers flexed, as if he meant to reach out to her but knew better. "If anyone understands that, it's you."

Ella huffed a resentful laugh. "Come, Highness, your situation will not be half so dire. Lady Locke cannot interfere with a prince's business. She will have no power to direct your actions, no control over your purse." It was not as if Lady Locke could toss him out on the street the way she'd done with Ella. It was not as if he could have any idea what it had truly been like.

Silas's look said Lady Locke clearly had influenced his path.

And perhaps she had; perhaps she'd wrecked the entire direction of his life. But she had not killed his father. At least, not yet. Such a thing could not be put past a Locke. But she'd be a fool if she did, for there would be no one left to cover it up. "Once she's tied to your title, she will be forced to act with decorum. Her station and society will demand it. And besides the rest, Lora is not as bad as her mother. It will not be such a trial. She is as great a beauty as the kingdom has seen." It was not an abundance of comfort, but it was all there was to be had. Lora would be no chore to look upon at the countless ceremonies required of a prince. She would draw the interest and admiration of all at court. Ella shrugged. "Even you cannot deny she's perfect."

Silas stood too close. His gaze roamed her face, her mussed hair and dirt-streaked skin. Every part of him seemed desperate to reach for her. She could barely tolerate it. Voice low, he asked, "Perfect for whom?"

Ella's chest squeezed. She tried to look away, but he would not let her.

Silas took her chin in his hands, holding her in place as he vowed, "I will never marry a Locke. Tell me you understand."

"I am not the one who is confused."

The words were soft but felt all the more brutal because of it. His fingers slid from her chin. "You cling so hard to every single other creature that touches your life, but for this, for me, you choose to give up? To run away?"

The pain in Ella's chest grew. She could not let it take over, and the only safe emotion she could reach was anger. "Perhaps. But you cling to nothing. Capering about as if there's naught but pleasure-seeking to be had. As if you've nothing to lose."

Silas leaned in. "I clung to you, Ella. For years, despite being punished for it, despite that you thwarted my attempts to reach you at every turn. *You*."

"Because it could never work. You have to know that, Silas. You have to see."

"What is to stop us? What can they do, punish us? They would do it anyway because of who we are. My father, society, they will only ever seek to keep us in line." He leaned nearer. "But we are not children any longer, Ellenora. And years from now, I am to be king."

Ella felt the blood drain from her face. Too late, she understood how her reaction might look. Not that of a woman who lived in fear of grief, who could never be what he needed and had secrets that could bury them both, but the reaction of one who could not face the man that Silas would be forced to become.

His expression shifted from anguish to anger. "Yet you hold back, the same as ever. You win, Miss Morgrave. I yield."

Then he shook his head and strode away.

From his spot in the eaves, George let out a sad, birdy croak.

Ella lurched forward, unable to prevent herself from chasing after, unable to grasp good sense. But as Silas reached the archway, he spun to face her. Expression dark, he strode back.

A small, quivering sound tried to escape Ella's chest. Her barriers were going to crumble if he said a single gentle word.

His jaw flexed. "We still have to go to the mausoleum."

Ella's mouth opened, then closed. "What?"

"The mausoleum. It's why I came." When Ella only shook her head, he scrubbed a palm over his face. "It was in the letter."

She stared at him.

"The one I sent this afternoon. To tell you I was coming."

"Silas, I didn't receive a message from you."

As the realization settled that it was the third missive Ella had not received, they both fell silent. Silas had gone a little pale. He took hold of her hand as if to drag her away. "You have to leave. The inn isn't safe."

The reminder of Lucian and the other guards on watch chafed. "And what? Hide like Harold? I've no reason nor means to do so. Let them come for me."

Silas's brow softened. "Ella, please. There are others missing. Lord Pembrook now."

Dread swam through her. It was Lord Locke, then, hiding witnesses and making plans. And she could not tell Silas, not without implicating his father. There was nothing but to wait for it all to fall apart. "What am I supposed to do? Abandon Henry and Blackthorn?"

"They'll be fine. I'll send someone to check on them and—"

"They won't be fine," Ella snapped. "Don't you see? They have to stay near me. I can't just leave them for long periods. They're tied to me, Silas, like everything else."

He stared at her.

She crossed her arms, furious at the shame of it, her every emotion raw and wanting to break away. "That's right. I'm not clinging to them because I'm the desperate, lonely girl who cried so hard and grieved so deep that she dragged unspeakable magic into the world. It happened—I brought this problem upon us all —because I was desperate and lonely. But now they are stuck with me, part of me because of the magic. They cannot exist without me, and I cannot return them to the state they were before." The only one she could leave for long was her mother, who was tethered to the tree, and Ella had still not let much time pass between visits, lest the magic become more unsafe. And the more the magic drew from Ella, the less control over it she had.

Silas did not ask what might happen if Ella did abandon Henry and the others, and it was all that saved him from the last shredded bits of her wrath. He simply said, "Understood. So they come with us. All of them."

# CHAPTER 16

Silas had moaned, "There's a *shrew?*" as Henry helped Ella gather the creatures lodged at various locations around the inn, and by the time she was climbing the stable rafters to retrieve George, he had absolutely lost his composure. Ella hurriedly penned a note to Grace, tucking it inside one of her last remaining books, then loaded everything she had left into the single small satchel she'd long ago borrowed from Finn, along with a battered trunk of clothes.

In the small hours, Ella knocked on the Spinster's door.

The Spinster answered the door in a finely embroidered dressing gown, her dark hair falling in waves around her shoulders. She did not look surprised to find her scullery maid dressed for travel, but she did look at least a bit softer out of her daytime attire.

"I'm leaving," Ella said. "I know it's unforgivable to do so on such short notice, and I will always be grateful that you gave me a chance at the start. I've put together a list of potential replacements who are in search of work. They're the good, reliable sort and shouldn't cause you any trouble." She held forward the list, written on fine white paper.

The Spinster crossed her arms. "You knew better than to get

mixed up with the lot that wronged your father, and here you are, apologizing for leaving the inn short-staffed, as if that should even rate in your concerns. Your morals are about to do you in, Ellenora. I will be disappointed should you let yourself meet the same fate as the High Cinder."

Ella stared up at her, for even in stockinged feet, the Spinster was rather tall. "You knew?"

She made a little huff of laughter. "The inn is crawling with undead creatures and you've a prince hanging about our back steps. Do you think it would escape my notice?"

Ella wet her lips. "I have to go. I have to try."

The Spinster nodded. "I suppose you do."

"Thank you," Ella said.

The Spinster reached forward and tugged the list from Ella's hand. The corner of her mouth lifted as she closed the door. It may have been the only true smile from her that Ella had ever seen.

※

As Ella stepped from the inn's back entrance for what was likely the very last time, a guard dressed in Silas's cloak rode away in the opposite direction. A distraction, one of many Silas had planned.

The animals were settled into crates, nested tidily in linen scraps and straw, and Silas conducted them to the carriage, muttering about menageries. The carriage was helmed by a single footman with Lucian standing guard. Ella had not indicated any issue with the guard's presence, despite the man's earlier deceit, and she was fairly certain Silas had no idea that Lucian had trapped Ella to deliver her to the king. So Ella allowed Lucian to load the crates into carriage.

Then, as Lucian's back was turned, Ella calmly said, "Henry," and stood witness as the guard was felled by a short-handled coal shovel.

A shocked Silas whipped around, but as he went for his weapon, he seemed to recall—with an obvious sense of betrayal—that Blackthorn had taken it to clean. His gaze shot to the valet, who held the weapon at the footman's neck. To be fair, he had actually polished the blade first.

"Get into the carriage," Ella said.

Silas's shoulders drew back.

Henry lifted the shovel.

"Menaces," Silas growled as he began to climb in. "The both of you."

Ella stopped him, gesturing toward the body of his guard. "Take him with you, if you please."

"Take him with—" Silas shook his head, questioned aloud his sanity, his judgment, and the decisions that had brought him to such a fate, then grabbed hold of Lucian's shoulders to drag him in.

Henry might have helped, as the dead were unaccountably strong, but instead he held the badger as Ella stepped in behind the prince.

Lucian was shoved into the seat beside Silas, head slumped, and Henry settled Magnus in Ella's lap before taking what was left of her seat, straightening his jacket and wedging his boot against the carriage wall beside the crate of creatures before asking, "Ready, miss?"

Ella nodded, and Henry tapped the roof with his cane.

As the carriage began to move, Silas leaned forward, peering out the front window to find his undead valet on the coach box with the driver. "Are you going to tell me what's going on and why you've tried to kill my guard?"

"No one tried to kill him. He isn't even knocked out, just playing one of your little tricks." Ella kicked the toe of the man's boot. "Go on, Lucian. Tell your prince why you've been knocked in the head with a coal shovel."

Lucian's dark eyes lifted.

Silas's surprise returned, but he could not seem to decide

whom to blame for it. Magnus grunted then bared his teeth at the guard; Silas's demeanor felt vaguely similar. "What does she mean, Lucian?"

Lucian stretched his neck, his attention on Ella. "I would not have taken you for one to break a king's trust."

Silas was quick, his hand smacking into Lucian's chest to yank him straight. "I asked you a question." Silas's jaw ticked. "And let me remind you that Miss Morgrave's safety was put into your keeping. If you continue to look at her in such a manner, I will throw you from a moving carriage and leave that badger to do the rest."

Magnus huffed, though it was unclear whether it was in agreement or offense. Undead badgers were notoriously difficult to win over. Ella wasn't sure about the live ones.

Lucian shifted uncomfortably beneath the threat. "After the ball, I was asked to bring Miss Morgrave to a private conference with the king."

Silas's grip went slack, his gaze darting between Ella and his friend. "And you did not see fit to inform me of this?"

Ella wasn't certain whom he meant to ask, but Lucian answered, "I was explicitly advised against it. Upon pain of death."

The prince sat back in the seat to stare at Ella.

His attention felt like an accusation, particularly after Silas's own confession earlier. Ella glanced down at Magnus as she ran an unsteady hand over his fur. Silas would not ask her in front of the guard what she and his father had discussed, but he *would* ask her.

Silas asked, "What do you plan to do with him?" with a nod at Lucian.

Ella shrugged. "That's up to you. Though I would prefer you decide before he discovers where we are headed, since it is clear where his loyalties lie."

Lucian shot forward in his seat, and Silas slammed him back. Lucian jerked his arm free. "My loyalties lie with the prince.

They always have. What would you have me do? Defy the king openly? Do you think I must disobey his every order to prove myself worthy of trust?"

"I will not tell you again, Lucian."

Silas's warning was low, but it seemed to only make the guard angrier. "You risk everything for her. Can you truly not see what danger she's put you in? Can you not understand that there's more going on than just—"

When Silas's expression went free of emotion, Lucian fell gravely still. The prince's voice was level when he said, "That is not up to you." Cold blue eyes pinned the guard to his seat. "And if you don't trust that I have good reason, if you don't respect my judgment, then there is nothing more to say."

The color drained from Lucian's face. The carriage was silent except for the rattle of wheels against stone, and even the crate of animals awaited Lucian's response. Finally, he vowed, "I am with you, Highness. Come what may."

---

AT THE END of a long tree-lined lane, the carriage drew up to a small cottage tucked between tall oak and chestnut trees. The cottage was charming and appeared well-kept despite that Blackthorn had noted the staff was only occasionally on site. Ella stepped from the carriage, coming to stand beside Blackthorn and the footman, the latter of whom had evidently come onto Blackthorn's good side during the drive.

Ella said, "It's lovely, Blackthorn."

He smoothed the front of his waistcoat, unable to entirely put away his pride. "Thank you, miss. It is good to be back."

She squeezed his arm.

Silas stood near the carriage, palm on his chest and gaze on the cottage. Behind him, Lucian handed down a crate to Henry, and Fritz and the shrew, who had not particularly cared for one another since the start, leapt free to bound over the soft grass in opposite directions.

"Be careful," Ella called. "Don't go too far."

Fritz gestured a reply at her while Magnus rolled onto his back for an enthusiastic scratch. Lucian watched as the badger emitted a happy little churr, then he looked to his prince, as if searching for confirmation that something was very off about the entire scene, but Silas's attention was still on the cottage.

"Come in," Blackthorn said. "It's nearly time for tea."

Silas seemed to snap back at the words. He met Ella's gaze, but she only lifted one shoulder in a subtle shrug. Blackthorn had begun to seem more settled, his movements relaxed in a way they had not been before and his conversation flowing more easily. He chatted with the footman, pointing out the pond and a few of his favorite spots near the trees before the man retreated to tend the horses. The group entered the cottage, leaving the door cracked for the animals to come and go as they wished, and Blackthorn immediately set to his task.

Beside him, Ella took down three fine teacups painted in floral patterns, then felt unconsciably rude for not preparing any for Blackthorn and Henry. She caught the valet's eye, but he only gave her a playful, knowing sort of look. It made Ella feel as if it were the first time she was seeing through to the Blackthorn he'd been before his death. She smiled, and he returned to his work.

Around a small wooden table, Ella, the prince, and a member of the royal guard sipped their tea in uncomfortable silence as Henry whittled down the new growth on his cane and Blackthorn sorted through a small box of drawings he'd taken from a tall cabinet.

Silas ran a hand over the table's smooth surface. Lucian said not a word.

The scratch of Henry's knife was the only sound until he paused to lean nearer the drawings Blackthorn had placed to the side. "Is this the cottage?"

Blackthorn nodded, sliding another page toward Henry and tapping the corner of a sketch. "There was a massive yew tree beyond the pond. Gone a decade or more now. Root rot."

Henry nodded sagely.

Blackthorn laid another atop the stack, pointing to a grassy spot along the edge. "This is the area I was thinking of when we spoke of drainage before."

Ella and Silas exchanged a glance.

Henry picked up the sketch. "Can we go down to see it?"

"It's a bit of a walk."

Henry patted a hand on the thigh of his trouble leg. "I think the new one will stick. If not, you can carry me back and we will try the bolts. I'm eager to see the tool shed anyway."

Silas's brow pinched and Ella gave him a small shake of her head. She asked, "Blackthorn, did you draw these? They're remarkable."

"Yes, miss." He took another out of the box, a sketch of a pretty girl with a round face and a mischievous gap-toothed grin. "My daughter. She's grown, gone away to live by the seaside for nigh on ten years now."

Ella passed the drawing to Henry as Blackthorn pulled out another portrait. He said, "And this one was by a young Silas."

Ella took hold of the fragile paper, its edges a bit creased and the charcoal smeared. Lines went this way and that, jagged and unsteady in a way that made it hard to be certain if the animal depicted was a cow or a dog. It was awful, truly, and Ella struggled to contain a delighted grin. "Is it holding a sword?"

Silas frowned. "Of course it's a sword."

Ella turned the page over to find a sketch of him as a boy in a tall, stiff collar, expression solemn and hair cropped short, the lines clearly produced by Blackthorn's hand.

Blackthorn's voice grew contemplative. "They kept him locked in that room for so long, no one his age around. A child needs to gambol, to learn their legs. Especially one so curious. Sometimes I would sneak a few pages in, to give him something besides language and law, a bit of fancy. Had to stop though, after they found the charcoal on his fingers. Princes were not to be soiled or fanciful."

Silence settled heavily over the table. Ella could not help but look at Silas. He held her gaze.

The stillness stretched, then Blackthorn said, "Miss, we'd best prepare."

"What for, Blackthorn? We've just arrived."

"Well, tea, of course. With the king."

A low sound came out of Silas that might have been a curse.

Ella patted Blackthorn's hand. "We will, Blackthorn. I've just a few things to discuss with the prince before we leave." Blackthorn's expression turned wary, and Ella added, "He's not to come along. Please don't fret. It will be just you and me." When he nodded, Ella drew a deep breath. She looked to Silas, whose eyes were on Ella's hand where it rested over his dead valet's.

She said, "The king offered me my father's title."

His gaze snapped up.

"He believes the Lockes would be willing to relinquish any claim on the estate and the office now that they have secured a higher rank." Silas was no fool. His father had been planning to appoint someone else. He would know that Ella would not be granted all they thought she wanted without surrendering something in return. Ella said, "I have decided to accept his offer."

Silas stared at her for a very long moment before pushing up from his seat. He stood there, seemingly torn between the notion of storming out and flipping the table.

Ella leaned back against her chair. "I cannot stay here forever, in hiding, as lovely as that sounds. There is endless treachery at the palace, but it is not as if I could sit idly by knowing what it would mean for the office of High Cinder. The king's choice would affect every Cinder for decades to come. It would impact the safety of the kingdom. Something needs to be done. And I have to find a way to contain the magic I have wrought, even if it only means standing guard over the hazel tree. Even if it means starting over without a scrap of my father's work."

Silas's jaw flexed. He wanted to tell her she couldn't; it was as plain as the glower on his face. "And when you're exposed?"

She cleared her throat. "Working directly under the king without anyone discovering what I've done will be difficult, but less so should I take possession of the estate. Henry and Blackthorn can be relocated there, and I will engage the trusted household that was let go last year. It will be worth the risk."

"Do they know what will happen? Should you get caught?" Silas's gaze did not flick to Henry or Blackthorn, only stayed fixed on her. But Ella understood whom he meant.

"They do."

"We've decided to support her," Henry said. "Miss Morgrave needs our help."

The nod Silas gave said, *I see it's already decided* in no pleased way. He understood far more exactly what Ella risked; he'd been raised at court. He walked from the room without a word, through the open door and past an undead badger lounging in the shade.

Ella drew a slow breath.

Lucian watched her. Then he took another sip of tea, stood, straightening his uniform, and followed Silas out.

Henry cut another notch in his cane. "They'll come around, miss. Too sensible not to." He brushed a thumb over the smooth wood. "Isn't that right, Blackthorn?"

The words seemed to draw Blackthorn back a bit. He nodded, absently sorting the sketches as he said, "He always came back. No matter how she might have turned him away. Kept a close eye on her, all those years. The king didn't approve, of course, but Silas always made certain the Morgraves were well looked after. Said Lord Morgrave was too good a man not to and, well, someone needed to, didn't they. Too absorbed in the work to do it himself."

Ella froze, teacup halfway to her mouth.

"Prince Silas knew Ella's father?" Henry asked.

Blackthorn closed the lid on the box, leaving a handful of sketches and empty paper out. "Of course. Stopped by his office at least once a month, even though it was in the bowels of the palace." As an aside, he added, "Cinders were never given much status, you know. Only the High Cinder, who stood at the king's side. The rest were meant to remain unnoticed, like any other palace staff." Then his gaze went distant. "Torn up when Lord Morgrave died, he was. Started asking questions, kicking up a fuss. King Julian didn't like it one bit."

Ella carefully returned her cup to the table. "Blackthorn, do you remember the accident? The fire that took hold the day my father died?"

He blinked, gaze turning to hers, mouth coming open as if he meant to reply, then he took in Ella's dress. "Oh, miss. You cannot wear that."

"Wear what, Blackthorn?"

"All of it. Wouldn't be appropriate for tea with the king. We'll have to get you something more suited."

Ella slumped against her chair, exchanging a glance with Henry. She said, "Don't fret, Blackthorn. I'll change straightaway."

---

THE DAY PASSED, and after a quiet dinner, Henry and Blackthorn sat at the table making sketches and talking through drainage and irrigation by lamplight while Lucian flipped slowly through a book of poetry and Silas fussed with the fire. Fritz was nestled in Ella's skirt, nudging her every time she attempted to stop running her finger over his head. He missed Cybil. Ella did too. She wrapped her hands gently beneath him, then carried him outside, where she deposited him in the low grass near the steps. He immediately picked a tidy bundle of grass, twining the blades into a braid for chewing.

Ella smiled, dropping a handful of seeds onto George's perch, gave a wave to the footman where he was posted to keep an eye on the road, then wandered past trees tinted blue in the moonlight to the clearing beyond. The air smelled of primrose and honeysuckle, as well as woodsmoke from the cottage chimney. Light reflected off the pond in the distance while night bugs chittered and croaked. Ella kept on until the muffled voices in the cottage were lost to the song of the night, then she settled onto the cool ground.

In the soft grass, she leaned back on her palms to gaze up at the trees. She sat alone for nearly an hour, thinking about what Blackthorn had said, and about the man's sketch of young Silas. And there, so distant from anyone she might endanger, Ella allowed herself to remember her father and how he had long ago inquired about her feelings for the prince. How Ella had told him firmly that she never wished to hear of Silas again.

How he must have taken the girl with wounded pride at her word and kept any association to himself.

Ella would never know how her father felt, because someone had made certain he could never be brought back. Ironic, given that the king's entire purpose for his Cinders was to call up the dead as witness. And yet not a single soul had been able to provide testimony after the fire.

None but Lord Locke.

Only the sudden silence of the crickets warned of Silas's approach, and she tried very hard to rein in what magic had escaped.

He stood for a moment beside her, as if taking in the sky and lake, not the unnatural way the grass flourished beneath Ella's palms. When Ella did not chase him away, he slid out of his jacket, offering it to her as he settled quietly at her side. He crossed an arm over his knee, his long fingers dangling in the pale light.

Ella drew the jacket around her shoulders. It was warm and

smelled as if Blackthorn had very recently refreshed it. She said, "Thank you for what you did for Grace's family."

His lips pursed as if he might deny even knowledge of the act, but at Ella's look, he inclined his head.

They were silent for a while, and with nothing but the birds, the bugs, and the breeze, Ella was reminded how much life was in trees. She was reminded that she missed her mother dearly, and of the ache to be able to let her go. She pulled the jacket tighter around her.

In the distance, a badger flung a rock into the pond. Ella watched as the Magnus-shaped shadow waddled along the bank, stopping to explore every new log or den. The first few weeks out of her family home had been difficult for Ella, and not simply because she'd lost her father, her income, and her home. She had cherished their land, its freedom and isolation. Her work as a Cinder had brought her close to many types of violence, but there was something very different about the casual cruelty of society, the creatures they became when they were packed together in an excited mob. Ella had saved Magnus from the pit. She still could not say exactly why she had brought him back, only that it felt as if it had to be done. That he needed more time.

Beside her, Silas said, "What my father did to you was unforgivable."

Julian's decision had nothing to do with Silas. But Ella could understand how he might feel as if it did. "He's trapped you into marriage. I suppose whatever he's done to me is not much worse."

He frowned, then ran a hand over the back of his neck. "Are we to both be unhappy simply because he says it is so?"

"He wears the crown." Ella's words were subdued, no matter how much she did not want to accept them.

They were quiet for a time, so close their shoulders brushed. His presence was comforting and consuming at once.

As the night wore on and the air turned cold, the feeling of it all ending pressed down. Ella would have to face what had been done. It would very likely rip her to shreds.

Silas's hand closed the small distance they held. His fingertips grazed hers, softly, inviting Ella to draw away. She did not. Sitting side by side, he tangled their fingers, then lifted Ella's hand to his lips. Gently, like the brush of a moth wing, Silas laid a kiss on the bare skin of her wrist. It stayed there, so very long, so long that it began a low, throbbing pain in Ella's chest.

He did not look at her as he pulled away, only stood, his face lifted toward the trees.

Ella stared up at him, his profile lit by the moon. He was so beautiful it hurt. Beneath her palm, the grass warmed with magic. She asked, "What happens now?"

Silas's gaze stayed on the trees, hands in his pockets. "The crown's purpose is to protect and provide for the people. That is why I can never let a Locke be queen." He drew a slow breath. "It is my responsibility to ensure it. And you, I suppose, will have challenges of your own."

Ella would. Keeping a Locke from her father's title, to put a finer point on it.

Silas said, "Someday, when we are old and I am king, we might stand together before the court. King Silas and Lady Morgrave, his High Cinder."

He looked at her then, a challenge, and Ella did not have the courage to reply. She could see it, the same as he, and the very many painful things that scene would require. Ella would have to accept his father's bargain, would be beholden to Julian's every whim. Her secrets would remain buried, whatever the cost, along with her morals and any notion of justice. There would be no trust between herself and that future king, only the threat of secrets revealed. The rot within the court would grow, just like the magic that had taken hold of Ella.

They both knew it could never be allowed to happen.

Silas said, "Goodnight, Miss Morgrave." Then he turned and walked toward the cottage.

THE NEXT MORNING, Ella woke early, pulled back her hair and tied on her apron, then quietly entered the front room. Because they did not need sleep, Henry and Blackthorn had spent the night on the porch, on watch should anyone have not been fooled by Silas's scheming. The sitting room was dark, the cottage was cool, and the prince lay sprawled atop a tufted sofa. Ella could not prevent herself from pausing to look. He was in shirtsleeves, one arm tossed overhead, the other resting flat against his chest, his jacket folded neatly over a nearby chair.

His expression was soft, breathing steady, and Ella had the unsettling urge to climb in beside him. Then her eyes adjusted to the lack of light, and she realized Lucian watched her from the corner.

She cleared her throat quietly, then crossed to the kitchen where Blackthorn was already warming the kettle for tea. The footman would likely be up as well, caring for the horses, and Ella had a number of undead creatures to hunt down and make certain all were accounted for and safe.

"Good morning, miss," Blackthorn said as he began unpacking the bread and preserves someone had evidently filched from the inn.

Ella smiled. "Good morning." She gestured toward the stack of new sketches scattering the table. "It looks as if you and Henry have a great deal of projects planned."

"Yes, miss. He's quite clever, and this old cottage is in need of updates."

Ella slid a foot stove diagram aside to stare down at a sketch of a palace room, its previously bare corners strewn with Henry's ornamental metalwork designs. The room was familiar, one of the libraries on the lower floors, seldom used but a resource the necromancers had accessed nonetheless.

Because it was situated across from her father's office.

At the top, above a wide doorway, the pediment bore a thick

crown tangled with thorny vines. Ella went cold. "Blackthorn, what is this?"

He leaned to look. "That's the Rose Library. Famous for *The King's Falcon*, hung in pride of place on the south wall. I used to sit outside of that room whenever Silas was in with the High Cinder. That corridor had the most uncomfortable chairs." He went quiet, as if recalling the memory. "Oh, but the office is burnt now, isn't it? Such a shame."

"A falcon?"

"Yes. Quite the story." He laid the knife on the counter. "But, well, you should get dressed, shouldn't you miss? We'll be late for tea."

Ella looked up to find Silas standing in the doorway. Silas, who had inadvertently revealed that the rose and king was to do with his father and a strangely drawn falcon. Silas, who had not let on that his dealings with Harold were in any way related to the High Cinder. "You knew." Knew that Ella's father had been murdered.

"Not at the start. I only suspected."

"When?"

"Harold's message not to cross the rose and king."

Ella felt the blood leave her face. "How many others?" How many men were killed because of her father's death? How many were involved in the conspiracy to cover it up?

Silas came into the room, stopping before the table. His fingers curled overtop a chair rail. "Henry, for one, though it is clear they were aiming for Harold. A palace messenger. And more, I suspect."

His gaze shifted to where Blackthorn stood, back turned as he prepared the bread. When Silas's gaze returned, Ella recalled his reaction when she had revealed Harold's words in the glasshouse. Harold had not just sent the prince a message. He'd sent it in a way that Ella would not understand. And Silas hadn't told her.

Ella wet her lips. "Who is responsible for the men pursuing you?"

"I cannot be certain."

If it was a Locke, their pursuit would immediately cease, because Lora was engaged to the prince. Yet Silas had made certain to plan distractions when they'd left the inn. Ella sank heavily into a chair. "Last night, you said we were to go to the mausoleum."

His jaw ticked with some emotion that did not seem to be anger. "That doesn't matter now. You're to become High Cinder. Once you're instated, your every act will be made on behalf of the crown. All you do will become legal."

Legal and on behalf of the crown were not precisely the same thing, but Ella did not argue. She could not decipher whether she or Silas was being played by the king, precisely whose hand the man was trying to force. Perhaps both. She looked up at him. "I still have to accept the position."

Silas held her gaze. "I know."

Blackthorn precisely placed a plate of bread and preserves in front of Ella, then frowned at the prince. "Highness, the state of your cravat is so unsuitable as to be intolerable. Please do try again."

## CHAPTER 17

Ella followed three paces behind Lucian as he strode in full uniform through the palace corridors. She had no intention of marching straight to the king and accepting his offer, but she could not gain access to the palace without at least the pretense. Their path wound through endless rooms and corridors that Ella had only visited once since her father's death—the day she'd been permitted audience with the king—and that was merely out of respect to Emeri's station. It had been made clear that unless the new High Cinder gave her license, Ella would not be allowed back.

Even then, Ella had not been given leave to visit the wing where her father had died.

Past the many offices and workrooms of kingdom officials, they finally reached the area that housed the rooms used by Cinders. The faint scent of damp ash still clung to the corridor. The tapestries had not been replaced. The stone would be scarred black nearer the fire. The books that had lined her father's office walls, a lifetime of study, gone. Ella felt a bit as if she could not breathe, her chest constricting and her neck damp with sweat. Lucian exchanged words with the posted guard, then he and Ella walked on, past the workroom where Ella had trained and the large chamber that would likely house the new High Cinder. Lucian stopped in the corridor outside the library. He turned to stand beside the entrance.

Ella stopped as well, staring at Lucian because she could not gather the courage to look toward her father's office.

His dark eyes made no judgment, but that was fine—Ella had plenty of judgment for herself. She said, "I can see why Silas likes you."

The corner of his lip twitched in annoyance.

Ella drew a deep breath, then turned to walk into the library.

The room was large, sparely furnished with a few long tables and chairs. The walls were covered in shelves from floor to ceiling, broken only by dark wood and thick, sturdy railings on the stairs and the upper level. It was not a space meant for leisure. She strode forward, her fingers trailing over a table's smooth surface.

Memories assailed her. The endless hours of study and research, the way necromancy had consumed her father's attention and time. Other Cinders had thought Ella favored by a partial father, that her greater skill was due to an unfair advantage. They had not understood how necromancy had touched every part of her life, how she had been steeped in it since the day she was born. Perhaps it was why the magic had turned bitter and rebelled. Perhaps Ella should have spent more time away from it.

Her fellow necromancers had never had the same sort of connection to it. When the group had gone out on complicated assignments, Ella had held back because emotion made her magic volatile. It was more they had not understood; it had looked as if Ella and her father thought her above the worst of the work. If she were to become High Cinder, she would have to either win them over or lead ruthlessly.

Her fingertips grazed a bound volume of tracheal anatomy. It had not taken a great deal of effort for Lord Locke to poison them against her after everything that had happened. She would have much to overcome.

Lord Locke, however, would never be granted license to practice again. He would be lucky if he lived past the end of the month.

Ella swallowed bile at the thought of the man, every recollection worse now that she stood so close to where the fire had raged. She walked forward, toward the south wall and the painting of the falcon, evidently long-ago gifted to the king. She had never paid the scene particular mind and, staring up at it, could not find any especially interesting details that might have drawn her in. She was fairly certain the birds were meant to signify power or success. But then, Ella had not studied such things.

"Lucian," she asked. "What do falcons symbolize?"

From a good distance behind her, he said. "Eagerness in pursuit. Relentlessly so."

She hummed. "And so what was the king's goal?"

Lucian was silent.

"Silas said it was a jest between his father's closest friends. Surely, there must be an interesting story behind it."

"Surely, you would not expect me to reveal a king's private jests, even if I did know."

"I suppose not." She turned. "Well, best we set to task."

Lucian's gaze was level. He had not been in favor of the plan, but, after having withheld information from the prince, his objections held considerably less weight than they otherwise might.

They exited the library, and Ella could no longer avoid the sight of her father's office door. She crossed slowly, then stood, palm pressed flat against the wood. Ella closed her eyes and whispered a painful farewell.

When she drew away, Lucian stood at attention, face forward and eyes on the opposite wall.

Ella cleared her throat, then nodded, and they strode toward the room near the end of the corridor.

※

THE HALL that held the Cinder work stations was large and dark. Ella and Lucian carried a pair of oil lamps through the space, slowly illuminating three rows of tables and desks. Glass decanters, surgical supplies, scales, and tubes scattered the surfaces in a manner that made clear that Ella was not the only Cinder who had not been allowed back. She did not want to think about what that would mean for the accumulation of cases when the necromancers' work finally resumed. It was never best to wait; an undertaker's preservation magic only lasted so long.

At the far end of the room sat the largest tables and Ella's desk. "There isn't time to linger," she whispered toward Lucian, who'd slowed to stare in either horror or fascination—it was too dark to be certain—at the contents of a large glass jar.

"I know that," he hissed back. Then he grumbled, "Never met anyone like you," very much not in the tone the prince had used when he'd said the same thing.

Ella placed the lamp on her worktable, trying hard not to focus on anything aside from the need for haste. She unlatched the fine metal box that held her tools then withdrew two bent picks and a long, thin knife with a carved handle.

Lucian had come to peer over her shoulder. He stepped back at the sight of the blade.

"Bring the light." Ella crossed the space to the desk on the opposite side of the room. She knelt before it, gesturing for Lucian to come closer as she shoved a tool inside a drawer's lock.

"Have you done this before?"

She did not glance back. "Are you offering to do it for me?"

"Just wondering precisely how criminal the woman I'm currently aiding is."

The lock clicked open. Silas was right—anything Ella did

once she became a kingdom official could be done under the protection of the crown. But this could not wait. If there was any chance to find evidence without surrendering to the terms of the king's bargain, Ella had to take it. She slid open the drawer of Lord Locke's desk. It stank of him, the musk and amber scent that clung to his clothes and the parchment and vellum he insisted on toting about. Even the sight of his handwriting made her angry.

Ella stood, lifting the stack of writings out to rifle through. Case notes, research theories, observations. Two more drawers, and more of the same. Lists of medical texts, formularies, inventories.

Nothing. It wasn't a shock, as Locke wasn't fool enough to leave behind evidence if he could help it. But disappointment rose nonetheless. Flipping through the final few pages, Ella tried to tamp down the shaky feeling in her chest. Then a word caught her eye. *Amnesia*.

Her fingers paused over a page of seemingly unrelated notes. She scanned the precise lines, a list of botanicals that would not be out of place in a necromancer's work. Beside the last, a poisonous plant marked with a simple short dash to set it apart, and the words *disorientation, amnesia, coma*, and *death*. Beneath that, in Locke's neat hand, a single word: *astringent*.

There was only one reason Locke would care if a toxin was bitter. The magic that brought bodies back was not a cure-all. It bypassed natural processes to return motor control, so there was much it could overcome, but it did not affect the mind. If a poison caused a memory issue, it could not be quickly eliminated by an undead body. The process could take months. It was impossible to know. Poisonings were uncommon, and no one had kept a body animated for long. Not when it was illegal, and not when the magic would continue to draw on the practitioner the entire time.

"Oh, Blackthorn," Ella breathed.

The words fell out of her in quiet lament, but Lucian did not seem to notice, his attention on the door. Voices echoed from far down the corridor. He whispered, "Time is up, Miss Morgrave."

Ella shoved the parchment into her bodice then pushed closed the drawers. She did not bother locking them. Not since, once she accepted the post of High Cinder, Lord Locke would never be allowed to return.

❦

THE PRINCE STOOD at the end of the corridor, blathering to the posted guards. As Ella and Lucian approached, he turned.

"Ah, Lucian. I've been looking for you." Silas's hands clapped together in a show of impatience. "I need assistance with a task. Rather urgently."

Lucian's gaze cut toward Ella; Silas's presence had not been part of the plan.

Silas waved dismissively. "Whatever you're about with Miss Morgrave can wait. Let her sit in a fine palace chair while we handle our business. Come, both of you. Make haste."

They followed Silas down one narrow hall then another and finally into a smaller, private room. The space was scattered with plush sofas, fine vases atop ornate pedestals, and little else.

The prince walked to the opposite end of the room to stand beside the sole table, where he removed a small square container from his jacket. He placed the container on the surface of the table. The breath he drew seemed resigned. He flipped the tiny metal latch, the lid flew open, and Cybil launched out in a fury. Silas stepped back a pace as the mouse skidded his direction, tiny arms flying in a collection of the rudest gestures Ella had ever seen.

"Cybil," she said.

The mouse gave one final glare to the prince, then turned toward Ella to wave. Lucian blinked.

Silas crossed his arms. "I found her on my dressing table digging through personal effects."

Ella stepped closer. "What were you doing in the prince's dressing room?"

Cybil shrugged innocently. It was overplayed.

Silas's glower flicked to Ella. She leaned forward and scooped the mouse into her palms. "Well, I'm glad you're back."

Cybil stood on her hind legs, her tiny hands coming up to dig into her mouth. A scandalized sound came out of Lucian when the mouse pulled a wad of paper from her cheek, unfolded it, then held it up for Ella to see.

"What's this?" Ella's insides went cold, because the scrap of paper held only two letters, but they were recognizable as her father's hand.

After a great deal of gesturing, chittering, and an elaborate impression, Cybil rested back on her haunches.

"Show me." Ella's voice was calm, but Silas and Lucian must have recognized the gravity of it, because as Cybil ran down Ella's skirt then across the floor, Ella behind her, they followed without a word.

ELLA, Silas, and Lucian followed the mouse through a half-dozen corridors to a narrow, dark-paneled room near the stairs often traversed by the Cinders in their work. The room appeared disused, drapes over the furniture and shelves empty of books or decor. Cybil darted over the hearth at the foot of a grand fireplace, its mantel decorated with battle horses and a great many flourishes. The grate was empty, the box clean and dark, but Cybil scuttled beneath and drew out another scrap of paper, its edges charred.

She handed it up to Ella. With trembling fingers, Ella took it, kneeling before the hearth. Her heart felt hollow, sick and sharp and a thousand emotions she could not let tear free.

Silas came to stand behind her, though Ella was not certain he would recognize her father's script. Cybil ran up Ella's arm to perch on her shoulder, gesturing determinedly to the prince. Silas cursed.

Then he turned, ordering Lucian to help him search the room. It did not take long. Yanking a drape aside, they upended the cushions to reveal a dark brown bag.

Ella sank to sitting. Silas laid the bag reverently into her hands. Her father's satchel.

Empty.

Lord Locke must not have trusted the fire to burn the documents completely. Or else, he'd needed some part of them, some piece of information that Ella did not know. Perhaps for blackmail. Perhaps for something else.

Her chest heaved in something of a sob but it, too, was empty.

"Watch the door." Silas's words were low, and Lucian followed the order without question. As the door closed behind the guard, Silas knelt beside Ella.

Her fingers traced over the satchel's worn stitching. If Silas placed his hand over hers, Ella would lose the last of her control. She had to do something. Anything to relieve what was roiling inside her.

Worse, she had to tell him.

She swallowed hard. The breath she drew stung her lungs. There was so much pain she could not find a place to focus besides the fabric beneath her hands. She said, "Insulting to be bested by someone so inept."

Silas did not laugh.

Ella drew another breath. "The day my father died, before the fire, Lady Locke was in the back garden, overseeing the new roses she'd ordered in. She had the head gardener digging up the old ones, a few workers carrying bundles to a pile for burning. Mama never came to the house. I thought, foolishly, that she couldn't. Looking back, I suppose it was simply too hard for her to be there, to see her lovely home being taken from her like everything else. And maybe she knew my father would be angry at what I had done. Upset at how wrong things had gone. Whatever the reason, it had evidently been her choice to stay away, nothing more. But that day, with the gardeners tearing out roses that had grown since before I was born, a thin pillar of smoke rising behind the manor, and Father's new wife bullying the staff, she just... appeared."

"Lady Locke went apoplectic. Of course, anyone would. But she understood more deeply. She had married a Cinder, after all, even if she had no respect for his work. She knew the dead did not rise on their own. And there stood her husband's late wife, a woman she'd been systematically uprooting any trace of for a year. Every loyal servant, every portrait of our family, every napkin she'd embroidered and tea set she'd painted, Locke had seen it gone. She knew who it was with only a glance. And that she'd never been rid of her at all."

Ella drew a shaky breath. "My father was in his study. He never had any idea of what I had done. I was too afraid to tell him when doing so could mean he might lose his title, the estate, even his life if the court looked upon the situation badly, if they believed, as Lady Locke did, that Emeri Morgrave, High Cinder, had stashed away his long-dead wife." A short, humorless laugh escaped her. "In the end, those were the very things we lost. And all at my hands." All because she'd been a fool. Because she'd thought she had time to remedy it.

Her fingers tightened into the material of the satchel. She could feel the weight of Cybil where she'd settled on Ella's shoulder to smooth a lock of hair. "I was down the hall reviewing an anatomy text, always searching for a way to detach the magic, when I heard the shrieking. I came into my father's study just as Lady Locke's violence was at its worst. Apparently, my father had bolted to his feet, ready to run to the window and see his wife rather than to listen to Locke scream. She thought it another betrayal. There was crashing glass; my father was hurt. He looked up just as I came in, and somehow, in that simple glance, my father knew I was to blame."

A shudder rolled through her at the memory, the guilt and grief and the horror that followed. "He did not tell Lady Locke, not when she'd already vowed to turn him in. He took the brunt of her anger, all the responsibility. And I... It still shames me to say it. I turned and ran from the room."

"I spent the night in the clearing, beneath Mama's tree. It had taken so long to return her to a state of peace, to drag her from the garden where she'd been ripping out the new roses, her fingers deep in soil, and to tether her to the tree so she could not escape again. She had so much anger, and once she was sleeping, I was too weak and sick from the magic, too afraid to go home." She glanced at the door to the chamber, still closed, Lucian outside. "That was why I wasn't there when the king's men came. Why I didn't know that he'd been killed."

Ella drew a tattered paper from the pocket of her skirt. Her thumb gently brushed the edge before she held it out to Silas. "That was when I found the note. Evidently, Lady Locke had thrown herself into the carriage and was off to tell the king and court. He did not have time to find me, to help with Mama, so he hid a hasty message in the pocket of my cloak."

Silas glanced up from the paper, his gaze sharp. "He knew someone intended him harm."

Ella nodded. It felt like a secret too big to hold, and yet she knew nothing, not truly. Only that someone was blackmailing the king, that Lord Locke was making bargains and fooling with corrupt magic. A witness was dead and the High Cinder had been caught in the middle. Her father had suspected someone was coming for him, strongly enough that he'd warned her in the note. "If I'd only returned home, he would have told me. I would know exactly who he'd suspected or exactly how he'd found out. I might have some leverage. Or I—I could have stopped him from leaving. Stopped him before the fire."

"Ella—"

"Let me finish. I need to have it done." Silas went quiet, and Ella pressed her eyes closed. "He did not go straight to the king. Evidently my father had no intention of stopping Lady Locke. He knew how she was. She was not going to forgive him. She would never understand. So he gathered up his papers, the ones he mentions in the note, to send to me for safekeeping and to prevent the very disaster that has come to pass. His last words to me were that I must take his place, should anything happen. That he'd left me instructions on how to proceed. But the documents never made it to the scribe. That night at the pleasure gardens, Harold said the satchel burned up in the fire along with everything else. He saw it in my father's possession. And here it is, which means someone kept it aside." The fire had been no accident. But a single empty satchel was no real proof, not when the witness to even the satchel was on the run.

"Lady Locke never knew about the tree. She never discovered I was the one responsible, so she does not know that my mother still roams the estate. She assumes that when my father died, the magic died with him. Lady Locke saw only a betrayal. They had a contract, she said. He owed her." Ella scoffed. "That was how she spoke of their marriage, as if it were a settlement. Before his ashes were cold, she threw me out of the house with nothing more than the shoes on my feet. So I never told her. I just snuck back on Sundays, checked the tethers, and stayed out of the Lockes' way."

Silas's voice was calm and even, but Ella could feel the

concern beneath it when he asked, "What happens with the tree when you become High Cinder?"

"I tried to destroy it before. It nearly killed me. If I hadn't stopped, I believe it would have. And when I died, I would become something like my mother. Only stronger. Infinitely more powerful, more dangerous, and there is no way to know whether the magic tied to the tree would be set free." She bit the inside of her lip hard. "My father didn't know about the tree, but he knew I struggled with the magic, with letting go. When he was here, he was able to anchor me, to help release the dead from their tether to my magic. I hoped to find a way to anchor myself, to practice and learn and... I don't know. To find a way before it unleashes something worse."

"What about the other Cinders? Can they not do the same, this anchoring of the magic?"

Ella shook her head. "I'm not sure who might be capable. My father studied for nearly three decades and had the ability to focus better than anyone I know. His craft was flawless. But they won't help, not when Lord Locke has poisoned them all against me." If she were High Cinder, though, Ella might be able to teach them.

"Lord Locke," Silas repeated.

"Yes. The man your father intends to name High Cinder."

"And you think he's responsible for..."

Ella met his gaze. "He killed my father. I know it. I only need the proof." Her fingers tightened again into the material of the satchel, empty of the proof her father had saved, and she felt sick and angry all over again.

Silas was silent for a long moment. When he finally spoke, his voice was soft. "And if you're hanged?"

What happened to the magic if the king discovered what she had done, he meant. If Julian decided to rescind his offer and the tree was not severed. "I don't know," she admitted. "But I suspect we may find out soon."

Silas stood, offering his hand to Ella where she sat before the hearth. She took it, and he drew her to her feet.

He did not let go of her hand. Ella pulled free, as if she only meant to join it with her other where it clutched the satchel.

Silas's eyes stayed on her. "You know I cannot let you accept the post of High Cinder with this hanging over your head."

"Yes, of course I do," she snapped. "Why else would I have gone along with your fool scheme?" She drew a slow breath. "There's something else. Another reason Lord Locke can never become High Cinder."

"Does it explain why my father is determined I wed the man's niece?"

She pressed her lips together. "I suspect... I suspect that Locke has promised the king some sort of corrupt magic. Something that might prolong life. Something near immortality."

The expression that crossed Silas's features made clear he'd had no such suspicion. "Can he?"

"No, not Lord Locke anyway. It would take someone with a great deal stronger connection to magic. Someone capable of funneling magic unceasingly to another being. For years on end."

Silas stared at her, the one person who could do just such a thing. "Is there... anyone else?"

Her fingers clutched harder to the satchel. "If there is, he will find them."

They stood in silence for an eternity. It was not as if Silas hadn't known his father was a man of shifting morals. But the idea he would take it this far was likely a great deal to process.

"Silas." Ella's words were quiet. She was almost afraid to ask. "What's in the mausoleum?"

He breathed out a sigh. "I found another body."

## CHAPTER 18

No one was permitted inside the mausoleum aside from the royal family and the appointed members of palace staff. Ella and Silas left Lucian, who aided by diverting the attention of the posted guard, so they could sneak into the narrow passage that led to a tunnel Silas meant to use to gain access to the mausoleum without being seen. Deep in the palace, Ella always felt the sensation of a great weight of stone surrounding her, as if at any moment she might be crushed. She had never particularly liked it, and even then, she'd never been quite so deep.

They paced silently through the passages by the light of a single lantern until eventually the weight seemed to ease, and Silas brought Ella through a small door near a well-maintained courtyard that held the mausoleum. The stately building stood in the center of a square of trimmed shrubberies surrounded by oak trees. There was a tall gate at the entrance to the square, but no locks on the mausoleum door. Leaving the lantern, they crossed to the building then slipped into a chamber with a tiled floor and a low ceiling. Silas glanced back at Ella, and she gave him a small nod.

They walked forward, into the main chamber, sculptures and

columns lining the space. Placed evenly in the center of a space illuminated by a pair of stained-glass windows rested a half-dozen tombs topped with effigies of kings and queens lying on stone pillows and holding symbols of their office. Ella was overcome with the feeling that it was a place she should not be. It would be the greatest folly to wake a dead king, even accidentally.

The enormity of what Silas had said settled over Ella. If someone had hidden a body in the tomb of a dead king, they truly wished it to never be found. She took hold of the edge of his coat. "Tell me it's not inside one of these."

His mouth remained in a grim line.

Ella groaned. "If we are found out, your father will create new and exceptional tortures for the misdeed we are about to commit. You realize that, don't you?"

"Entirely."

She cursed. "Which one?"

He pointed to what Ella believed was Silas's great-grandfather, carved in stone atop a tall tomb.

"Why?" Why would anyone do such a thing? What would possess a person, drive them to such ends? The rising dread in her did a little flip, because wasn't Ella just desperate enough to open the same tomb? Sweat broke out in places Ella did not know she could sweat.

"I think it was an accident."

"An accident?" she hissed. "How do you accidentally stuff a body into a dead king's tomb?"

He gave her a measured look.

She glared back.

"I believe the murder may have been an accident. Not the stuffing of the body." He gestured toward the entrance. "It's not as if there was a way to remove him from the grounds without being seen."

"Him?"

Silas drew a breath, then he crossed to the tomb. They stood beside it, shoulder to shoulder, and Silas gestured toward the small triangle of material sticking out from beneath the lid.

Black, trimmed in gold thread. The colors of the office of Cinder, with a manly sort of flourish to the design. Ella's knees gave a little jolt, as if threatening to buckle. She locked them in place. "How did you find this?"

"Trust that, had I any choice in the matter, the mausoleum would be about the last place I would want to look. Workmen repairing the crimson hall remembered seeing an altercation in the courtyard."

"Right." She breathed. "Do you know how much these lids weigh?"

He nodded.

"So whoever did this either had a team of men or a single man of unnatural strength."

"I didn't know if someone who was undead would be strong enough to ..."

"Definitely," Ella said. "Which means that whoever did this was also a necromancer. And whoever is inside knows precisely who is to blame." Her heart felt a bit fluttery at the idea of finally having a witness, even as she knew what they were about to do was the worst sort of bad idea.

Silas's fingers flexed. "How do we get it open?"

She wanted to say, *We don't. We tell the king. We let the Cinders investigate.* But they could do no such thing. So she said, "The oak trees."

༺༻

ELLA HAD DONE DELICATE WORK. In the past, she'd tested the magic in small ways countless times in order to learn how best to apply her skills in complicated situations.

She had never moved a slab of stone meant to house an ancient king for eternity. "If this cracks and splits, I'm fleeing the kingdom."

Silas ran a palm over his chest. "I hope you'll allow me to come along."

She blew out a steady breath, focusing on the narrow scraps of dead wood they'd wedged beneath the lid and the base. Cybil abandoned her spot on Ella's shoulder, leaping onto the lid, where she scurried down its side to check each piece was firmly in place.

Ella pressed the magic into the wood, slowly levering the lid from its base. Wincing at the sound of scraping stone, she paused, drew a steadying breath, and adjusted her stance. Cybil chittered a few suggestions, and Ella nodded. Silas ran a palm over his face.

Ella pushed harder, and the lid rose. It wobbled, Cybil chirped, and Ella sent more shoots from the wood to stabilize the stone. It was a slow process, and Ella was just beginning to realize how difficult it would be to clean up should they have to hide what they had done. She hoped, very hard, that the man inside had answers.

Silas placed one of the larger branches they'd collected in the courtyard against the floor, leaning it toward the lid, and Ella braced it before bringing the lid nearer. Eventually, the tomb interior was revealed.

All drew a deep breath—at least, those who were living. Ella and Silas stepped closer.

Silas frowned. "Is that enough space?"

"As long as he behaves."

The prince's eyes closed for a long moment.

Ella used the time to survey the man inside. He was tall and had broad shoulders with an otherwise narrow build, before the bloat in any case. That was the problem with murders—no proper burial preparations had been made. There was a gash on his head, and his dark skin had gone grayish. He hadn't been dead long.

"Do you recognize him?" Silas asked.

"It's Lord Pembrook. Did you not say he told you how to find Harold?"

"Blackthorn met him in my stead."

"Oh," Ella said, in a manner befitting a mausoleum. The guilt that Silas carried was suddenly very present. Ella could not bring herself to voice what they both now knew about Blackthorn's death. So instead, she said, "Lord Pembrook was a Cinder for twenty years or thereabouts."

Silas leaned nearer to peer into the tomb. "Were you close?"

"No, he was... He wasn't very pleasant to work with." She glanced up at the prince. "But no one deserves this."

Silas gave a single nod.

They stood looking down at the man. Silas said, "Are we really going to do this?"

"It was your idea."

"I don't know that I said—"

Ella drew the wand from her skirt.

"Right." He stepped back, glancing only briefly at the entrance before finding a spot out of Ella's way.

Cybil darted into the tomb, and Ella hissed, "Don't touch a single jewel on that king!" before the mouse popped her head back up and gave Ella a wounded look.

"Not one button, not one thread," Ella warned. "There will be entire investigations, should we live through this. I will get blamed."

Cybil lifted a careful finger to point at Silas.

"No. We shall not blame the prince. Leave the dead king alone. I mean it."

The mouse huffed irritably.

Ella took the braided string from her pocket, winding it through her fingers to begin the song.

Silas whispered, "Next time, I'm leaving you in the box."

Cybil wagged her head mockingly, then performed a vain little imitation of the prince.

It was too impressive to be angry about, honestly, and Silas just crossed his arms, shifting his focus to Ella as she completed the outer circle. Her voice rose, the magic sparked, and for the first time in her life, Ella woke a man capable of waking the dead.

※

Lord Pembrook immediately tried to sit up. His shoulder and chest struck the tomb lid, knocking him flat, and his wide gaze shot through the room. "No," he breathed as his eyes finally landed on Ella.

"I'm sorry, my lord."

The prince shifted from his spot, and the man's expression turned wary. Beneath his line of sight, Ella held a hand back to prevent Silas's approach. "It's all right, Lord Pembrook. He's only here to help. It's just the three of us."

Ella did not mention the mouse. She gave the man a few moments to take it all in.

He said, "I'm dead."

"I'm afraid so."

"He left me in a tomb."

"Yes, unfortunately."

Lord Pembrook closed his eyes, deeply distraught. "Am I on top of a king?"

"Let's get you out of there, shall we?"

Once Lord Pembrook was settled, had a moment to right his clothes and be introduced to the prince, the three of them stood before a tomb covered in oak.

Lord Pembrook stared at the growth, then Ella. "Miss Morgrave …"

"I know."

His chest moved, then he lifted his hands, as if experimentally. "I never thought I would experience it from this side. It's quite awful."

"Is it?"

"Well, I am deceased."

She nodded gravely. "True. But otherwise?"

Lord Pembrook considered. "It's so much stronger than I expected, the connection between us."

"I cannot say whether that is the usual. You see, my lord, my magic does not seem to want to let go."

His hands dropped, all experimentation in the new version of his body seemingly stilled. "How do you mean?"

"We can discuss it later." When he frowned, Ella rolled a look at Silas. "There really are much more urgent—"

Lord Pembrook's posture went stubborn, a bit like a strong-willed mule, or a man in full confidence he was owed whatever he wished.

Ella couldn't stop him from acting the mule, but she wasn't about to pull his rope. "I've a bit of trouble with returning the dead. The connection does not want to sever, and I find myself tied indefinitely. High Cinder Morgrave used to anchor the magic, to help me let go, but he's gone now."

He stared at her. "Fascinating. Does this not drain you? Indefinitely, you say, but for how long, specifically? Have you tried to—"

"Lord Pembrook," Silas started, but the lord entirely ignored the attempt.

"—and what of the circle? You just hold whatever entity you've returned inside of it until you've sorted an anchor?"

Ella bit her lip, not wanting to launch into a thorny explanation of how she had no one to act as anchor now that her father was gone, that her long-dead mother was magically tethered to a tree, or that Henry and the others weren't anchored at all, only tied to Ella by way of her magic. Lord Pembrook would never trust the undead outside of a circle, let alone let them sleep in his suite. She said, "Something like that."

He leaned back in awe. "Miss Morgrave, we knew you were powerful, but this is—" He turned, snapping, "Do you mind?" at Silas as the prince again attempted to interrupt.

"Highness," Silas said. When Lord Pembrook only glared, Silas repeated, "It's 'Do you mind, Your Highness?' And yes, I do mind."

Ella shot Silas a look that she hoped conveyed *what have I told you about picking fights with the undead* then said, "Lord Pembrook, I realize this is dreadfully rude, but we're in a bit of a difficult situation at the moment, and I'm afraid we'll have to hold off on discovery until we can deal with said situation. I promise to answer all of your concerns the moment we're able."

"Situation," Lord Pembrook repeated.

Ella pointed to the tomb. "Situation." As Silas pinched the bridge of his nose, Ella asked Lord Pembrook, "Would you mind terribly helping us out?"

Lord Pembrook knocked the oak aside, brushed the ledge clean, then slid the lid back onto the tomb with one hand.

Silas went still. His palm, for once, did not find the hilt of his sword.

"Thank you," Ella said when Lord Pembrook turned around. "Now, if you would be so kind as to tell us how you were murdered."

Lord Pembrook's hands folded neatly over his middle. He made a bit of a face, smoothed the front of his robe, then looked back to Ella. "He told me the Cinders had been recalled, that the king had summoned us for a private meeting, wanted us here, every one. I knew Lord Locke was vying for the title of High Cinder, and, though I thought the request strange, I came." He glanced down at his wardrobe. "Look a fool, don't I, now that the truth is out. Won't forget that. Is he dead yet? Have you killed him?"

"I have not."

He made a noise of disapproval. "Needs to be done straightaway if you ask me. I mean, look at this." Lord Pembrook gestured to the tombs. "Desecration, never mind the oath we all swore."

Silas glanced at Ella. She said, "Yes, Lord Pembrook. It is a horrific violation, truly. And I'm sorry to bring it up again, but you've been murdered, and we do need to gather a clear statement. I can obviously not act as an impartial witness in this case, but Prince Silas is here if you could just name, for the record—"

Lord Pembrook glanced disdainfully at Silas. "Feels like something we ought to bring to the king, not a prince."

Ella wet her lips. "My lord, to put a point to it, you're recently dead."

He shrugged.

"And you've not seen an undertaker."

He drew himself up.

Ella lifted her hands in surrender. "Not at all. Please, yes, let's... take this to the king. Prince Silas?"

Silas gave her a disbelieving look. She gave him one back that asked if he'd like to stand there and argue until dawn. His asked if she'd lost her senses. Hers asked if he'd seen the man move the tomb lid. His, reluctantly, said he had. Hers said this was just the sort of thing his father needed to see, so that, for once, the man might understand what precisely they were dealing with. His said she had definitely lost her senses. Hers said that was fine; she'd simply accept the king's offer to make her High Cinder and bring their witness to the king herself.

Silas glared at Ella before inclining his head toward Lord Pembrook. "Yes, by all means. Let us take this to the king."

## CHAPTER 19

"I am here to see my father," Silas announced to the guards posted outside the hall that held the king.

The guard looked past him to Ella and the dark figure standing a good way back from the door. "It is not a suitable time, Highness."

"I didn't ask if it was a suitable time. I implied that you should move aside."

"The king is not taking guests."

"I am not a guest."

"Perhaps you'd like to—"

Silas's voice dropped. "You have three seconds to move."

The two guards conferred for at least two and half of those seconds. A familiar laugh sounded from the chamber beyond.

"That's him!" shouted Lord Pembrook.

Ella cursed. Silas spun to look at the pair of them, and Ella reached forward, but it was too late. Lord Pembrook was striding forward. Ella rushed to stop him, to lay a hand on the man before he could bust through the doors, but another guard came from behind—evidently suspecting Ella was rushing the prince—and yanked her to a stop. Silas shouted, the guards took up their weapons, and Lord Pembrook walked right through.

The doors were possibly the thickest and heaviest Ella had ever seen. They had not stood a chance.

"Well," Silas said as one of the remaining hinge pieces clattered to the floor. "I hope you're pleased."

Ella was not pleased. But she did hope the king would finally understand what he was toying with.

To the guard, Silas snapped, "Let her go."

The man stared at the doors but did not resist when Ella jerked her arm free. She ran into the hall behind Lord Pembrook, then stumbled to a stop.

She had expected the king to be stationed before a long table with a council of advisors, signing declarations or sending orders out for the various kingdom offices, or even simply reading or receiving reports. What she found instead was a wide bright room lined with windows, its balcony doors open to the afternoon air, its tables dotted with arrangements of cut flowers.

Centering the room were three fine sofas in pale hues, a full service of tea and sandwiches placed neatly on the table between. One sofa held the king and queen. Another, Lady Locke and her daughters, sipping tea. Perched on the third, staring at Ella in a manner that did not bode well for the next quarter hour's events, sat Lord Locke.

Somehow, it felt like a betrayal. Her accusatory gaze shot, embarrassingly, toward the king.

He was not looking at her. He was looking at the undead man in Cinder robes staring down Lord Locke on a fancy settee.

For his part, Lord Locke seemed prepared to leap to his feet. He wouldn't try it, Ella guessed, with a man so fast and so strong within easy reach. He may have been immoral, but he was not a fool.

Ella bit down on the words that wanted to spill forth. She had not meant to actually endanger the king. It had never entered her mind that he might be sitting beside the single man Lord Pembrook wished dead. "Lord Pembrook," she whispered. "Perhaps it would be best if we—"

"Lord Locke," Pembrook said. "I would like a word."

The room fell silent except for the dispirited sigh that came from the prince. "Mother," he said, "to me, please."

Queen Amaya unfolded her hands neatly from her lap, then stood, gracefully inclining her head at Lord Pembrook before crossing the room.

Lord Pembrook bowed.

King Julian leaned back in his seat. "Miss Morgrave's doings again, I see."

Ella wished she had some grounds for denial. She dipped into a curtsy. "Majesty."

Julian snorted. "Well, go on. Tell us why you've broken two of the palace's best doors."

Ella stepped carefully forward, dipping again for the queen, then momentarily met Lady Locke's gaze. The woman was purple with outrage. Lora and Lena merely stared at the corpse in necromancer's robes. Lora looked a bit as if she'd gagged up her tea. Ella stopped beside Lord Pembrook, ready to lay a hand on him should the need arise. "This is Lord Pembrook. You may remember, Majesty, that he was a necromancer under my father for nearly twenty years."

"Twenty-one," said Lord Pembrook.

"Twenty-one," said Ella.

Julian gave her a flat look. "Why is he here?"

"We've interrupted your"—Ella gestured toward the other sofas, biting back every nasty word she wanted to use regarding whatever the king and queen were about with the Lockes—"your afternoon, as we've discovered a grave crime against the crown."

Lord Locke did shoot to his feet then, but King Julian said, "Sit." The word hung in the air for a heartbeat or more, Ella could not be sure, as hers were running wild, and some deep part of her wanted Lord Locke to attempt to run.

He did not. When Lord Locke resumed his seat, Ella said, "Lord Pembrook has come to serve as witness."

"I'm about to have you arrested, Miss Morgrave. Best make this worthwhile."

"We found him in the mausoleum," Ella said.

Julian's expression shifted. His gaze slid slowly to the undead man.

Lord Pembrook never took his eyes off Lord Locke when he explained, "Lord Locke asked me to meet him at the records room. But when I arrived, he wasn't there. I had come sooner than he anticipated, I suspect, as I received the message not at my country estate but here, en route to another meeting. I had my robes with me, as I've done since the day we lost our High Cinder, as I was quite eager to return to office. And so, I donned the wardrobe and came immediately. There would be, after all, a great deal of work to be caught up." His long fingers curled into his fists. "One of the guards said they had seen him passing through the courtyard, so I thought to find him. Make him aware that I was available to get started on any tasks. Find him, I did, but he was meeting with another man, so I held back, not wanting to interrupt."

Lord Locke had gone pasty. His brow was dotted with sweat. Lady Locke had lost a bit of her color as well, but she looked as if any moment she might burst out into objections and accusation.

Lord Pembrook went on. "That was when I heard the argument."

"Your Majesty," Lord Locke started, but King Julian only said, "Silas."

The prince squeezed his mother's hand, then crossed the room to stand behind Lord Locke. From the way Locke's posture stiffened, it was clear Silas's sword point was at his back. Perhaps digging in a bit. Ella hoped so. Julian lifted an eyebrow at Lord Pembrook, indicating he should go on.

"As I was saying. The pair bickered, throwing about allegations. Lord Locke said, 'You weren't supposed to kill him—the more people dead, the more likely an investigation,' and the man replied, 'It was only a valet.'"

There was a brief flash of shock in Silas's expression before it hardened.

Lord Pembrook said, "That alone would not have sealed it. I had worked with Lord Locke for years, after all. I did not immediately suspect he was the sort to murder. But they went on, and it came out the valet had been killed because he'd discovered the pair were trading in poisons. That Lord Locke intended to brew one into a tea." He shifted. "If you forgive me for even repeating such a suggestion, Your Majesty, I believe I heard correctly that the tea was meant for 'the king'."

Lord Locke shot forward, shouting, "How dare you!" but he did not make it far. Silas's hand rested on the man's shoulder, his blade clearly deeper than it had been before. Silas's restraint was admirable; anyone else would have likely already run the man through. Perhaps Silas had a preference for slow torture. Ella would not find the idea particularly distasteful in this case. Through gritted teeth, Lord Locke growled, "You've not a shred of proof."

Ella stepped forward, tugging the parchment from her bodice. She shoved it toward the king.

Julian pressed the bridge of his nose. "Miss Morgrave, please."

The *please* could have meant anything at that point, really. But Ella did not have time for decorum. She shook the parchment. "Do you wish to know or not?"

King Julian plucked it from Ella's hand. The queen strolled forward, coming to stand behind Julian as he read through Lord Locke's notes. Ella said, "Written in Lord Locke's own hand, those notes reference the side effects and bitter quality of a toxin, one that would be verifiable upon exam. You may recall my friend at the inn, Majesty. His name is Finley. He was recently taken into custody without due cause. I believe he can identify the man who was working with Lord Locke. In exchange for the information, you'll dismiss Finley of any charges." She did not explain that the assumption was based on the way her undead mouse had reported the man had smelled, that Locke's poison victim was currently making tea at the summer cabin on his estate, or that Ella suspected Lord Locke had killed the apothecary and used his corpse to open the king's tomb. It was difficult to say where the apothecary's body was currently, given that Lord Locke had a preference for keeping witnesses from being able to rise again. Shoddy work, leaving the edge of Lord Pembrook's cloak out. Ella wondered if the man had done so on purpose.

Julian's tone was dry. "I am not accustomed to taking orders, Miss Morgrave."

Lord Locke's gaze trailed from the parchment to Ella, as if he wanted to yell that she'd cheated. Ella said, "Go on, Lord Pembrook. Tell them the rest."

Lord Pembrook explained how he'd intended to confront Lord Locke once the other man had left. How Lord Locke had drawn the man into the mausoleum on the pretense that they might speak in private before they were overheard and how, when they had not come out, Lord Pembrook had followed them in. He explained the scene he'd found, Lord Locke standing over the body of the other man, how he had rushed to help, thinking the man must have a had a weak heart, some issue triggered by the argument. He had knelt near the man and found a fine scalpel driven into the base of his neck at an educated angle.

When Lord Pembrook told how he had turned just in time to see the statuary coming down on his head, the queen's expression went dark. The king folded the parchment and turned his gaze to Lord Locke.

"He is not a reliable witness," Locke said immediately. "Look at him. He's clearly conspiring with Morgrave's daughter. You know what a mess he made of things. I've told you—" Lord

Locke winced as, Ella suspected, Silas's sword pierced the meat of his ribs.

"Majesty," Lady Locke said breathlessly.

King Julian lifted a brow, daring her to go on.

She did not. Mouth agape, frozen in whatever denial she meant to spew forth, Lady Locke only stared back at the king.

Ellenora said, "Majesty, Lord Locke killed my father, your High Cinder." She did not say *and I think you know that*.

Lora made a disgusted sound. "Our father died too, Ellenora. Men die all the time."

Ella's jaw went tight. She did not look at her stepsister. "Your father isn't dead. He's gone to the seaside with his mistress."

Lady Locke shot to her feet. "How dare you! Emeri Morgrave was a stain on this family. The man raised up his dead wife! It's obscene! King Julian should be grateful that he is gone and you" —she nearly spat the words at Ella—"you should have gone with him."

"Petty of you, Lady Locke, though perhaps I should have. Poor planning on your part to say the least. Quite like the plan you concocted with your brother when you realized you could not report to the king what you thought my father had done. If Emeri Morgrave were stripped of his title and estate, you would be as well. So you thought to replace him—a little murder and blackmail to see your brother installed as High Cinder, and you could keep your station while clawing your way even closer to the king."

Lady Locke shrieked and launched herself at Ella. Lord Pembrook's arm shot out, and Lady Locke ran full into it, knocking herself backward. She landed on the floor at her daughters' feet. They had not reached to catch her. Lena took a slow bite of a ginger biscuit.

"Enough," said Queen Amaya. "This display is embarrassing, truly. Silas, wound Lord Locke so that he might not escape, something clean if you would; this rug is new."

"With pleasure."

The sword twirled in a flourish, and Lord Locke made a sound not unlike his sister's shriek before he fell to the floor unharmed. Behind the settee, Silas shrugged. His blade was still clean, having never touched the man currently crawling across the palace floor in a cower.

"May I?" asked Lord Pembrook.

Ella shook her head vehemently at the king. Pembrook would play no such games. King Julian said, "Best we wait," and called for the guard.

Lord Locke was taken into custody, and the king suggested Lady Locke and her daughters would feel more comfortable waiting out the investigation at the palace, no reason to trouble them with leaving should he find a reason to arrest them as well. There was a great deal of indecorous protestations and weeping, which Ella tried not to let herself enjoy too much, as it was likely her own detention was forthcoming.

Once the room was cleared of the Lockes and the guard, King Julian gestured toward the settee. "Miss Morgrave."

Ella crossed the distance, leaving Lord Pembrook to stand respectfully before the proceedings, and Silas came to sit on the third settee, recently vacated by Lord Locke.

Ella and the king took each other's estimation. Queen Amaya sent Silas a speaking glance.

Ella said, "I wish for leave to speak freely." Julian gave her a look that said if that wasn't what she'd been doing already, he would be surprised. And also that he was out of patience. She nodded. "I will not accept your offer."

Julian huffed out a humorless laugh. "The offer no longer stands, Miss Morgrave. Not after this."

"Regardless. What you did to my father was wrong, not merely while he was in office but once it became clear the circumstances of his death were suspect, and I find that I cannot allow myself to participate in situations where such things are likely to continue." Ella could not stop him from what he had planned, but she would be no part of it.

The king's brow shifted in something of a warning. "You question my rule as you sit here before a man you've dragged back from death uninvited. You have not come to this with no wrongs of your own."

"More than you can imagine. But the Lockes attempted to blackmail you, and if I had not intervened, they would have succeeded. A murderer would hold the office of High Cinder."

The queen's gaze turned sharp.

Julian said, "That is a bold opinion to toss at a king's feet."

"At your feet is where I am, Your Majesty. That much cannot be helped."

He barked a short laugh. "Miss Morgrave, that tongue of yours." He gestured toward her, sending a glance to his wife. "Do you see why strict discipline is so important? This is what comes of letting a child grow free of restrictions."

Queen Amaya said reasonably, "Your son is holding a blade for that young woman, my love. Perhaps you've not noticed in your bluster."

"Bluster," he muttered. To Ella he said, "The Lockes were able to maneuver a great deal, putting myself and several members of court into a difficult position. I find, as someone who is not permitted to sully his reputation or dirty his hands, that those difficulties are best resolved by the people who surround me. You chose to join in those machinations against my wishes. If you'll recall, I tossed you from court and banned you from the palace. If not for my respect for your father, trust that you'd have been tossed someplace far worse."

Ella bit out, "Lord Locke had dirt on you, so you handed him my father's title and his niece a chance at the throne. That smacks of disrespect, at the least."

Silas winced. The queen went a little pale.

Julian's tone turned hard. "I urge you toward caution, Miss Morgrave."

She stared back at him, as they both knew he had encouraged her father to wed Lady Locke in the first place. But she held her tongue.

He leaned back, releasing a breath. "What would you have me do? The fire has already burned any chance at recompense. Your father is gone, and I do regret the circumstance. But you refused the offer of his post and the title and estate. You may go free. It is all there is left for you. And because your father served the kingdom well, I will grant you his property, whether that satisfies you or not. You will be Lady Morgrave and all that entails, assuming Lady Locke has not emptied the coffers."

"I want everyone who aided in covering up my father's murder punished." A dark part of her wanted to add that it was what Lord Pembrook wanted as well, but that seemed like a bit too much of a threat, given the manner in which the man hovered. Besides, Ella did not wish to remind him exactly how deep her power ran.

"You've no weight to negotiate."

"She has me," Silas said. "How much do you suppose I weigh, Father?"

"Yes," said Queen Amaya. "Lady Morgrave has made quite the presentation. I believe I shall lend her my weight as well."

"Mutiny." Julian's word was tinged with disgust.

Ella said, "I never wish to be under threat from a Locke again. Remove any chance of that—reveal his crime, cast them from society—and I will leave the rest be and live out my time quietly at Morgrave House."

"I've already announced the engagement. I cannot back off my word."

"Nothing will induce me to marry a Locke," Silas said.

"It's not your choice."

"I would love to hear your plan to ensure I behave. I'll remind you the man murdered my valet."

"Cease this bickering," the queen said. "Children, the both of you. Of course Silas cannot wed the Locke woman. She's clearly unfit. Julian, you should be ashamed for even suggesting it."

"I will not go back on my word."

"Make public that Lord Locke has been arrested, and whatever any of them speaks against you will appear a desperate attempt to protect their reputations."

He threw up a hand. "There was a ball. Specifically in honor of the announcement. Need I remind you of the precarious state of public opinion? Fickle as the weather."

She sighed. "Then he will marry Lady Morgrave."

Every soul present, including Lord Pembrook, turned their stares on Queen Amaya.

She shrugged. "Is a stepdaughter not a daughter? It satisfies your conditions."

Alarm lit through Ella. She dared not look at Silas.

Julian grunted. "Look at him. Do you want the future king mooning over a lady necromancer for all the court to see? It's beneath us."

"Beneath us? Everyone is beneath us, Julian; we're the king and queen. Are you truly so threatened by a single woman?"

His gaze narrowed on the queen, and Ella suspected he might be considering whether he was under threat by a particular woman at that very moment. Possibly, he was considering how useful it might be to keep Ella and her magic close at hand.

Silas leaned forward. "If... I may..." When he had the attention of the king and queen, he said, "Ellenora and I will decide to whom and when we are to be married, should we be so moved."

The queen smiled obligingly at him. "Of course, my darling." She stood, leaning forward to pat Silas's knee. He sat warily straighter, as if the gentle pat were a weapon. And perhaps it was, because Amaya said, "Until then, you will pretend. Just a year or so, then we will decide." She dusted her hands. "Now, that is settled. Lady Morgrave, would you be so kind as to return Lord Pembrook to"—she glanced up at the man—"well, not to the mausoleum, obviously, but wherever is best suited. Perhaps the undertaker." Then she inclined her head toward Lord Pembrook and swept past, calling, "See you at dinner, Majesty," over her shoulder.

Ella stared after her. When her gaze returned to King Julian, he was giving Ella an especially ungracious look. "One more thing," Ella said softly, and his expression pinched even further. "I would like to recommend Lord Abbot for the post of High Cinder. He is, perhaps, not the best skilled, but he excels at teaching and command and would do well by the crown. A bit stodgy, but I think capable of becoming accustomed to the many ceremonies required of the office. I believe he would have been my father's choice, if not for everything else."

Julian's mouth shifted into a begrudging non-scowl, and he waved a hand in acquiescence and dismissal. "I'll take it under consideration."

Ella stood, bobbed a quick curtsy, then swallowed hard and skirted the keen gaze of the prince with nothing more than a, "Highness."

Lord Pembrook turned to follow, and they strode from the room. Silas did not run after them.

# CHAPTER 20

After a lengthy conversation with Lord Pembrook, rehashed half a dozen times as he'd demanded Ella bring in other Cinders for consultation, they'd run a few trials with tethering and releasing Ella's magic. It turned out that one of the newer Cinders had a talent for holding fast to the magic, and he was able to provide a bit of insight into the process of anchoring. With Lord Pembrook's help, and the promise to soon be returned to work, the Cinders had come together in a manner they had not in years. It revealed just how much damage Lord Locke's maneuvering had done, eroding the trust between lords and ladies who possessed a bit too much arrogance and independence even on the best of days, Ella included.

Discovering what Lord Locke had done to their High Cinder caused them to rally in a way they'd never been inspired to before. It gave Ella hope that the king's desire to grasp hold of a near eternal life would never come to pass. And it was how, only weeks later, Ella stood in the clearing beyond Morgrave House with a line of Cinders at her back.

"Mama, do you remember Lord Pembrook?"

Her mother looked at the undead man in Cinder robes. Her

pale fingers fluttered toward her throat, as if dismayed by the state of her own dress. "Of course. Goodness, he worked with your father for—how long was it, Lord Pembrook?"

"Twenty-one years, my lady."

"Twenty-one," she breathed. "My, time does escape."

The hollow feeling scraped at Ella's insides. "He's going to help us, Mama. Lord Pembrook and the others believe we can get the magic under control and you will finally be free."

Her mother's eyes trailed slowly from Lord Pembrook to Ella. They were so pale, so soft.

Grief thick in her throat, Ella said, "I only have to let go."

"Oh, my darling girl," her mother cooed, pressing a gentle hand to Ella's cheek. "I'll be right here. No matter if I'm gone."

Ella collapsed into her mother's embrace, and they stood, holding on, until Ella was finally strong enough to draw away.

Then Ella's mother took both of Ella's hands in hers and nodded. "Come, it's time. Show me what you've learned."

---

The sun set on the hazel tree, now quiet of all magic and populated with a few brave birds, as Ella sat alone at her mother's grave. The hollowness inside of her had eased, a great deal of herself and her magic returned. She had underestimated how much the sensation had weighed on her, and it felt as if she could truly breathe for the first time in years. The hollowness was not entirely gone, but it was so much less painful. So much more bearable.

She laid a careful hand on the soil to wish her mother farewell. Her magic had not encouraged the grass to flourish; the grave would surrender on its own terms. Ella stood to walk back to Morgrave House, as she would do every night now that it was again her home. She had set to work regaining the house staff and ordered the most offensive of Lady Locke's decorations removed. There would be a large portrait of her mother and father in the sitting room, where the windows overlooked the spot that had once held their favorite garden. In time, the damage done to the estate, and to Ella's heart, would heal.

Days later, with the help of the other Cinders, Ella returned Lord Pembrook to rest in a ceremony that spoke of the respect and dignity the office deserved. She exchanged farewells with the men and women she'd worked with and strolled from the palace on a winding route that brought her too near the glasshouse and memories of Silas. She'd made excuses to avoid thinking of him for weeks. Sorting out the magic with the Cinders. Restoring the house. Making arrangements for, and explanations to, Grace and Finley.

She was out of excuses. There was nothing left but to face it.

Fortunate, that, because Ella was fairly certain Silas was right behind her.

In a secluded section of the winding path, surrounded by climbing roses, their leaves dappling the stone with shadows, Ella stopped, then turned around.

Silas rocked back on his heels a bit, coming to stand too close before her. The edge of his mouth tipped into a smile, as if he couldn't help it.

"Are you following me, Highness?"

He learned forward to whisper, "Silas." When Ella did not respond, he said, "You've been avoiding me."

"I had matters to attend."

His expression fell. "I am sorry about your mother. That can't have been easy."

Ella nodded. "This is better. She did not deserve what I had done."

They were quiet for a long moment. The finches cheeped at each other sharply. A bee landed on a nearby rose.

"Is Harold safe?"

Silas seemed to shake himself. "Yes. He's been discharged with full pay."

"Discharged?"

"He was offered the position back. He said he'd rather eat live ants."

Ella choked out a laugh.

Silas watched her, as if taking in every detail, as if he'd never seen a thing such as mirth. His blue eyes met hers. "I've missed you."

Her mouth went dry. When Ella was not thinking of her mother and her tasks, she'd done little more than worry over the queen's plan. Her voice was soft. "It feels like a very bad idea, to pretend for the whole kingdom."

"Will it be so terrible?" He shifted impossibly closer. "I will get to hold your hand wherever we go. Slide my fingers over your ribbons. Lift you into carriages."

"Everyone thinks you're a rake."

He hummed agreeably. "Think of how much more they'll allow me to get away with, then. We might be able to brush shoulders. Sit too closely and touch thighs."

"You do not seem to be taking this very seriously."

His gaze dipped to her lips, his voice low. "What am I to do, Ellenora? I am merely a set piece for the crown. As you said, they think I am nothing more than a rake." His gaze lifted once more. "They will say you have tamed me. And all the while, you, the wild and chaotic beast, will be allowed to run free." The tip of his nose grazed her cheek as he slid his mouth to her ear, sending a shiver through her. He whispered, "Let me kiss you."

The breath that came out of her was slow and deep. Silas drew back to look at her, and she reached up to take hold of his neckcloth. There was a flash of surprise in his expression. He did not appear displeased. Ella said, "I liked you better without a cravat."

He snatched her up. "However you wish me." Then he kissed her, full and deep. Like a man who'd been waiting for years.

# EPILOGUE

*(months later)*

"Make haste, Lady Morgrave, or you'll be late."

"Coming," Ella called to the steward, neck bent as she shoved the last pin into her hair. She rushed from her room, grabbing a shawl and taking the stairs two at a time.

"Careful!" shouted a maid.

Ella waved. "Have a good break, Clara. Thank your mother for that recipe for me."

"Oh, I couldn't. It would go straight to her head."

Ella laughed. Across the entryway, the footman handed Ella her cloak. "Safe travels, my lady."

"Thank you, John. Do take it easy on that ankle. An injury like that can cause trouble for years."

"Of course, my lady."

"I'll keep an eye on him," the steward called from the top of the stairs.

"Thank you, Miss Finch. We couldn't do without you."

"Don't I know it," the woman murmured as Ella yanked open the door.

Silas waited, standing on the top step. He turned, grinning the moment he saw her. "Lady Morgrave," he said suggestively, drawing out the word as his gaze traced every part of her.

"Grab my trunk," Ella said, darting past him toward the carriage.

Silas chuckled, chasing after her when the footmen beat him to the trunk. He climbed into the carriage, shoving in beside Ella and her bulky bag. The bag made a growl of disapproval. "Still hates it?" Silas asked.

Ella moved the bag to the floor and flipped open the latch. The badger poked his head out to give Silas a scowl. Ella said, "Of course he does. But it's necessary now that he might be seen." She shot Silas an accusatory glance. "Quite a bit more traffic past Morgrave House these days."

He hummed as the carriage door shut. "Everyone wants a look at you."

Silas was looking a bit long himself. Ella asked, "What?"

He leaned forward, voice low. "I haven't kissed you yet."

A grunt of complaint rose from the bag, which was roundly ignored.

Sometime later, the carriage came to a stop near a line of new trees, and Silas jumped out to assist Ella down. The footman gave him a look. Silas lifted a palm. "I will let you get the trunks, if you like."

Ella elbowed him in the ribs.

"My lady."

Silas tucked Ella's hand into the crook of his arm, her bag in the other, and they strode the short distance to the door. It came open just as they stepped onto the cabin porch.

"Blackthorn." Ella smiled, setting down the bag as Magnus climbed out. "You look well."

Blackthorn inclined his head. "Thank you, my lady. Do come

in; the tea is ready and I'm just finishing up the biscuits you love." He shot a disapproving glance at Silas's cravat but made no comment.

Silas's shoulders straightened nonetheless. His hand slid to Ella's lower back as they entered the cottage, recently redecorated and scattered with sketches of all kinds. Diagrams, landscapes, even portraits of Ella and the prince. A newly framed drawing of Magnus rested on the side table. Silas shook his head.

"Henry is in the workshop," Blackthorn called from the kitchen.

"Still working on the guttering?" Silas asked.

"Finished that. He's moved on to decorative molding. Wants to fancy up the windows some." Blackthorn settled a platter of breads and pastries on the table.

Cybil and Fritz darted through the open door, scrambling up Ella's skirt then over her arms and shoulders. She laughed, lifting her hands so they might find a spot to settle. "Have you two been up to no good?"

They launched into a dozen complicated gestures, chittering and laughing, recounting every interesting thing that Henry or Blackthorn had done in the days Ella had been gone.

"Traitors," Blackthorn muttered.

Ella grinned. "Truly, the worst sort of secret keepers."

"How long are you here for?" Blackthorn asked as Ella set the mice onto the table.

Ella took a deep, relief-filled breath. "Two full days."

"Well, we are pleased to have you. Will Finn and Grace be visiting as well?"

"Not this time. Finn is moving with his sister into their new apartment, and Grace has a visit planned with her mother and sisters."

"Just the two of you, then."

Blackthorn's words were polite enough, but Ella could not help but feel a bit guilty about all the swooning and casting of sheep's eyes the man was about to be once again subjected to. Silas, however, slid his hand around Ella's waist and tugged her closer to his side. "Yes, just the two of us. Flaunting our joy about until it makes everyone absolutely sick."

Fritz made a gagging sound, and Cybil laughed uproariously.

Silas gave Ella a look. Ella only shrugged.

He reached down, snatching a handful of cookies from the tray. "Come. I can tell when we're not wanted." He took hold of Ella's hand, dragging her with him as they headed briskly out the back door, telling Blackthorn, "Lucian may show up Sunday, once my father realizes we're gone. Feel free to entertain him however you like."

Blackthorn's response was muffled by the breeze as Ella and Silas crossed the field of tall grass. Ella waved at Henry in his workshop, apron tied over his clothes and punch in hand.

He called, "It's getting close, my lady!"

"Silas can't wait to see it," Ella called back.

Silas threw a glance at her over his shoulder. When they reached the massive tree, three arm-spans wide and just as tall, he grabbed Ella about the waist and tossed her up.

Laughing, she took hold of the ladder and clambered the rest of the way into the shelter they'd built amid the limbs.

Silas wasn't far behind her, tumbling through the door and onto the pile of cushions they'd laid on the floor. He peered out the window where Henry was still visible in the shop. "Are you certain we've built far enough away from the cabin?"

Ella leaned onto an elbow to look with him out the small door. Beyond the workshop sat the cabin, the tree George had taken a liking to in one direction, and in the other direction, Magnus's favorite pond. Everywhere Ella looked was something she was dearly fond of. She turned toward Silas, taking hold of his jacket—somehow already unbuttoned. "This is perfect. Just where we are."

His expression softened. "Perfect?"

"Not a single complaint. Nothing you could do could make me happier."

Silas's mouth slid into a playful smile. "Ella, sweetheart, that sounded perilously close to a dare."

Ella laughed and Silas pushed her to the pillows, climbing over her as he tugged free his cravat.

# ALSO BY MELISSA WRIGHT

### - STANDALONE FANTASY -
*Seven Ways to Kill a King*

### RIVENWILDE GASLAMP FAIRYTALES
*Beyond the Filigree Wall*
*Within the Hollow Heart*
*Upon the Riven Throne*

### GRAVE MAGIC AND OTHER FORMS OF COURTSHIP
*A Necromancer's Guide to Grave Mistakes*

### - SERIES -
### BETWEEN INK AND SHADOWS
*Between Ink and Shadows*
*Before Crown and Kingdom*
*Beneath Stone and Sacrifice*

### THE FREY SAGA
*Frey*
*Pieces of Eight*
*Molly (a short story)*
*Rise of the Seven*
*Venom and Steel*
*Shadow and Stone*
*Feather and Bone*

### DESCENDANTS SERIES
*Bound by Prophecy*
*Shifting Fate*
*Reign of Shadows*

### SHATTERED REALMS
*King of Ash and Bone*
*Queen of Iron and Blood*

### - WITCHY PNR -
### HAVENWOOD FALLS
*Toil and Trouble*

### BAD MEDICINE
*Blood & Brute & Ginger Root*

Visit the author on the web at
https://melissa-wright.com

www.ingramcontent.com/pod-product-compliance
Lightning Source LLC
LaVergne TN
LVHW090040080526
838202LV00046B/3907